Outbound

A Novel

by

G.A.Chamberlin

Titles by

G.A.Chamberlin

The Handmaiden Legacy
Cultural Attache
Rare Earth Element
Outbound
Somma
Unintended Consequence
The Particle
The Kneeling Woman
BLACKBIRD SECRET
EXILE

Kathleen The War Years

Outbound
Printed in the United States
ISBN 978-0-9904027-2-5

Crown Eagle Publishing

Distribution by Ingram

Cover Design by Jennifer Chamberlin

Rare Earth Element

climate, culture, commerce...Too important to ignore, too well written to overlook. And too technically suspenseful not to wonder about...

* * *

The Handmaiden Legacy

The Handmaiden Legacy is a contemporary thriller full of corporate interests, beautiful seas and ancient legacies...
>---*G.A. Chamberlin is an International Thriller Writer!*

>"International Thriller Writers ...that will surprise "
>--Agent, Thriller Fest, New York City

* * *

Cultural Attache

"...Amanda Wells is lecturing on the historical integrity of medieval works at the University when she is informed that the original manuscript of a major work...has been stolen from the vault.

I will guard you, keep you from all woe
and harm. Softly, gently I will rock you,
resting sweetly on my arm. May you
slumber e'er so softly; dream of visions
wondrous fair...

Traditional Welsh carol

Outbound,

An International Thriller

".... As wife to the new Diplomacy Emissary in Washington DC, Amanda Wells gets to enjoy the Nation's Capital and all its delights while revisiting the sites of her childhood...

Amanda is thrilled to be of service to a Senator on the Hill... But she discovers that in designing a financial framework, an older truth must be unearthed, one built in a stone structure left by colonial venturers trading in waters off the shores of an old world ...And she must shelter a fugitive

This is Amanda Wells at her finest...

Outbound

A Novel

G.A.Chamberlin

Chapter 1

Long Island Sound

"Can we make it?" called out Charlie, his body at the helm of a sleek forty-foot sailing yacht.

Ten. Nine. Eight. Seven...

From the forward position of the boat, the jib tender turned to his skipper, his face thrashed by wind, and he gestured with a clenched fist.

Charlie understood instantly. They had served together.

"Tacking!" he shouted. "Tacking!"

Six. Five. Four...

"Coming about..." he bellowed. "Heads Up! Heads Up!"

The crew scrambled to the halyards and heaved hard. The metal mast screeched in protest and shuddered against her bulkhead now filling with thunderous sea-spray as propulsion spilled from her powered main sail. Slowly the massive boom began her swing across the deck, leaving the crew splayed and panting with relief.

"I'm sorry. *I'm sorry!*" wailed Charlie. "It was too close to call..."

Three of his crew gave him the bird.

Safety First. Above all Charlie was a lawyer, they knew. He looked out. The start line was far from clear.

"*Starboard!*" boomed a voice from another vessel.

Charlie ignored him. No place for *Right of Way* here. His crew had managed. But the wind picked up.

Delays to start the race had been a mistake. The Race Committee made their decision on a bay that could deliver unpredictable wind gusts.

This was the start line. Too late for change...

"*Starboard!*" persisted the voice.

Charlie took in the situation about him.

Vessels had converged to the start line and the cannon about to discharge. The gust had thrown them into disarray. To hell with jockeying for best position. This was surviving the start of a race to Bermuda.

No question. In less than 20 minutes, the weather for an ocean race to Bermuda had turned foul. No longer a feat for positioning, it was a hazard for collisions and many skippers were pulling away to restart. Costly on a clock. He thought about it.

In the world of sailboat racing, the Bermuda Race was an event that held many to months of preparation. Through the winter, it was the conversation of skippers and boat crews, family, friends committing themselves to the feat with the fervor of a corporate asset of a major investment. And not without reason.

Neither were these inexpensive vessels, nor could technology have been any more challenging in a risk-averse world of insurance, certification, updates and fierce competitors now arriving from all parts of the world. Still, for many it was a family tradition harking back to the local boat race up the creeks and back, following by a lot of summer fishing, crabbing and family picnics. *The Tempest* was no exception. She had been handed down as the name of the household boat with children learning from happy fathers taking the family out for a sail. Today, it was high-end, go-fast tactical training seminars in hydro-dynamic sponsored racing by investors and eager owners.

Charlie and his friends had been sailing together for years. And not until recently, with a job earned from years of certifications and sophisticated learning, did he take a mortgage to buy a boat that had some meaning to enter the Bermuda race. *The Tempest* had been entered in the Bermuda race. For this, his friends came from computer jobs in the city to crew, and practice. The actual race was days away.

But today was different. What should have been respectable effort at the start line turned into a stunning disaster for many. The trick was to get started and get the boats out to sea and into the gulf stream where the weather was predictable, if a little unsteady. The last thing anybody wanted was to damage a boat. Collision, they all knew, was to be averted at all cost. Right of way rules or no. The sea was the sea. Every skipper had to use his head. That was the mariner's rule always.

Charlie had made his choice. Jeopardizing the boat in close quarters was his call. Besides, as he would late explain, he didn't want anybody to get hurt.

For now, the crew was still furling rope, the crisis averted, and they were off guard. The race, they all said, was cancelled.

But the assault came out of nowhere, a dark beast breaching upon them with screeching force of wind, steel and a pitching sea.

"Oh my God..." squealed Bill at the stern. "Charlie, watch out!"

"*Get out of the way you sonnovabitch!*" bellowed the skipper of the oncoming vessel. "*Starboard!*"

"Jesus!" cried Amanda.

"He's calling for Starboard...I'm out of room to maneuver!" *yelled* Charlie. "Tacking!"

The jib sail thrashed free up the 40 ft mast with a whipping that could flip four strong marines off a deck like fleas.

Charlie spun *The Tempest* upwind to luff the sails, his momentum gone.

The dark hull lurched forward and tore past reaching a full speed with sails full and wheezing power.

The vessel spun about, searched for an opening amongst boats all tangled at the start-line.

If found a hole, dipping into the pack with a thunderous tack, technically able to demand of right of way, and leaving a snarled fray of boats bellowing in protest...

Such barging tactics were against the rules. But the start-gun shot went off and nobody could argue as the vessel timed a perfect tactical entry for a strong start. It pulled in its sails and took off at close haul.

"Head's up! Head's up!" screamed Charlie as the mast lurched with such force that the boom tore free like a Master Executioner about to relieve all crewmen of their heads.

The tangle at the start-line compromised the entire fleet of sailboats. Most were disabled and would not compete.

"Assholes!" cheered the Skipper of the dark hull as it surged ahead, sun glinting off its stern transom, *Outbound*.

"Everyone alright?" said Charlie, having fouled his own chances for a strong start to avoid collisions.

By now the wind was gusting.

They all gave him the thumbs up.

"Okay. Do we go on?" he asked.

They all nodded.

"Okay. We were tossed over line prematurely and we're a mess. So it's 360° about penalty; tack to port and off. Everybody in?"

"*We're in*" responded Bill.

"Go! Go! Go!" shrieked Amanda "He ain't seen nothing yet!"

They picked up speed, gathering taut sail and sheet lines.

In a swirl of silver sea spray *Tempest* spun handily around, puffed up her sails, and closed-hauled for an upwind stretch across a sea of glittering diamonds.

The race was on.

"Oh my God!" said Amanda, later at the bar. "I thought we were out of the race!"

"So did I" repeated Bill.

But it was Paul who looked squared at Charles and said "But you made the right call. You're made a good judgement, skipper."

"Damned right!"

"Your boat could have been up in a sling at Jebens with a dry dock repair bill for $20,000" said Amanda.

"To the race then?" said Charlie.

"To the race!" they all cheered.
Later that evening and back at home in Washington, Amanda told Trevor what happened.
"Not a bad call for a staffer at the Supreme Court..."
They chuckled.

**

Washington DC

It was warm for April. The Nation's Capital was in full bloom and the scent of spring filled the night air on Pennsylvania Avenue.

A motorcade of Limousines approached 12th Street and New York Avenue, stopping at the red carpet where a brass railing and bright lights flashed brand names; sponsor flags; media broadcasters and celebrity journalists in a tide surrounding the gold-domed National Museum of Women in the Arts.

Some guests arrived in private cars, valets accepting their keys to park below. Patrons, wearing black tie; fur and jewels disembarked to applause and photographs. The Charity Fundraising event was for the Museum Annual Gala.

Tonight the guest list included icons and personalities from across the globe, here to patronize the Arts Museum which, over the various political Administrations, held political overtones of support for women worldwide.

Hosted at the Mezzanine level and surrounded by portraits of recognized statesmen and industry leaders, early guests viewed works of Arts created by women down through the ages, later to be auctioned for charity.

Trevor and Amanda MacDonnell arrived late. In a party driven from the Chancery gates on

Massachusetts Avenue to the Gala, the Embassy chauffeur had a car full of beautiful ladies, as Trevor put it.

Barbara from New York was wearing a hot pink chiffon *Sherri Hill* ball gown. Lady Totteridge from London sat draped in red velvet and black lace. Amanda's crystal stiletto heels peaked out from a silk Lauren ball gown shaded from ice-lavender to silver pearl with petals.

Trevor poured to each one a glass of campaign for a toast, and they cheered the festive moment just as they entered the procession of vehicles.

The media was everywhere now, and they waived as they approached.

Amanda noticed Trevor's ear firmly fixed with an earbud off his cell phone. Smiling as he was, she knew he was conversing with his government. The sun never set on Greenwich Mean Time for Trevor MacDonnell, now Emissary to the United States.

The car came to a halt. The doors opened, and Trevor offered the Ladies on his arm pride of place for the media. Amanda smiled, relishing the moment of flashing lights and questions. She glanced at her husband and saw a fearsome look within his eyes that told her his mind was elsewhere.

"Delighted to be here!" said Trevor to one party.

"Hello!" waved Amanda to someone.

The ascent up the steps to the Main Entrance was spectacular. Corinthian columns marked the granite portico of Renaissance architecture befitting a Capital City, and ornate wrought-iron gates flanked a portal of the great classical period.

Baroque gilded-sconces and crystal chandeliers glittered above marble foyers that ran the length of the structure, a vast marbled grid-work of marquetry flooring was bordered by brass registers for ventilation, Roman style.

They talked, meeting and laughing as they checked coats, and Amanda's silk floor-length gown dazzled, less from its ornamentation as from its form on her slender body and natural beauty. She looked at ease and comfortable. The photographers had a field day for their headline news and tabloids.

The crowd moved forward and Amanda found herself nudged to the perimeter as parties surged. She paused, catching her breath, the air close.

Then just as Amanda shifted her weight and lifted her foot she was edged off balance. She stopped suddenly, her foot rooted to the ground. Her heel had sunk stubbornly into one of the floor brass Registers.

Instinctively, she lifted the hem of her gown and looked down. A woman behind her bumped into her. Trevor was two paces behind her, and he caught her arm.

"Oops, sorry darling!" he exclaimed when he realized what had happened.

Amanda laughed nervously as Trevor bent down.

Those besides her chuckled, offering good-humored advice. And like Cinderella she slid out of her glass slipper wedged there in the teeth of a wrought metalwork.

Finally, the stiletto heel was rescued, as Trevor put it, restoring full confidence and composure to the ladies with a chivalrous smile.

"Thank you!" whispered Amanda.

The halls filled with more guests arriving, and the access ways jamming up in the throng.

Suddenly out of nowhere strode in giant Mimes. High on stilts and dressed all white in face and hands, they loomed over guests with red lips and red noses, bowing and striding with terrifying splendor.

To some guests in the crowd, their appearance was alarming. But to one guest, a rose was presented; another received a kiss and a handshake. One mime pulled a magic act, producing a silk scarf from nowhere.

Ping.

Ping.

Three banks of elevators arrived to ferry guests to the Upper Galleries.

Ping. Next party up!

They all shuffled in, their group giggling and cramming festively.

"Oh...oh... my hands!" husked an elderly lady "Oh... look at my hands!" she cried, rubbing them clean, her pitch rising with anxiety.

Moist and crimson colored coating appeared on her hands. "I'm bleeding. *Oh my God...*"

"Here!" said someone, procuring a napkin come forward, the elevator hot.

"Oh Ralph! Ralph!" she said, "I'm bleeding...Help!" She searched for her husband.

"No!" admonished Trevor. "It's the paint. The clown's wax-red paint on your hands...You are safe!"

"Oh...Oh...Oh" she repeated. "The Paint?" her face was distraught and her husband held her elbow.

The elevator doors opened and the throng dispersed. Trevor held back as the two found a railing to rest and clean off.

"Are you alright?"

"Yes. She is fine..." said the husband, his face flushed and alarmed at the condition of his wife. He looked about, as if searching for a steward.

His wife leaned against his arm, her face worn and pale.
"Is there something I can do?.. A doctor perhaps?"
The husband nodded.
The evening progressed with some confusion and periodically Amanda eyed her husband, his hand reaching for his earbud. He was having a conversation with someone on his device. Evidently, he was knee-deep in an incident of gathering urgency.
The Auction of the Arts on exhibit was to occur in the ballroom where dining tables glittered with silverware, glass and gold-rimmed china.
An orchestra strummed out melodies to provoke care-free dancing at the center of the ballroom, interrupted only by a Master of Ceremony who came forward to announce progress of the bidding sequence.
Clearly the bids grew and a marathon ensued with auction offers for art displayed in the halls by Lot Number, and the charity was off to a strong start with generous donations for the Museum.
When finally seated at the dinner table, Amanda was actually hungry, she had to say. And she was proud of Trevor. He was ignoring his phone and conversing with others at his table.
The food was excellent, and the wine changed vintage at every course. She so wanted to dance. She looked at Trevor who was engaged in conversation with two gentlemen and a lady at the table.
"We are a poor State!" insisted Mrs. Giordana across the table, referring to their home state of Rhode Island. "As a Chapter, we cannot raise funds for the Museum other than a few family donations..."
Amanda listened.
Clearly she'd had a few servings of wine.

"But we are a generous family!" she added, picking up her bread roll and buttering it.

Senator Williams sat at her side, eating from his plate a good slice of roast beef and skewering one small potato. He looked up at her, dabbing his mouth with his napkin.

"What we need..." he said "is a resurgence of economic activity that has... a life of its own in our region!"

"Oh?" asked Amanda.

"Yes, something that would generate fees, income and activities for the less institutionalized markets of New England!"

"Umm... Boston is a wonderful city" said Trevor, a polite smile on his face.

"It is indeed. Thank you. But languishing!"

"That's because..." interceded Mrs Giordana everything is rr-regulated to death"

The Senator drained his glass of Bordeaux and turned to her "What line of business are you in?" he asked.

She grinned, in her eye the sparkle of a good retort.

"Liquor" she said, her rouged lips pursed tight before peeling with laughter.

"We have...a chain of licensed stores" intervened her husband, his face in full earnestly.

"We came from New York" ploughed on his wife "Years ago...from little-a-Italy in New York..."

"Florence" interrupted her husband, to blunt his wife's talk.

"Where are *you* from?" she asked the Senator, unblinking.

He looked at her.

"I am the retiring Senator from Rhode Island, Ma'am. Formerly Chairman of the Bank of Boston; and Board of Governors of the Federal Reserve. My parents were Scots."

"Ohh..." she said, looking down.

With table conversation stalled, Amanda leaned in mildly to offer the woman some shelter.

"Have you thought of a local Jobs Board, Senator?" she asked.

"That's exactly what we need!" he said, lifting his fork in the air from across the table.

In the chatter that followed, Amanda noted Trevor's cell vibrate, and she knew he'd need to excuse himself. She covered.

"As you know Senator, I'm working on a think tank at the University, and we're exploring some economic model possibilities that meet SEC guidelines. I can send you the latest, if you'd like?"

"Really? I'd be most interested. Send them to me will you please? My staff and I were discussing just such a prospect not long ago..."

The ballroom filled with noise as the band surged.

"So. We have to go!" said Mrs. Giordana, fairly hoisted from the table by her husband.

Trevor got up. As did the Senator.

An invitation to the dance floor beckoned, its tone flirty.

"I...I send you money!" said Mrs. Giordana.... And soon...for this wonderful Museum..."

Trevor grabbed Amanda's hand and tugged her to dance.

Too late.

Someone came over for the dance with Amanda, and Trevor conceded. The night was not over, his eyes told her...

By 9.30 pm, the band had been playing and the soiree moved with abandon, raising fabulous amounts of money for the Museum, as the announcements claimed. .

Only once did Amanda get a chance to dance with her husband.

"Do you know how beautiful you are tonight?" he whispered in her ear.

"Oh really?" she answered.

"Umm. That dress...I can't wait to ease it off and..." he looked up "Yes! Hello!...Lovely? Yes! Nice to see you too!" he waived. Behind her the Spanish Emissary's Aide swirled past with his wife in a cloud of feathers and tulle.

"Well..." said Trevor, returning to the gaze of his wife. "It's this business of ...of this...err, this most beautiful bare shoulder that I want to touch ...with my lips" he brought his mouth close, his look travelling down her neck "...and kiss!" he said softly.

Drawn into his eyes by a magnetic pull, his breath warm breath across her face, Amanda succumbed to a swirl of longing and watched his mouth draw closer. But he averted his eyes suddenly.

A figure was approaching.

Senator Steve Williams had spotted her and come forward with relentless determination.

He tapped her shoulder, the very shoulder Trevor would kiss and...

"Is there any chance, Amanda, that you have the time to Chair a Commission on developing that concept? Especially for the Boston area?"

Her head was spinning, her toes ached and she was in her husband's arms just now.

Amanda looked at him, aware of competition from K Street where Lobbyists would seize this man's cause to earmark political interests, and her thoughts scrambled for ground. This was Washington. Neither could she shrink from his call to serve, nor could she abstain on grounds of credentials. Still, this was not her crusade... And what she really wanted to say was that her life was full with...with...Trevor's career, that's what she wanted to say. And it was what she relished doing just now, she wanted to say.

But her answer was definitive. Instead she responded "There is a desperate need to find solutions...If I can help..."

"Right then! I'll have my staff confirm? Set up a small operating budget, commission members and support staff for you" He looked at Trevor and grinned, pressing first his hand, then hers.

"I'm at the National Press Club tomorrow giving a luncheon speech. May I say that we have something in the works then?" he asked her.

"You may say that of course. But allow a little time before bragging rights...There may be people better qualified than me to do this...Its too critical to play around with, and solutions so needed..."

"Check your schedule Amanda. I need this very badly! More importantly, the people in my constituency are hurting...They need solutions to keep the economy alive at the grass roots level...Please! I'm asking?"

"I'll call" he said, and left.

"Persistent little prick..." muttered Trevor, smiling gamely.

For Amanda to shake her head would be a bad sign in public, she realized. Instead she looked directly at

Trevor who gazed determinedly ahead as he reached for his buzzing cell phone.

"Excuse me" he said, and walked to the sidelines.

God, was there no way they could be allowed to have a relationship in peace?

The tempo changed, and Amanda was swept into the moment of festivities. She would check on her guests. Between her many invitations to the dance floor, and her introductions of eligible bachelors for Barbara -- who was having the time of her life, she was beginning to wonder what happened to their other Houseguest:

Lady Totteridge was not without fans, she discovered. She had sailed around the ballroom like a ship docking from table to table making "new American friends" as she called them.

In one free corner of the dance floor she found Trevor's hand give her a twirl, and then before she could say anything, a couple approached them.

They were a stunning pair.

"Trevor!" called out a man from the crowd, his arm waving, "I saw your boat... there off our Point... and I say 'for sure it was you!'"

Trevor was surprised.

A Museum Gala event of international appeal in the Nation's Capital saw the presence of diplomats often. But Gregor Vuoli, a man with a dark complexion, thick hair and ocean-blue eyes was a Russian who would be noticed anywhere.

And he loved boats.

Trevor grinned. "You should have hailed! I would have brought over a drink!"

"It looked like a raft party, all of you, at dusk...I *so* envy you!" he stamped his foot, beaming.

Trevor MacDonnell knew that the Russian Embassy kept a Dacha on the Chester River in the Chesapeake Bay. It was a beautiful point of land, and he sailed often in those waters.

"Yes! The kids had a great Regatta. We were suitably stern as their Committee Vessel…" said Trevor, his face intimating a fearsome expression. "But it's good for them to learn the rules. And safety, of course."

They laughed.

"How nice to see you Gregor… Please allow me to present my wife Amanda Wells" said Trevor.

"But of course" said the Russian "We have all heard of the lovely Mrs. MacDonnell…" he bowed slightly, her hand to his lips.

"And…My guest Ladevine DeBerle"

"Pleased to meet you" said the woman, "I am Russian" She proffered a few fingertips to touch.

She fixed her gaze on Trevor by way of a survey.

Average height, her face with eyes exquisitely brushed in dark shadows, she peered above a sustaining smile as if delivering a magical potent. From her neck hung a teardrop sapphire gemstone set in sparkling diamonds, large like a third eye.

Gregor, spotting a waiter, lifted two glasses off a passing tray, handed them first to the ladies, then two more for him and Trevor.

Judging from the pallor of his face and loss of words, Trevor seemed dazzled. Amanda saw him twice glance at the jewel laying softly against the olive skin of the woman's breast.

They chatted animatedly, the party crowd thinning as guests started to leave.

It was a remarkable piece of jewelry, Amanda had to admit. Especially as the woman displayed the gemstone, framed by a tightly draped bodice and bare back – her dress was entirely held together by a single clasp to show off the jewel.

Amanda sipped her champagne as the men talked.

Of course, it could have been costume jewelry, but the chain said it all. It hung from silver links like capstans threading a delicate hawser-line. The teardrop sapphire was real.

"Ah, There you are!" bellowed Lady Totteridge "I don't know about you, but I'm having the most marvelous time. Thank you so much for inviting me!" She spoke at length of her encounters, determining who from which Embassy had entertained her at their table, and there were several...

The band arrested all chatter with an announcement.

The crowd was moved on to the final event of the Art Auction, the *Piece de resistance*. By the third round of bidding, it became abundantly clear that Trevor was avoiding them, thought Amanda.

A new price was announced for a painting, and it solicited much applause from the audience for the cause. Museums could not live on grants alone. Amanda looked back casually at the tables behind them.

Twice Barbara waived at her, usually from the arms of someone she was dancing with...

Amanda smiled back, an accusatory leer in her eyes, leaving Barbara to chuckle.

Returned to their tables, Amanda spotted the Russian coupled seated at a table in the rear, its centerpiece a glass-encased candle arrangement emitting gossamer rays between tall wine glasses. Yet there it shone, the jewel at the chest!

They were not seated side by side. But Gregor was clearly having a wonderful time. She sat, perched like a golden eagle fixed on prey, a shadowed spectator to his storytelling.

She did not flinch, wave or smile when Amanda looked at her.

Amanda turned away, pulling her silk shawl slightly closer to her shoulders. The woman's eyes were fixed on their table, and judging from the introduction, Trevor was her target.

When the time finally came to conclude the event, Amanda's shoe pinched. The back strap of her damaged shoe had been wrenched, forcing her weight forward all night upon toes that now ached. Under the dinner table she had lifted her skirt several times to tighten the strap, but to little avail between invitations to dance; or to stand for a short applause as she walked onstage to announce the winner of a donation...

That, plus "a kiss from the beautiful Mrs. MacDonnell" as the MC announced.

Amanda was there as consort to her husband Trevor MacDonnell, British Emissary for Special Finance Affairs. But she had her own field of admirers.

She wrote a column in a respected newspaper, a weekly article replete with intellectual analysis on policy, if laced with good humor and encouragement for their hard work. Making decisions, she was known to say, was the hardest thing to do because choices always came at a price... She was known for her quips and insight, and she was popularly read.

It had been a long night.

Amanda looked around. Trevor, who must have now done his share of walking and dancing, was not beside her.

Neither was it easy to spot him in the crowd, nor to disengage him from those still chatting, even as the waiters began stacking the chairs...

* *

Located at the top of the hill on Massachusetts Avenue was the US Naval Observatory was the official residence of the Vice President of the United States. Next to it was the British Embassy compound.

A large sprawling office complex, it constituted one of Britain's largest overseas posts. The gated compound stood back from the boulevard, landscaped by trees and a modern glass rotunda. Not theatrical, by any standard, but it represented, up there at the top of the Avenue as a steadfast European bond. It was a hub of Euro-American interests that included all manner of state affairs from trade to trust; from policies to prowlers and, increasingly, intelligence.

Within the compound, the Chancery at the Diplomatic Embassy was a large structure - a classic brick Georgian architecture, and it housed the Head of Mission.

In a city of world players in transition, this place was a stage of acts from the center of power. Not measured in epochs - like a London or a Rome, but in political cycles for the longer view of the postmodern world. Especially since America held the Western standard for democracy, and the dollar now the world's currency.

Like the British, this avenue of Embassy row was base camp for all who labored for the greater good. And it was perhaps this tacit understanding that so puzzled tourists, sightseers, students and foreign bureaucrats who came visiting. For all the tumults, here, diplomacy could settle all, including the building across the street, a modern Embassy for the Vatican.

On the other hand, while a city of monuments, it sheltered with normalcy the motions of ordinary people doing ordinary things. Like walking a dog on along the Potomac River. Or jogging to work across the Smithsonian Mall. Or the Museum of Indian Affairs.

Here, people had lunch at the Crystal City Pentagon Mall. Or cheered at the Caps Center, or assembled peaceably at the steps of the Capital before Congress. Living in Washington DC was much like an endurance tour of unrelenting page-turning events, and here everyone worked hard.

Amongst those who had stayed at the Chancery House of the Embassy compound was Winston Churchill. His bronze statue, in open stride, stood just beyond the wrought iron gate. He had especially used his days in residence pleading with Roosevelt for aide in the WWII effort in Europe.

Other Royals had been housed there, including Edward VII on his Washington visits. His private collection of wines were still locked in the Cellar, it was said.

The Queen of England, Prince Phillip and members of the Royal family made it their home when visiting the United States.

Prince Charles with his wife Dianna had stayed there briefly. And it was not far from the bronze of Winston Churchill that Washingtonians expressed their unending sentiments of sympathy at her death, leaving flowers at the gate in spontaneous gesture, until they became a sea of blossom so large as to fill the boulevard sidewalks.

Amanda Wells, a working professional American, was frequently found in the Embassy offices collaborating with staff on topics ranging from trade to finance;

from modern art to colonial history. She was known as the *working girl on staff.*

But it was Trevor who insisted that they not live in the Chancery, citing Love as the reason for choosing instead to live in a Tudor house in Chevy Chase bought by his parents on their honeymoon during WWII, a home still owned by his family. It was a home kept warm, safe and updated over the years by a groundskeeper, Timothy Watson and his two sons.

The structure was a large comfortable home with cathedral ceilings. The structure, built by stonemasons during the decades of Cathedral construction was embellished with crenellated stonework; deep-timbered eves and large French doors. Within were porches and great rooms for spacious entertainment, the rooms finished with cabinet-carved paneling and overhead beams of mortice and tenon woodwork. Outside, rimmed by a brick wall that surrounded the perimeter, a garden lawn, old oak and elm flourished simply. Nothing could have suited Amanda better.

April, a Welsh springer, was staring with one eye patched in deep rich brown fur, the other in glossy white, and her tail wagging fiercely as she watched. Amanda would come around... She lay down and waited patiently. Amanda played tennis and swam at a local club. She especially loved to jog, often stopping at local shops. Washington, as far as she was concerned, had so many mature trees it was like living in a Park. And the life of an Emissary's wife was nothing but enjoyment in her favorite city. After all, she was American-born.

Not that she was letting Trevor down, she told Barbara, with their decision not to live at the Chancery. But she wondered if it were appropriate living in the suburbs like regular staffers, somehow abrogating their obligations.

Trevor assured her it was alright. As had his mother, when they called her in Scotland, and told her of their decision.

"*Acht* ...It's been a long time since Ah lived in a house..." she said in her playful Scottish accent. Something Amanda had to explain to her friend Barbara who had first asked about Trevor, long ago: What it was like to be married to a Scottish clansman, she had asked. Did he, for example, have a "wee-Scottish cottage"...? Or did he live on the *highlands*?

Amanda remembered that conversation well."No. It wasn't like that at all... They did have a home. Just not a house!"

"What then?" quizzed Barbara from New York City.

"It's a Castle."

"A Castle?" giggled Barbara

"Yes. As in...a long family tradition of the Glen... like a family ranch" she explained.

"Might it have plumbing...?" asked Barbara.

"Of course it does! The kitchen is..."Amanda gave up. But she almost laughed out loud. "It's..."

"*What*?" insisted Barbara.

"Well. Ok. It's just that we had a fight there, his mother and I... No. I mean, a food fight. See, she was loading this powdery flour into a bowl, and the kitchen staff told her it was already sifted for making patties - that's pastry...Only she sneezed, and I tossed some back at her...She looked up and went for it ...and by the time

Trevor walked in we were both standing there looking like a pair of Pillsbury Dough Boys...*Oh never mind!*"
 Silence.
"Barbara...?" Amanda asked.
Barbara was having quiet fits of laughter.
"It's the haggis thing that I can't quite do yet..." finished Amanda.
"The Haggis? ...Jeez!" giggled Barbara "I won't even ask..."
"Anyway, I'm coming home next month. With Trevor. He's been posted there!"
Then it occurred to Amanda that there was something that needed to be said. She paused thoughtfully.
"Barbara?"
"Yes?"
"Look, I never wanted to ask. But you said you were married once. What happened?"
A long pause followed. "Well, I don't know really. Perhaps because of family assets of inheritance ...In the end, her son made his choices!"
"I'm sorry Barbara. I didn't mean to pry...It must have been a very difficult time in your life"
"Oh..." sighed Barbara. "It was a difficult time. And...thank you for asking! I appreciate that you care."
So Chevy Chase it was for Amanda and Trevor.
And April, their newest puppy dog.
For now, the children were in England. The two oldest were in boarding school; the youngest still with her Nanny and Grandmother in Scotland, and due to arrive in a month. Arrangements were still being made.

Whatever little interior decorating she added to the old house was mainly restorative since it held midcentury seating; mirrors and art deco fixtures.

Only one faulty overhead lighting fixture in the main room needed replacement. So Amanda ordered an art nouveau sculptural Murano chandelier and hung it like an ornament above easy textures and neutral clustering of furnishings.

With a few large plants by the bright windows, the décor of the mid-forties appeared glamorous and not overwrought.

Both of them had settled in nicely, Trevor driven to work by the Embassy car, and Amanda filling her days with work and play – and exercise with April. But she would have liked to work more. This, she explained to Trevor one morning as he read the newspaper.

"*Umm*," he had said.

His work and *her* play, she laughed.

Umm, he said again. So she tore down his newspaper and landed in his lap. Those were halcyon days.

No more.

Those were the blissful days of *before*, the days *before* the Gala.

Until that night of the Gala, this had been their dream world. That is, until the last hour of the Gala when she raced down the steps and hailed a cab to take to the Leow's Hotel for the night, alone.

Why?....

It happened so unexpectedly. Almost when they were leaving, really.

Amanda had been searching for some time when she found him, and when she did, she was shocked.

Amanda had gone down to the Foyer where guests were leaving and collecting their coats.

She had checked the Great Hall beside the Coats Cabinet and opened a lateral broom-closet door.

She stood there, dazed.

He was not alone.

They were together in the narrow cloakroom, Trevor and the woman Ladevine DeBerle.

She, facing the door, had one arm aloft almost over her head, reaching for Trevor's head at the back of her neck, her face burning with pleasure and her gown loosened with a hand holding up only the bust and the sapphire gemstone.

"Darling!" he said, flushed, looking up from behind her. The woman lifted up her bodice and tucked the unzipped dress back up under her arm.

Amanda closed the door on them and stood outside, breathing softly.

**

Chapter 2

It was not what it seemed.
Trevor explained himself a dozen times.
The face that stared at Amanda from the newspaper picture was unmistakable. The woman she discovered in a cloakroom closet with her husband was listed in the Obituary section of the newspaper.
Not that the last two weeks had been easy.
The sudden and awful disorientation that attends doubt and betrayal were bad enough, even as logic must fight its way through all the facts... but what threw her were thoughts of anger as she pulled herself together.
The shock of seeing them together in that posture seared itself onto her consciousness like no other image could.
The evidence, as Trevor kept saying, was before her.
Thank God!
Perhaps in a few months she could smile, if not laugh it off, but at the time it all seemed too real and left her somehow damaged.
Still, the loss of life of the woman DeBerle was not what she expected to see in the morning newspaper.
Murdered, the article suggested, citing her as being a Russian visiting America.
What happened to the woman?

Why?
Did Trevor know anything about it?
The newspaper article said she was murdered in her apartment at the Watergate, an elegant apartment complex overlooking the River.

**

It wasn't until the next morning, when Amanda was pouring coffee that she realized she had forgotten something. A phone message, for Trevor. Mrs. Carlos the housekeeper had picked up.

"Signor, he say he have a package of materials he want to give you personally. Kendall, he say his name. He spoke with accent?"

Trevor put down his morning newspaper.

"Never heard of him!"

It was raining. From the library window the garden looked grey.

Amanda found it difficult to absorb.

They had talked.

The account of what Trevor said had happened seemed so far away, so distant in time, and so unlikely that she felt like an intruder.

She returned to the desk.

Yet, as she turned the sheets of the estate's inventory, she knew deep down in her heart that Trevor was telling the truth. He would be home shortly, and perhaps they could talk.

Barbara called.

"You got yourself married to a man from the old-world you know, from where all ye 'huddled masses' fled to land here at this very spot" she said invoking the immigrants of Ellis Island responding to words writ upon the Statue of Liberty.

…"An' it ain't gonna be easy - all them stiff-necked affairs of the Britts!"

Barbara had a talent for speaking directly, if with the heart of a Jewish grandmother. Barbara was always right of course, even as she was walking downtown New York City in her dark-shadowed eyes and trendy haircut. "But he loves you babe! I wouldn't worry about it. Taxi! Gottago!"

Still, the catalogue of the paintings and treasure listed in the family inventory of Kaerney Castle were impressive.

It read like a picture album of history:

The Duke of Kavearness in 1714 laying his sword in fealty before King James; the Clansmen of Mount Eeasterling in full battle dress of kilt and dagger.

Portraits of women of their realms, no less stunning...All of them images of hung painting on the walls of Trevor's estate, now secured, insured, and in Trust.

Then Trevor showed her the inventory of the next-century sketches; paintings and treasure from antiquity of heirloom tradition.

Amanda turned carefully to the photographs of recent history at Kaerney Castle:

Visiting viscounts and monarchs prior to the Coronation we imaged at the Castle. The King of England; his Queen in womanly hunting-gear; children and animals splayed out in happy gathering at their feet, all of them relaxed after an event – a Stag hunt in the hills of Scotland.

There, in their midst, was the family of her husband Trevor MacDonnell, monarchs themselves of their Scottish Glen tradition.

His grandfather and great aunt. Seated in a white cane garden chair, Trevor's grandmother, aunt and his parents; then, he and his brother as young children, their sister still a toddler...

The story was sad. A scandal really. In the collection of the leather bound album was a *Thank You* letter written by the Queen, along with a picture of herself wearing the full necklace:

> *"I never got a chance to wear this again, but in your efforts to search, you might find it helpful to see the necklace for identification purposes. Please do keep us informed if it should turn up on the premises of Kearney Castle. Again, with thanks. We had a wonderful time!"*

The necklace comprised of a rope of drop-sapphires; diamonds and pearls. It matched a small tiara upon her head of drop pearls. The necklace had been given on loan to be added to the Crown Jewels from her great Aunt, the Grand Duchess, a beloved monarch in another state - just prior to the socialist upheavals and unrest that swept Europe into war...

Amanda sighed.

Her hand touched the images, it was very quiet.

She looked carefully at the picture and understood the embarrassment that attended the account. The necklace had been stolen on that very hunting visit in the photograph of 1939.

Time had passed, and Trevor's family had never recovered the necklace. It was to be a disgrace that the MacDonnell family endured for generations, even causing the premature death of Trevor's grandparents, if not his Uncle who went to war insufficiently trained as an Airman. His father fought at Dunkirk.

Of course, with the benefit of hindsight, the necklace had in all probability been stolen by a member of the royal retinue that attended the royal visit, if not a spy.

At first, incidents of theft revealed spies intent on stirring discord and disunity amongst the royal households, heads of power themselves. Mainly it was to achieve public embarrassment.

Later, as the unrest grew worse, dastardly ploys seen by the Metropolitan Police were found to be financed operations specifically designed to arouse political suspicion and distrust of the monarchy by socialist provocateurs.

Thus, the lost necklace was kept quiet.

Soon, England was caught in the full grip of wars: The First world war and the overthrow of European monarchs, followed by the Second world war where survival of the nation became paramount.

Amanda looked carefully at the picture for the hundredth time, even using a magnifying glass to examine the image closely. There was no doubt.

No doubt at all.

On the table was the jewel.

The sapphire gem set in diamonds of drop-pearl shape before her on the table - was the same as those on the full rope of pearls worn by the Queen in 1939...

The royal image showed the necklace, each cluster arranged in a setting, hung from a neck-string of matching sapphires, and complemented by a matching broach; bracelet and tiara.

She picked up the jewel.

What Amanda had in her hand was one section of the whole. It had been broken down, the sapphires separated from the neck string.

Yes they talked.

"Oh, it's authentic all right" said Trevor later that night. "I just had it examined by a collector who wants to buy it!"

"Does it have much value?" asked Amanda.

"Oh my God, yes!" said Trevor, standing up brusquely and pouring himself a Scotch from the decanter on the sideboard.

"The collector consulted jewelers in Philadelphia and New York who identified the pattern, the diamonds; even the hand of the maker at the turn of the 18th century!"

"How sure can you be...?"

"No question. It was the one given to the Austrian Imperial Prince in the last century by the Dukes of Savoy as a gift, then passed to the Czar's family of Russia. By WWII, it was inherited by the Duchess, widow of the Czar's uncle, and sent to the Bank of

England for safekeeping and for use as a Crown Jewel...That's when the Queen wore it. It brought luck on the hunt, as the saying went amongst family..."

He walked to the window. "The Queen wore it only once!" He drained his glass, an old family wound worth drowning.

Amanda inspected the jewel. It lay there in a black velvet pouch, the leather case produced by those who examined it in New York.

Trevor was right on one matter, it was the same jewel as that worn by the Russian woman, Ladevine DeBerle, at the Gala. And if Amanda was to accept Trevor at his word, the moment of her appearance was indeed a compromising view of something that happened in earnest. Trevor was above reproach.

Apparently, the woman had wanted to give him the item, but as the chain from which the jewel hung was neither unbent nor reliable, she had tied it fastidiously around the clasp of her dress at the back of her neck.

She found it difficult to dislodge without loosening the stubborn clasp of her dress. The evening gown, which revealed much skin, gathered in a clasp at the neckline. They were at the coat-check counter when she realized she had to negotiate her fur coat; her bag and her dress to give him the jewel.

Trevor suggested she pop into the closet nearest the coat-check area with the idea that she would have privacy to take off the gown and rearrange her dress. But she could not unfasten the clasp, she asked him for help. He went inside to assist...

Unfortunately, the clasp did not come free easily. Trevor had to set his teeth to it, and as she lifted her arm to hold up the back strap of her dress, Amanda walked in to find her husband with his teeth closed on the clasp at her neck...

Amanda almost laughed.

No, it did not look good.

But it was remaining as a dark moment for both of them: For Trevor it brought back the memories of a a painful scandal against royals to whom his family was bound to honor and defend; and for Amanda, a failure of trust between herself and the man she loved with all her life.

Later that night, they vowed to search for reconciliation, even if it should come slowly.

For now that was all they could manage...

Still, the overriding question that refocused their attention, even after discovering how much the loss of the sapphire necklace had become to the family over the years, was *why* had the woman found Trevor, or even chosen to wear the jewel that night, let alone give it back to him...

And why was she dead?

That she was murdered in the city less than ten days later left more questions than answers.

Westminster, London

They executed the King on January 30th 1649.

Until now, for over a millennium, the Holy Roman Catholic Empire had held dominion over all kingdoms; all skills and trade - such that craftsmen, seamen, shipbuilding, trade merchants, licenses, armies, resources and discovery - lay firmly in the foundations of royal allegiances appointed by the Pope.

All kings became Rome's territorial holders of their kingdom's public treasure in tithes, gold, resources, land, manufacture, human laboring and all works of public industry and invention.

Spain amongst them, if not chief of the Holy Roman Empire of Europe and the world, acquiring gold from the Spanish Mexican colonies in great abundance.

Yet, since the sinking of the great *Spanish Armada* - a challenge to England posed by King Phillip of Spain, there resulted new opportunity for the English in territorial expansionism.

The execution of Charles I of England in 1649 occurred because he refused the Reformist ways of Protestant England. He held for the Catholic Papal authority over his realm: At his trial, Charles I invoked his *Divine Right* to rule as King, Papal-ordained by God, and claiming his right to reign as Absolute Monarch.

The English Civil War followed.

Under Oliver Cromwell, the country became *de facto* a republic under Protestant leadership.

Britain, from Roman-roots through medieval catholic empires of monarchy, had just enjoyed a century of Protestant rule since Henry VIII; followed by his daughter Queen Elizabeth I.

During that period a blossoming occurred of an early modern world offering individual agency for trade, and a burgeoning domestic consumption economy.
Yet the regicide of Charles I took its toll on the English, a people customarily led by royal sovereignty...
To reconcile factions, the monarchy was to be reinstated. The King's son, Charles II was declared the rightful heir to the throne of England.
However, having defended the cause of his father in the civil war, he had been defeated in battle, and Charles had II fled.
As a political crisis followed the death of Oliver Cromwell, Charles II was officially invited back to England in May 1660. A period of restoration of the monarchy followed, all legal documents now asserting that he had succeeded his father as King in 1649.
Charles II died in 1685, and was succeeded by his younger brother, *James II and VII*.
James II ruled England like his father, a Roman Catholic monarch. Predisposed to vapid liberality, he was deposed in *The Glorious Revolution* of 1688. He would became the last Roman Catholic monarch of England, Scotland and Ireland to rule the British Isles.

Parliament, descending from the ancient Barons of England as a legislative body, wrote now the laws of the land as Acts of Parliament, remaining a system of governance of the state deriving democratic legitimacy from its elected constituency representatives.

Parliamentarians were Protestants and Puritans, and it was their way to encourage civil laws and rights; independent license for individuals, merchants of venture and trades. In so doing, they were ending dominion of the Roman Empire, and embarking on independence for an early modern world of Western democracy.

It was radical.

In the colonies, New England with its Puritan settlers comprised of supporters of Oliver Cromwell in the civil war, known as the Commonweath and *The Protectorate*. They were reluctant to accept reinstatement of the monarchy. But they they did one by one, if reluctantly so: Rhode Island declared in 1660; Massachusetts in 1661, New Haven and subsequently Connecticut in 1662.

Maryland was a Catholic bastion until defeated in the Battle of the Severn in 1655 by Parliamentary forces. Its Governor aimed then to seek an early independent republic for the state, separated from England, a movement that would lead to the American Revolution in the next century.

Virginia remained loyal as a dominion of catholic monarchy, but declared for the Anglican Church of a Protestant England in 1660, chiefly on account of its merchant trading.

Finally, the Province of Carolina was given a concession by King Charles II in 1663, increasingly under pressure of an England divided and hungry for new domestic trade, growth and territorial expansion.

* *

Amanda jogged across the main street and walked into Starbucks where she ordered a coffee. She strolled up Mill Street, and came to the park.

Truro Park, surrounded by colonial houses, was an historical landmark of an old Tower. Small in size as towers go, it stood on a mound at the center of the grassy knoll and commanded a high spot.

Peeking between the houses, Amanda could tell there must have once been a wide view downriver on the one side, and across the point of land on the other. Perfect place to defend a Fort, and to keep Watch, she decided. She sat down on the park bench, sipping her Cappuccino, and watched the sun herald a new Atlantic Ocean morning.

A modest low black fence had been built by local devotees. A preservation club of sorts. It surrounded a structure that nobody understood. She leaned over and read the monument.

Evidently, many had tried to research it, and speculation abounded. But there were no answers in definitive terms. She leaned down to read the inscription once more. It was a Tower. Unfinished, or in remnant condition...A legacy, said the inscriptions from....

From when?

It had been standing here for 350 years!

Older, it was, than America.

How odd, she wondered. Who put it there? What did it represent?

Anyway.

She went back to her Hotel in downtown Newport. She had work to do.

Find ways to describe money in ways that have modern applications for Rhode Island and its economy.

That was her task.

Rhode Island was his Constituency. That was his State. Certainly, it had a long history. Could she find characteristics from its statutory legacy as a foundational colony of the Crown before it became a State? Could money be achieved in ways newly defined?

She wanted instinctively to ask for what purpose. But it was assumed that what he wanted to redefine language, perhaps to help his constituents make money and get jobs locally.

Obviously, that was his purpose. How silly of her to ask!

Money then, she supposed, should be described as the operational realities of the modern fiat monetary system in the United States, using the understanding of *Monetary Realism.* (MR)

OK, she grinned. How hard could this be...?

* * *

The New World.

George Lawton applied sand and water to his mix. It would meld the stone together.
His came from a London company, a Merchants' Guild that sponsored a settlement in the colony of Virginia founded by John Smith and his party.
But these were difficult times in the colonies, some called it the *Starving Times*.
Up here, the English had long fished in these waters. Thus, a treasure storehouse would be built within the mill tower of the Fort settlement. Just as he had done in the old world, he would build one here. The new settlement was called Newport, a seaport to Massachusetts.

It was 1619 when they convened an Assembly of governance at Jamestown. The next year, colonists arrived in Massachusetts.
 Already, Peter Minuit the Dutchman purchased Manhattan, calling it New Amsterdam. The Dutch West India Company was conducting trade in New York.
Above all, fur trade with the Indians was flowing in great abundance for merchants. In Maryland and Virginia, Englishmen grew tobacco, and sent raw materials like timber in return on ships...Then
Passage berthing for any wanting to come to the new world for venture, or opportunity, or independence.
Customs Agents tarried adroitly, full with exploit and commerce on ledgers.
The Spanish Holy Roman Empire watched contemptuously at such gain. Especially at kingdoms

attempting to harness trade and wrest control of their territorial colonial expansion, like the Dutch, the English and the Swedes.

And the same time, a newfound domestic market was flourishing in Europe. Ships sailing to the orient, the middle east, the colonies, all bring goods for their consumption, especially savoring products from faraway climates and consuming tobacco that unloaded off ships in bails.
For trade, coin was minted; copper was stamped, money exchanged, and gold was mined in the new world by the savage, as the Spanish put it.
In the battles for colonial territory and settlement rights by sovereigns, shipping traffic was plundered at sea, captured as prize in acts of tactical piracy.

The English had enemies. Marauding fleets could sail in and slaughter a colony. These were dangerous times, and the fortification of the colony was paramount. This, George Lawton knew. As was self-preservation...
Lawton peeled the scrapings off the stone and added shell lime, mixed with sand and gravel, to make mortar.
Slate and stones were all jagged and ill-shaped, all would have to be chipped and refined to fit together and stack firmly in reassemble for a strong column, just like a Roman colossus before it was covered over. He labored, and some in the town came to observe. The fitting and positioning was of close precision for a reason, he told them. Not only was it a load-bearing column, but finished, this Tower would have to shine

out. It had to hold its secrets. And it had to hold treasure within its stone creviced chamber.

Lawson had come from England to build the tower. From Chichester, where he had just completed another, up along the great Roman Fosse Highway, that was his tower too.

He liked the colony. His work not go unrewarded. Here the independent venture prevailed. In the new world, and they paid him well for his labor.

It was a masterful work, with enduring quality.

Later, in the will of Benedict, first Governor of Rhode Island, great grandfather of General Benedict Arnold of the Revolutionary war, the Tower that Lawson built at Newport, with its eight columns, would be listed as "my stone built Wind Mill" in 1651.

Lawton had positioned eight supporting pillars of the tower to face the main points of the compass. Many of the apertures were precisely aligned with astronomical stellar indicators.

At the summer solstice, the setting sun would shine through the west window onto a niche next to the south window.

An angle from the east window, through the west window, was 18 degrees south of west, the southern extreme moment of moonsets during the lunar minor standstill.

But the smaller windows formed alignments with cosmological surveying positions. These alignments should explain, for a stone mason like himself, the pattern of the windows and their *mathematical* celestial bearings, either in short form, or if projected, in long form to define the projected direct line to any particular place on the latitude and longitudinal lines of the earth: A fixed position for moving seasons, seas, and stations on the compass, as they would say in navigators terms.

Terms, that through the ages, represented the very latest in technological advances. And also, survey markers.

And here it was, centered in this tower. Here, the builder would meet his Master's expectations. In times past, such a Tower was the Keep of King's treasure, plate and grain.

Here, he decided, was the heart of a new kingdom. Markers of a survey territorial claim.

* *

Amanda returned from Boston. The Senator had asked for her report, and she would deliver it. Precisely what the Senator had asked her to do.

Today she would consult anthropological readings on labor and the history of community manufacturing and business, of all things. Especially early laws, and measure new regulation of business.
Nation-building depends on trade – to quote Jefferson.

The Senator called. He wanted to know about what she was finding. And she told him, in as simple terms as she could find, even as she was quick to point out that her findings were still inconclusive...
"What's the issue?"
"It is not a conflict. It is merely a refinement" she said.
"Go on..."
"Free Market capitalism is a doctrine that advances our society, right? It's about the way we do R&D, develop markets etc... it's all part of that matrix..."
"And...?"
"Well Sir, coupled with that premise is the accountability of *defending* those efforts!"
"You mean Defense? As in defense of the nation?"
"Umm... Not exactly. What I mean is this: When left without reasonable *protection*, then local labor and jobs and training are affected..."
"How is that?" he asked.
"Trade Agreements. Compliance. Corporate Taxes. Regulation. Copyright and Patents...They're our intellectual property which as a commodity. If left unprotected, it can do damage to the local economy!"
"Exactly how?" he queried

"Because the seduction of global-scale is too tempting for companies. They won't hold back for local hiring!" she blurted out.

She regretted her words. It was an opinion.

He paused. "Explain!"

She was reluctant.

"No. I mean it, explain more fully ..." he insisted.

"Local talent...They're unable to compete for the-job-next-door, chiefly because the employer is searching a 'field of global hires' to achieve cheap labor and more profit!"

There, she said it. And he was waiting for more.

"Further, technology makes remote activities more viable..."

"Is that so bad?"

"No. It's a good thing. I mean...Without protection, there is risk of cyber-theft of our stuff across the highways of the Internet by unregulated foreign interests..."

"Hacking?"

"Well. Its more than hacking. Its software predators and spider-crawling and data-mining."

"Amanda, these are well financed global information Tech companies, and they are doing well..."

"Yes Sir. Yet infiltrating our source material; resources and intellectual products for their re-marketing...It's big business. Big commerce. And big profits!"

"Especially good for us stockholders!"

"Yes Sir. Still, our financial landscape holds assumptions for mainly in two tiers of thinking: One risk management for international investment strategy; and the other free flow of capital."

"Isn't that what our business schools teach?" he asked.

"Yes! But with a prejudice. While these practices attract endowment-dollars for big name universities, especially liberal and Jesuit Institutions touting ethics and progressive policies, they don't put the American national interest first!"

"What about Union laws?"

She paused, never thinking that he was a banker himself.

"Labor laws don't dictate finance. Nor do they set doctrine of national interest...That's not relevant here entirely."

"But they *do* affect local labor regulations" said the Senator. "The policy of government is my responsibility, isn't it?"

"Yes Sir. It's just a "creep" of things that occur with advancement and technologies."

He was about to ask her for more, she knew it. But she did not want to go further. These were her thoughts, and she didn't think they belonged on a policy paper for the Senator. If necessary, it was for him to change laws...

He understood.

Instead he said "What do you recommend?"

"Just more local hiring of geographic American talent, and training! Training that amounts to trade certifications, applying the best of American thinking for local participation. Especially with so much unemployment. It will pay off...I'm confident of that."

"How does Regulation affect my state?" he wanted to know "So, err...make that more clear for publication, will you?"

"Yes Sir."

"I want this to go before the Senate Hearing!"

"Yes Sir."

"And then I want this behind me. Wrap it up quickly, will you please?"
"Yes Sir."

It wasn't much later that her Notes came in handy.
"The government plays a facilitating role in helping to regulate and manage the infrastructure within the system of money: If properly utilized, the government can be an extremely powerful tool in helping to stabilize and create efficiencies within the money system."

Her cell phone buzzed. Barbara.
"So.." she said "have you called him?"
Amanda paused and looked up at a crisp blue sky touch with the briefest of cloud.
"Thought so! And why not?"
Amanda opened her mouth, her thoughts a jumble and her heart still bruised.
"I'll call him when I feel ready ready..."
"Call him! You've shut him down!"
"I just don't feel..."
"When does a woman *ever* feel ready?" said Barbara in her twangy New York style.
"Call. You'll feel ready, trust me!"
"Barbara!" admonished Amanda. She was gone.
Of course she was referring to Trevor.
No, she had not called him since she left Washington.
She stood there, her thoughts a muddle.
She walked down the street, and zipped into a coffee shop. Barbara was right. She should call.
Later.
How she would have liked to discuss this with Trevor.
She turned away, then opened a bottle of water.

Then suddenly she knew what Trevor would say. She was having a crisis of confidence: She was on the right track. *Keep at it!*

So...Back to work:

"The monetary system exists primarily for private purpose in order to create a system for efficient exchange of goods and services. The private sector plays the lead role in helping to advance the well-being of society..."

**

George Lawton, the builder, knew things.

Perhaps for the noting of seasons and times, Amanda later wondered. She had contacted the club that tended the moment, and she got various versions of what happened here. But nobody could understand it. Still, she jogged there every morning, and sat at the bench.

She took out her cell phone. She would call Trevor and tell him all about this place!

It captured her imagination, something about this tower was telling...What was the builder *saying?*

Maybe something that society would count as pivotal to their survival, and resolve.

The landmark was resolute, beckoning her to consider things...things she was having to grapple with today.

In constructing the Tower, perhaps he relied on numerical landmarks and locations, territorial claims by expansionists, projecting linear extensions beyond the confines of this stone tower. What informed his motives, here?

She looked it up, and all around her, long before the settlement developed into a modern town.

These ideals, numerically expressed in architecture, had universal designations of mathematical measurement that had survived for centuries, if not millennium.

But how? Why here, and for what purpose?

Nor were these details unknown to the skilled.

Such technological understanding, beginning with the Egyptian builders of the pyramids, had been ascribed to many landmarks over the centuries, including some of the earliest civilizations of builders and masons.

Some of the oldest known stone-marked gathering places, she realized, like Stonehenge, were the measure of time and seasons centered: From it, all society revolved.

And it would have sacred, later religious and moral overtones for any community.

How else do you organize a society, a new world even? So definitely this had a purpose. Only, why was there no historical provenance? Had its price been too costly to recount?

But not at its founding. Amanda could only imagine what Lawson knew and what he didn't know.

So, what Lawson knew was that he was replacing with stone the previous tower made of wood. Its purposes here, on this spot, was therefore legitimate and carried official authority. This he also knew, having just completed one similar tower in England at Chesterton, in 1632.

Clearly, someone told him the winds here were fierce, shuddered Amanda, especially if it was used as a wind-powered stone mill, at first.

What did that suggest? An agrarian world? A central storehouse? A Keep of significance that was defended by a Fort?

For one hundred and fifty years, up to the American Revolution, this tower signified an authority!

 So, he built his structure upon eight towers rather than six as he had on the Roman Fosse of England.

Above open ground, defended by arches, two higher floors were upheld with timbers, their sockets still visible in the stone...

The lower stone floor housed millstones; a great spur wheel, and hurst-frame and sack hoist-rope passing through the floor trap, like that used at Fosse Way.

The upper chamber was therefore a mechanical hoist floor with a brake wheel; main gearing and winding winch. It had lifting power for dead-weight.

What could that be: For Arms? Cannon? Iron or other metals of value...

But whereas grain was stored there, an open timber staircase was also used as a watchtower and fortification – a storehouse for provisions and treasure.

Lawson must have considered that the arched tower should have an unusual winding gear, the cap possibly winded by a hand-operated winch having a spur and worm gears. Or, a circular treadmill below for oxen to pull for leverage?

But *what* was he *defending*, wondered Amanda. What was his world like? For what purpose, and how did they organize?

Medieval, yet teeming with opportunity, replete with assumptions of ancient law...

Since the Roman Empire, feudal Princes owned lands, resources and labor, the concepts of sovereignty were shaped by land resources. That was the motive of conquest.

Embracing early concepts of expansion, it was territorial land-lords searching for trade while proselytizing the message of Christianity.

At first, they were just Princes in the provinces of Europe that marked the early Holy Roman Empire.

Some key princes of Europe of the higher rank periodically nominating a high priest of God, a Pope. Thus it was his role to uphold their authority according to the scriptures.

Such a prince was a "Nominator" of the Pope. Such a titular legacy carried on through the centuries as a royal duty to perform with the title of certain territories.

Also, at their conclaves, if one Prince died, another leader had to be appointed for his territory.

Prince- Electors, Amanda knew, were members of the electoral college within the Holy Roman Empire since the 13th century.

Theirs also was the privilege of electing a principal King over the whole Roman empire. The King of the Romans was elected by Princes from the middle of the 16th century onwards, a title known as the Holy Roman Emperor.

Locally, markets were centrally organized for the survival of village constituencies. Some village laborers concentrated on foundry works, others cloth dying; food harvests; brick-making, or mining. Commodities of value for trade and exchange.

Further, as peasants gathered for central protection from their Prince, and as they were routinely summoned by bell-ringing for village proclamations, laws, and reminders for tithes, the authority of the church at the heart of the community grew in significance.

Especially as princes increased their demands upon communities, showing sanction from God, for aspirations of expansion, or levy, or conscription.

Here, what Lawson's Master did *not* tell him as he built this tower, was *who* they were, exactly. Nor what their intentions might have been.

Amongst those early "princes" were some from the territory known as *St. Clair*, or "Sin-clair."

One was named Hugh de Payns.

Married to the sister of the Duke of Champaine, Henry de St. Clair, Hugh de Payns had joined with a powerful prince and broker of the First Crusade.

The Crusades were ritual pilgrimages by princes to propagate the faith and engaged in traffic and trade of the ancient market routes, including the silk road caravans from the Orients.

Many returned with treasure, spice, gems and silk cloths and gold coin.

As disciplined knights with swords, they were sworn to defend the holy city of Jerusalem for their Faith of Christianity.

So what were the Knights Templar doing in the new world? Had they really come to America to exploit trade and wealth?

Amanda was far from finished, even as dinner was due in an hour. She needed to finish one more page of her Notes:

"In many market based sytems such as the USA, the money supply is essentially privatized and controlled by private banks that offer loans, this so as to build deposits in the vault."

Funny, thought Amanda. Most people think that it's the government that controls the money supply, or creates it!

* *

Washington DC

"HELL NO! WE WON'T GO!"
The marching protesters swarmed the steps of the
Capital at 9 a.m. under a crisp blue-sky morning.
Shipped in by bus, they occupied a platform ready-
made for marching protestors. Beside it were courtesy
sanitation bathrooms.
Here, they exercised their constitutional right to
assemble peaceably, as their MC put it.
And they were having some fun.
Wall Street had flayed the country, they shouted.
Laws established in the New Deal favored by Roosevelt
under the influence of a socialist movement had been
betrayed, they said.
They circled "Down with Wealth!"
Another round "Down with Wall Street!"
A big shout "Occupy... Or Hell No! We won't go!"
The police watched, wary.
The city was swarming with tourists for Washington's
Cherry Blossom Festival at the Tidal Basin
The marchers stopped at noon for a picnic lunchtime.
Tourists waved, some took pictures.

*****

She would just finish up some of her Notes, then leave she decided. Or, as Trevor suggested, explain the role of the Federal Reserve.

"The Federal Reserve (the central bank of the country)and the government have a symbiotic relationship and together they issue currency to the monetary system. That is, currency..."

She paused. Better explain:

"Currency, is something known as "outside money" – because it comes from outside the private sector..."

Amanda paused, how odd to consider that money was produced by the private sector, and that anything produced by the government was considered "outside" that paradigm.

She shrugged, then went on:

"That currency accounts for bank reserves cash notes and coins."

Trevor called. She told him what she just wrote.

"How the Crown would have liked to get its hands on that in the 17th century!" he laughed.

"The Fed, who issues the bank reserves, the US Treasury is the other issuer of outside money in the form of cash and coins. Household, business and state governments are users of public sector supplied currency, and also private bank made moneys..."

The Senator called.

"I'm not going in!" said the Senator to Amanda on the phone. "There's hell to pay out there, and we've decided to cancel the Conference meeting for the day. Make it next week, same time, if you will, please?"

Amanda was in the kitchen having coffee, not yet fully dressed to go into the city when she took his call.

The Conference was scheduled for the afternoon session of Congress.

She sighed, frustrated. Then she thought about it.

Frankly, the postponement suited her fine. Whatever it was that he said had "caused the disturbance" downtown didn't worry her much. These things happened all the time.

For Washingtonians, protest was something of a normal event, if not a flavorful color to city culture.

But the Senator did seem a little jittery.

She agreed, of course. As she was expected to do.

Was there something here she was missing?

Oh well.

And now she had the day to herself. A treat!

She thought about continuing with work anyway. Even if she stayed in place at her home office. However, having placed everything in readiness the night before, all materials had been packed and prepared to go: Her briefcase by the door was bulging.

Tomorrow, in more casual fashion, she would go in and chat with the staff.

So for now, Amanda decided she would catch up on some social calls...

Later, she would go shopping in Chevy Chase - she needed a fresh look in blouses for her suits.

Then she would drive down to Georgetown, park underground, and walk up to Dean and DeLucca for luscious things; things like blue bottles, wine, jam preserves and New York cheeses.

After that, perhaps pop in to visit her friends at the Antique Gallery in the Paper Mill.

Tonight she would prepare a delicious gourmet meal...

She sipped her coffee and smiled.

Today would be a fun, relaxing day...

* *

The Paper Mill was a red brick structure rehabilitated from a packing warehouse on the waterfront of the Canal.

There was a time when in those dark corners and alleys, it had shipped products and government paper all over a growing nation. No more.

The wars had taken their toll, and progress left them behind. Thus, like much of old Georgetown, it had suffered the vagaries of upheavals, disrepair and neglect.

Now it enjoyed its renaissance. The district constituted high-priced condos and elegant galleries for tourists and visitors to the nation's capital.

The Antique Gallery of Simone and Simone found its place there, across the courtyard from the old canal, once a barge causeway pulled by draft-horses moving coal and cargo.

The shop was framed by thick blossoms from terracotta containers, brick troughs of water fountains and natural side grass. It was elegant, cozy and not far from a riverfront of parks had been upgraded for joggers, perambulators and a public water spout.

Simone and her father owned the Gallery now.

She and Amanda had been friends in College, and later she earned her PhD in Art History. The History of French Theater, she said, was the topic of her dissertation.

Simone's knowledge of color, stage props and special effects through the centuries were her specialty.

Such elements had given Europe a richness and public splendor, explained Simone, and they were always part of her Galley exhibits.

Her father joined her. He came from France after her mother died, and together they managed the Gallery in Georgetown.

Known for its items from the curious to the splendid, their Gallery was garnering fame from Miami to New York. Mostly it was European Art, Austrian and French, if not Russian bought by Katherine the Great for the Hermitage in the 18th century that they were acquiring. But mostly, they were known for their congeniality and knowledgeable disposition.

Over the years, Trevor and Amanda had bought wonderful things in the store. And with them, a lot of happy memories.

Without Amanda, Simone often said, she would never had completed her program. And forever, to them, Amanda would be family.

It came as a surprise therefore, when Amanda found the Gallery dark and closed.

She was about to turn away when she noticed a shadow. It materialized at the door, Simone appeared.

A hug and a kiss on both cheeks, and their continuing friendship soon turned to a conversation that left Simone distraught.

"What happened?" asked Amanda.

"We've been burglarized! They came during the night, perhaps after the protest march. And they broke in and stole almost everything we had here!" said Simone.

"Your father..."

"Fortunately he is in France. I have not told him!"

"But what of the Alarm systems?"

"They were disabled...*Imagine!*"

"Wow, Simone. That sounds serious. Did you talk to the police?"

"But of course! They say we should stay closed. But I persuaded them to keep it out of the paper. Our business as you know, is by word of mouth and reputation. I do not wish it to be known that we are unsafe here..."

"Certainly not. Especially considering the rent you pay to be here!"

"*Precisement*" said Simone, her eyes betraying a touch of fear.

Amanda waited.

"Are you alright Simone? Would you like to stay with us?"

"No thank you! That's very kind. I have tons of work to do. Insurance claims...etc."

They had tea.

"So, if the alarm was disabled, and you say you had a theft, it would suggest not just random vandalism, but a premeditated act?"

"Mais yes!"

"What are you saying, exactly?

"Our entire *Russian* collection was stolen."

"Was it worth a lot?"

"A fortune! I could not afford to insure it. It was a gift, a loan, imagine!"

"Oh Simone..."Amanda gave her a hug. "What can we do to help?"

Simone took a minute, but she said nothing.

It was a sad indictment for the city, observed Amanda. The robbery had been specific and targeted.

Why?

They walked.

The traffic of students, tourists, shoppers strolling behind them was a normal thing in these parts.

They crossed over the Canal and up to Dean and DeLucca. They ordered coffee and pastry, commiserating over the details of the robbery.
Gradually, Simone relaxed.
Those that walked by left their shadow, it was an open-air café.
In this place of visitors, languages were spoken as they came and went. Here, the crowd would linger. Watching, waiting.
By the time they parted, Simone was much more cheerful. Amanda promised to call daily until her father returned.
The time with Simone had passed so quickly that most of the afternoon had waned.
Amanda had parked two blocks away, and she walked along M Street, its chrome and glass shop windows a brassy gossamer from a setting sun.
The figure that came twice into her line of vision did not surprise her. She walked on.
Only later, when she entered the book store and then reemerged, she noticed the same figure.
Then again, around the block towards the Garage...
The sun now danced between the trees, its shadows on the canal elongating.
She thought a second.
Impossible that she was being followed!
Perhaps a friend of Simone, just someone thinking they were still connected or something, a patron of the gallery wanting to ask a question. This was a city of questions. Tourists asking directions. Visitors asking for parking. Dog-walkers asking for water. It was as if Washington DC...
She turned the corner.
He followed.

Georgetown was on a hillside. She darted into the lower level of a reconstructed multi-tiered Mall. She ran down the steps to the river level and emerged at grade with Garage parking. She ran, silly perhaps. Just in case.

Thank God. He was gone!

She climbed in the car, paid her ticket, and drove up two levels up to pop out to the street, some daylight remaining.

He was across the street. Watching. Almost waiting...

She revved the engines and roared down to Jefferson Avenue, then on to the Parkway.

She glanced back only once. She saw him in the rear view mirror.

He had not turned away. He was still watching her car disappear. He was very recognizable in the distance. He wore a hood attached to his sweatshirt.

* *

Siam was a Blue point Siamese cat. His place was at the window perch of the kitchen where he paced like a sentry.

He was sent from Scotland by Trevor's mother as a gift for the household.

Though condescending enough with other household pets, Amanda wondered how it was that this aggressive breed could be so winsome for Trevor.

It came as no surprise when she discovered Trevor swinging his arm loose from the dining table and pass a table scrap to his cat without anyone noticing.

Or, how this feline poised its head to receive auto-strokes from Trevor. "Where's my alley cat?" he would say and get away with it.

For everyone else, it was a fierce blue-eyed gaze of disinterest from this cat.

Except when Amanda was on her knees gardening. Only once did the cat approach her, as if in appreciation of her efforts to redeem a flower bed.

Otherwise, it was disdainful respect and a steady pacing at the window.

So when Amanda came barreling into the kitchen carrying a crystal bowl of tall-stemmed orchids, her peripheral vision was totally accustomed to the shadowy sentry movements of Siam across the window perch.

But this was not Siam.

The apparition just stood there, a man in a hoodie, his face against the window, staring at her from outside.

Amanda could have dropped the bowl.

She could have ...except that he was too close to disengage from; his stare was direct and dark. He was clearly standing on their porch!

She was shocked.

Clearly, he was at her door, giving her time to respond. He could have opened the kitchen door himself and come in. Or, he could have knocked at the front door. Or, he could have ...

Instead, he just stood there. Waiting. Then he stepped back. Waiting.

She looked straight at him. He alarmed her, that's all, and she put down the vase carefully.

Perhaps he was a delivery boy. Perhaps someone lost, or too clueless to know better. ..

Perhaps...he was an intruder.

Obviously, he had come in from the back alley and opened rear gate, walked through the garden, and climbed the deck steps to the back house porch.

But he waited, if deferentially.

She opened the kitchen door.

He was soaking wet and tugged at his rain gear with a pale face, his hood over her head like a monk in a robe.

"Can I help you?" she said

Kendall, he said his name was. Was Trevor in?

Amanda paused. *He knew Trevor!*

"I need help" he said, his accent vaguely familiar to Amanda. "I'm in trouble and want shelter" he said. Just like that.

 "Excuse me. Err...what did you say your name was?" She was alone in the house. Trevor was in New York, Clara the maid gone, and it was six o'clock in the evening.

"No. I'm afraid he won't back until...later" she said.

The man shivered, his darkened eyes turning from pleading to fear, and his haunting demeanor looked intimidated. He seemed to be at the end of his rope.

"Won't you come in for something to drink?" she said, He did ask for Trevor by name, did he not?

He thought about it.

"No." he said "Thanks" and turned away.

A car drove him off. Or so it appeared. Until Amanda peeped out the upstairs window and saw him walking away at a distance. He must have talked to the driver however. Perhaps amicably. Perhaps not.

The car was surveillance.

*** ***

Chapter 3

In his official capacity in Washington D.C. Trevor did not like to keep people waiting.

He was on the phone at his desk where he and his Embassy staff enjoyed absolute authority of their sovereign government, with all guarantees of safety and security by their host country. That was the global practice of diplomacy. Or so it was supposed to be.

Sitting outside his office was the FBI of the United States. Being accustomed to having entry to premises anywhere, and for any reason, they had neglected to make an appointment. Yet they received every courtesy from the British, a close ally to the United States.

Trevor had to keep them waiting. On the phone was the Irish Representative of the Diplomatic Consulate in New York.

They spoke on a secure line.

"His name is Kendall. He got out of Dublin undetected. He is wanted by the Americans for local trouble, but I suspect it's his Intelligence information that they want: Names of tax-evaders; offshore banking accounts, and corporate shells that they want to get their hands on following the banking collapse in Europe."

"How is that?" asked Trevor

"He was a banker. He copied everything. Kept data. Hacked everything."

"That makes him quite a liability, certainly!"

"That makes him a high target loose cannon sitting on Europe's most sensitive data. Much of the Irish banking systems were tied in with Europe's main banks - also looking for ways to evade taxes..."

"Umm"

"It's a difficult situation, considering the political fall-out. The Americans are worried..."

Trevor also knew that the center-right Fianna Fail party has been in government for years, during which time Ireland became one of the richest countries in the world per capita terms. Something the Americans were quite happy to accept for a long time, until now.

"Why now?" said Trevor

"Ireland as you know became one of the biggest victims of the global financial crisis. This threatens the very basis of the Fine Gael...It's a mess, just now!"

Trevor knew the Fine Gael was another center right party that had pledged to push through the EUR 9 billion in cuts agreed to by the outgoing government, and under very contentious conditions.

"I don't pretend to know the full scope of things. But I suspect the darker sides to banking involve dangerous business with large entities..." said Trevor, looking at his watch.

"Of course it is! Underwriting arsenals for certain unfriendly nations etc...Perhaps to get around our official government sanctions. Anyway, this we must know about. Or at least, be the first to know about if it gets out..."

"Do you know where he is?" asked Trevor.

"No. Only one American does. His name is James Lloyd. He says he knows you. Stand by. He may be in touch. Let us know, will you please Trevor?"
"Will do!"
He hung up and leaned over to catch a glimpse of his secretary on the other side of his office door in the front foyer. He waved.

"The Emissary will see you now" announced Fiona in her social-secretarial voice.
The sweetness on her face betrayed nothing.
As far as she was concerned, there were just some things that had to be done internally before a host country could barge in with police...
Fiona Beasley was an old bird on the staff who had survived at the Diplomatic Embassy for years. This was not the first crisis...

> *"Last seen passing through Dublin Central on way out of the country ... straddles the main highway to Dublin airport. There they would have seen him and imaged him..."*

It was a message just posted to him by Fiona herself.
Trevor realized that for Dick Kendall to have evaded the authorities at that point was feat enough.

They walked in. If Trevor's official visitors found him seated at his desk reading his laptop, they were unperturbed.
Not an altogether rude distraction, while receiving visitors in one's office, but an allowance, so to speak, for only the most privileged diplomats in Washington.
Trevor stood up and came forward.

"So good of you to come! And I do apologize for keeping you waiting" said Trevor.

Fiona walked in, rearranged some furnishing fixtures, and turned to offer the visitors coffee or tea.

Trevor's office door was shut behind them, Fiona looking at Trevor directly.

Fiona returned to her computer. She was taking notes from a phone call. A phone call that might interrupt Trevor's meeting with the FBI.

She proceeded to type another message to Trevor.

Trevor toured his office with his visitors, showing them a few pictures, then offered them seating forward of his desk at a side lounge-seating arrangement comprised of leather armchairs.

He returned to a side seat with an low glass-top coffee table where he could glance at his laptop screen discretely, placed there by Fiona for his view only.

> "KINDELL TOLD THEM HE MANAGED TO GET OUT - ONLY HOURS AFTER THE FINANCIAL COLLAPSE OF IRELAND...

Fiona used bold lettering so that Trevor could read her words on his screen some feet away without appearing to take his eyes of his company.

> HE WANTED TO GET TO ...**BOSTON**.
> FAKE CONTACT AT HARVARD AS COVER...
> ID FALSIFIED TO ENTER THE COUNTRY.

They wasted no time in making themselves clear.

"We are interested, Mr. MacDonnell, in the whereabouts of Mr. Kendall."

Trevor nodded respectfully.

"And we...err... are concerned for his protection!"

Trevor nodded appreciatively.

They had been briefed, these two, with all the trimmings of Wall Street's polish and charm. *"Unofficially,* of course" said the one.
"Of course!"
Neither one of them was one hair away from the bloodhounds of Baskervilles. Trevor smiled graciously. He got up, offered coffee, turned around, and glanced at his screen.

"LAST OFFICIALLY WASHINGTON 12th OF THE MONTH...NO ALIBI..."
Trevor sat down and crossed his legs.
What they wanted, he knew, was to attain him; file charges and retain him for questioning.
He took two sugar dots and dropped them into his coffee.
"We'll do everything we can to help" he said, his eyes blue and shining above a great big smile.
Trevor's job was to get to him first; secure him for extradition procedures...
But he knew that extraditions could take a long time to effect, *conveniently* for the host country! At least they were diplomatic. And they were asking.
He nodded, careful to keep his eyes even.
"I'm not entirely sure where his whereabouts might be." said Trevor.
Had Kendall tried to make contact with him?
"He may be a dangerous threat, possibly armed..." said Mr. Todd.
"Umm" said Trevor.
"And the police should attain him ..." affirmed his partner Mr. Sampson. "So...you have had no contact with him?"
"No. It might scare the hell out of my wife..." admitted Trevor boyishly.

They grinned.

"As you know" said Mr. Todd, "He worked in Dublin..." he looked at his notes. He was at some leading banks... in their Accounting Departments"

"I see" said Trevor, glancing at the computer.

JAMES LLOYD. INFO, DOCS, INTEL ON WEALTH-DEPOSIT ACCOUNTS- VAULT BOXES REMOVED FROM SWISS BANKS THE YEAR EARLIER...

Mr. Todd was more than investigative officer for the FBI. He was an attorney.

This was no enquiry asking for his cooperation: This was informing him of his obligations as a matter of Justice on US soil, something that should have been officially channeled through diplomatic correspondence. Instead, they had walked right in and made their demands known...

"Ireland's economic troubles are largely due to aggressive lending by the nation's banks to property developers" proceeded Mr. Sampson, relishing the lecturer mode

"The cost of repairing the banks has risen steadily since 2008, and a further EUR 35 billion may yet be needed to recapitalize them -- much of it coming from American sovereignty funds!" he said with an upturn to his voice, clearly agitated.

"My God!" said Trevor, wondering how much also came out of the Bank of England, and curious that he failed to mention the balance sheets of US $14 Trillion at Central Banks.

Trevor remained politely attentive.

"It's that we need to find him and question him about ...certain information that he might have known about while there..."

A stalling tactic.

"Wow!" said Trevor "Of course! I understand completely your position. Your interests are valid. I shall do what I can to let you know if we hear anything at all..."

HE INFORMES ...THAT ONE OF THE BANK VAULT BOXES STOLEN HELD SOFTWARE OF LISTED NAMES, ACCOUNTS, NUMBERS, BANK ROLLS AND OTHER TRADING INFORMATION THAT CAME THROUGH IRELAND FOR EVASION...

No wonder they wanted Kendall.

HE ESCAPED CAPUTRE IN BOSTON WITH DATA/ DOCS. MAKING DATA COPIES, AFRAID OF REPERCUSSIONS AND INCRIMINATING MATERIAL OF BANKS AND ACCOUNT HOLDERS FOR TAX EVASION AND OFFSHORE ACCOUNTS...

"We want to bring accountability to the table" Todd was saying, with Sampson nodding.

"Of course!" said Trevor, knowing that lecturing by host countries was gratuitous crap.

What was more realistic was the hidden unemployment following the Irish collapse - a rate edging close to 24%.

Worse was the quiet despair...An exodus of 100,000 people leaving Ireland to find work elsewhere.

They were done with him.

"So, if you hear anything at all...we'd like to question him ourselves..."

"Yes!" said Trevor, deferentially.

I HAVE SENT HIM TO NEW YORK.

Trevor suddenly put down his coffee.

What he found so distasteful was the thirst for Irish blood, world wide, as long as it was tainted with money: Thank God that his last task before leaving for Washington while still in Britain was to offer an Act in Parliament that would *Stay the Rule* that stipulated that once an Irishman left the country, he would lose his right to vote - an outmoded law long overdue for reform!

-Money and distress was one thing, but to lose your soul was another, he had once told Amanda.

But this was America, as Todd and Sampson just explained.

-Not that the Europeans were any better, thought Trevor. Kenny's Irish government had negotiated with European leaders, including German Chancellor Angela Merkel, a fellow Christian Democrat: Ireland's debt problems had threatened the stability of the euro zone. Should Kenny seek to reschedule some of the debts of the banking system, it would incur losses for German and French banks, no question...

Even greater damage would be inflicted on banks from *outside* euro-zone countries, especially if the government were unable to repay its own debts.

Ireland was swimming in shark-infested waters. This, the British government was keenly aware of. Certainly the situation for Ireland was grim. But difficult as their histories had been, if you damaged Ireland, you were damaging Great Britain...

He got up and showed his visitors the door.

* *

He was a wanted man for damage to an Irish bar in Boston. And it would be all Trevor could do to keep Kendall from being taken into custody by the FBI, he decided.

Trevor had Yusef drive him to the Chancery. There was more to the story that he supposed.

And even though it was three weeks of effort to sort out with attorneys from the FBI and the Department of State, it was clear the man was seeking diplomatic immunity for reasons not entirely made clear.

Trevor understood why.

He had intelligence that he was trying to find a home for.

"From *where* is he?" asked Amanda, later that night.

"From Ireland" said Trevor over his Pasta primavera.

"What?"

"Yes. It's complicated. But the Banking meltdown and the financing deals that went down are of interest to the Americans..." he looked up, his fork aloft. "We need to see the first draft before the American's haul him up for fraud..."

"Woah!" she said, "Ireland?...Since when is Ireland the enemy?"

He put down his fork and raised his napkin to his lips, a wry look on his face. "Well... you'd be surprised m'dear...err...Well No. This is different. There is something *else* going on here."

"Like what?"

"He is wanted for murder..."

"Are you *serious*?"

"Well. He killed a man!"

"*Killed* a..." Amanda sat down. "When?"

"Last week. Slit his throat."

"My God Trevor..."

"Yes. But that's not what I am worried about..."
"So you're sheltering a fugitive who intruded our home..."
Now it was Trevor's turn to stare.
He looked like he had had a long day and needed time to sort through his thoughts.
"Don't worry. If he wanted to kill us, he would have succeeded. He's a trained paramilitary officer..."
She raised her hand to her mouth, searching for answers.
"No" said Trevor "Relax. He is *not* a threat. He came here for help. He needed shelter!"
"Shelter from *what*?...In our home, out here?..."
She regretted the words the second they were uttered, having assured him a million times that living in a home outside the Embassy was as safe as any other.
"I'm sorry" she said "I didn't mean that..."
He looked down, perhaps reconsidering their decision. Or perhaps elsewhere with his thoughts.
She waited.
"Alright. He's a Hacker. He's been *acquiring* intelligence... leaks"
Amanda's stomach tightened.
"It'll take a few months to come out..." he voice trailed off.
"Where is he now?"
"I sent him to New York"
"New York...?"
"Yep! He's safe and... in our custody up there. I want to offer him shelter till we get to the bottom of this..."
"What do the Americans say?"
"Well, they don't want him leaving American soil for one thing. And....err, well... They're mad as hell"
"Jesus!"

"They'll be watching the house 24-7" he added, getting up and walking into his Study, jerking tight the rope-belt of his housecoat.

** **

April was staring at her.

Amanda walked the dogs: One Irish setter and two Welsh Springer Spaniels. They were frisky, lingering at every fire-hydrant, post sign and corner hedge. Today they were especially capricious. One of them had to mark a car. The other...

Even the setter tugged at her leash. Amanda was tired of their yanking and untidy behavior.

"*No. No!*" she admonished quietly.

"Hey you!" yelled a voice from inside a van whose rear tire had been chosen as the target by April to sprinkle. Amanda apologized profusely, noting that it was drizzling...*ha, ha..*?

Round the block they all ran, and the van was still there, she noted.

She turned the corner.

A team of Latino housepainters with ladders, supplies, provisions and drinks populated the street curb. They were not just contractors. They were...*what*...doing something else?

The vehicle was laced with communications devices. Antenna, logo banners and even white bagged containers to match their overalls. They erected a small tent to shelter the workers from the drizzle, now a steady rain.

Ostensibly, sidewalk work was being improved, mainly as curb-appeal for a house being rehabilitated at the end of the street. Process of the Foreclosure bank, decided Amanda, prepping for an Auction Resale. The house had been vacant for years.

They waved.

She waved.

The dogs fairly pulled her up her driveway and into the side door with unbridled energy.

Amanda laughed all the way to the kitchen door. There, they each had food, snacks, water, toys.

She bantered, and the dogs wagged and played and stayed, drinking water and twirled all around. Off to one side were large-pillowed cradles for cool and private naptime, their favorite place!

Evidently, life was good for them.

House living suited them: They saw lush velvet oriental rugs; a stone fireplace hearth, wooly mats at bedside. On the first floor were clean pewter bowls always ready with food, water and snacks. In the library they liked soft matting ...complete with bones for chewing.

A long wood-floored hallway was used for a good chase on all four clattering paws. Plus, a screened porch for a lusty bark at a wayward squirrel. Not that any squirrel was deterred from chuntering...safely up the Magnolia tree in the back garden. But occasionally something strange would happen. Like a cat.

Or an intruder.

Or... someone unknown at the front door. The doorbell rang.

They came, both police officers. One, a woman holding a German Shepherd. Standing at her front door!

"Excuse me" said Amanda "But could you please secure your dog?"

They stepped back. The woman returned the dog to their police car.

Amanda withdrew to alert Carla their housekeeper, who was inside housecleaning. Carla should keep the dogs away.

Amanda stepped outside to talk with them.

"Mrs. MacDonnell?"

"We are with the City Homicide Investigation Services. May we ask you a few questions, please?"

"Of course!" she said, steadily. "What is the nature of your enquiry?"

Amanda looked at the woman who pulled out a small pad for notes, as if such a gesture were routine operating procedure. But it was poised, Amanda could tell.

She did invite them in. But they declined.

Amanda heard a soft growling in the background. Something none of her dogs *ever* did!

"You were in the company of a lady who died a few weeks ago. We'd like to ask some questions about the occasion of your meeting?"

It took a few moments, but Amanda suddenly understood the meaning of their visit.

The lady in question was the elderly woman in the elevator on the evening of the Gala.

The investigative officers wanted to know how long they were together; how close; what was said - by whom, and who else was there.

It was all Amanda could do to describe the events without adding to the panic of the moment, or the care with which Trevor tried to assuage her fears.

Before they left she discovered that she the woman had died of poisoning. And while no connections were made, or even implied, Amanda felt certain that the red paint on the woman's hands had something to do with her death.

She did ask the name of the bereaved husband, and was later on the phone to the Museum to get his address. She and Trevor would send flowers with condolences. What amazed Amanda was that not a murmur had been made about the woman DeBerle, found dead in her apartment.

* *

Barbara called. Trevor called. Boston called.
Amanda was at her laptop.
 "...the First Continental Congress met in 1774" she wrote quickly *"with twelve of Great Britain's representatives sending grievances to King George III."*
Carla Carlos, the housekeeper was asking questions about weekend provisioning and Amanda had an article to complete - even if was just an historical feature about the Nation's Capital City...
"...But it was the second Continental Congress that evolved into the first governing body of the United States Congress. The American Revolutionary War was commenced in 1775 by the thirteen colonies, and ended with Articles of Confederation. The Constitution was ratified in 1781, rendering America an independent Nation..."

The dogs would need feeding. And yes, the turf on the front lawn should be replaced if it was not responding to treatment with pesticides...
She turned to the keyboard on the laptop. Thank God it was just a quick article, a public relations blurb.
"The ratified Constitution finally gave more powers to the federal government and authority to establish a national currency and provided for the separation of powers, including divisions between the executive, legislative and judicial branches. It was finally signed in 1788"

Done. It was 3.30 P.M .
Already?
That's all they need for the article today!
Just one more thing. Something she read in the books at her elbow. Something that resonated with another

project she was doing at the moment...Tomorrow she would return to her work on the Senator's project. Thank God! No time today!

"The Articles of Confederation offered a unicameral body, but proved ineffectual with one veto each state. Nor could it collect taxes, regulate interstate commerce or enforce laws, principally so that that states remain sovereign and ignored legislation passed by Congress."

Amanda's thoughts went to the Tower in lovely Newport. A world away.
The dogs barked again.

"... A conflict of doctrine followed between federalists and anti-federalists about scope, power and role of authority, a debate that carries on to this day. But sovereignty of the states continued to hold sway until a Connecticut Compromise suggested that one house should send proportional representation, and other equal representation!"

She was staring at the words, somehow just imagining the turbulence and traffic on horseback as they crossed the countryside, all communicating and concerned with matters of forming a new nation. *What a task!* 18th century agrarian plantations rooted in English colonial structure would be challenged with *bloodshed.* Their women? Children? Workers? Food supply? Who would remember the 40,000 Irish evicted and indentured to the American colonies to labor on the southern plantations following the English civil war? So one century later, what was it like to be asked to be a Patriot, she wondered.

"Hello?" she answered her cell. "Yes. I'm on it!"

A Feature Article was what she was writing for the DC Council Tourism Outreach Issue.

Initially, they had asked her if a book was appropriate, but she recommended that a well written and intelligent article would be sufficient.

Further, it was easier for their web page, she said to the editor. And fun too! Something they could upload.

However Julie, in charge of publicity, was prodding daily about meeting the new deadline. "Before the spring onslaught of tourists" she said, leaving Amanda to wonder if she could fit in the work one week earlier than originally agreed.

Amanda knew about the Cherry Blossom Festival. It occurred at the end of March - always arriving in Washington as a surprise somehow, bitter winter winds ever relentless and a city gripped still by bright icy-blue days. Yet the blossoms popped out, and with them a crop of tourists, as colorful as they.

Julie was pressing Amanda. What was supposed to be a casual walk-through a Tourist Guide had become a compendium of history! Nor was this a city easily compressed: Round and round she went with the beginning of the account, the middle, and then an explanation of the city's function, background and landmarks...

She pushed away from the desk finally, tired.

"The city is ...fraught with American contradictions" she muttered to Trevor, later.

"Umm? Why?"

"Because the facts were often difficult...so contrary to the politics of a republic, yet set on a colonial stage... "

"And rightfully so!" he laughed in his patriarchal tone for all things pertaining to early colonial American history.

Amanda waited, her lips tight.

"Stick with the facts" said Trevor turning the page to his newspaper.

She eyed him suspiciously like a true Patriot should. But actually, she decided, he was right.

The facts then. Trevor would know. He came from London, a city state with a history of mercantilism expansionism.

But words failed her.

She felt pressed. Or pressured. Or politically compromised to make the shoe fit, somehow. Truth was, Washington was closest to Jackson in spirit, reflecting the age of the common man than to Jefferson, the poet of romantic reconstruction. Yet his words suited a nation of dreamers.

Just now, it was hard for her to ponder the matter and piece it all together.

She moved to the kitchen.

She would do it in increments, she decided. Then she could report to Julie.

The Senator, or the Retired Mr. Steve Williams, as she told Trevor, had e-mailed her, inviting her and Trevor to an informal dinner on Capital Hill, followed by a performance at the Kennedy Center. "*The Marriage of Figaro*" - with his party at his box.

Mozart!

She was already in his service for that day, and working hard. Was he pressing for something, probing even?

She replied that after the meeting with his staff, she would be leaving for the weekend.

Truth was, she wanted a quiet evening.

She and Trevor needed to get away together...
She replied to his message.
That was before she heard about Trevor's plans for the evening.

* *

It was five o'clock in the afternoon Friday before Amanda switched off her laptop. She took the dogs for a block-walk, and managed a quick shower before Trevor called from the office to say that he was running late.
Could Yusef come pick her up for their dinner engagement at the Italian Embassy that night?
Could she bring him a dinner jacket to wear, and they'd both be chauffeured to the event for the evening.
It was arranged that, since Trevor had the Jeep with him parked, they spend the night in the guest quarters of the Chancery, and leave directly for the Bay in the morning in the Jeep.
Amanda agreed to pack a weekend bag and bring it with her to load into the Jeep. The dogs would be fine with Watson, who with his son was arriving at 7a.m. to work in the gardens this weekend.

She picked a satin cocktail shift dress for the soiree.
It was black gauze at the shoulders with small diamond buttons down the side to match black evening sandals and clutch bag, each having a small diamond cluster.
She added the heritage silver-fox fur stole, a gift from her mother in law, made from an animal stricken down at their Glen in Scotland years ago.
Yusef the driver picked her up, and she stepped into the limousine.
Washington was in a rain storm, the streets shone like ice.
It would have been a long day had it not been for Eva Montaignon, always a favorite hostess for an event.

She was giving one of her small dinner parties at a newly built modern Renaissance building that served as the Embassy from Italy on Whitehaven Street, off Massachusetts Avenue in Washington DC.

A chamber music quartette greeted them at the entrance. "To add to the fun of the evening" said Eva, swanning forward in her characteristic way to welcome guests.
Champaign was served all round. Tonight was an evening for the Pantomime, she had announced.
Most of the frivolity came from two Court-Jesters clad in flop and folly caps of the Renaissance world.
"May I introduce Carinal Guiseppe di Valenna?.."
He bowed.
"... And Amanda Wells MacDonnell, wife of Trevor..." said Eva
"So pleased to meet you" said the tall Cardinal in black vestment and scarlet cummerbund.
"Amanda is writing a little something for the city tourism board and is fully informed on its history" said Eva.
"Oh really?"
"Yes. Just a little piece for their sightseeing program" smiled Amanda.
"How nice..." said the Cardinal, his brogue definitively Irish. "Washington is a city full of surprises!"
"It is" she said "both aesthetically and historically."
Trevor joined them and they bantered.
Amanda was served a fresh Champaign. Eva called Trevor over for an introduction to a new arrival.
"Are you a native?" asked the Cardinal

"My family is from New York. I am rediscovering Washington from a *different* perspective" said Amanda.

"Me too!" he said "I'm serving at Boston College for a year."

He contemplated his hands, until now folded over his vestment. "I lecture on Philosophy..."

The music started up.

"Do you read Kant?"

"No. I'm afraid I'm hopelessly illiterate on the defense of Religious precepts" she said.

He eyed her carefully as if contemplating her words, then he smiled.

"So. Do you guide your husband through his daily duties?"

"He lets me *think* I do!" she chuckled. "At the moment we are in observance of the Cherry Blossoms on the Tidal Basin. Have you seen them?" she added, keeping to safer subjects.

The jesters took to the floor and padded around in frivolity.

"Yes. I have! But actually, what brings me to the city is business of a nature that involved investments" he said.

"Umm" she responded over the growing noise.

The two clowns tossed hats to the ground and rearranged their colorful checkered uniforms of purple and gold, playfully poking over posture and tassels.

"How do you like Mozart?" asked the Cardinal.

Amanda was smiling "I love all things Renaissance, including court jesters!"

One reached for his viol as if about to wax poetic about love.

"Actually" whispered the Cardinal "they are not court jesters. They are the official guard of the Vatican!"

"I see" said Amanda

"Yes" he said, with a glint of humor "We are dressed in Medieval clothes, but we have very modern interests..."

She sipped at her tall-stemmed glass.

The music drowned them out as the Quartet strummed in, and the pair sang. One actually peeled off his hat to hit the tenor note that brought them to a gathering applause.

Amanda moved away from the Cardinal.

He seemed to watch her move around the room, as if in warning.

She chatted mostly with the wives of other delegations serving in Washington. Food, fashion and plans for the summer... For most of the evening she remained stubbornly behind the pillars of the main hall.

Trevor found her.

They left shortly after the Japanese Emissary sang a song from *West Side Story*, and to great applause.

"You sorry we went?" snuggled Trevor into her hair that night.

"With you at my side, I'll go anywhere!" she murmured.

"Umm..." he purred. She cuddled up closer.

"Fishing? Tomorrow?..."

And tomorrow, she decided later, she would bring up the business of the police visit.

* *

"Amanda" said the Senator. "I'd like to ward off any criticism for reliance on newfangled finance instruments. As you can see, Wall Street is hardly popular. Our case is to solve for employment opportunities."

Amanda listened.

"Since most of the Constituents from this district are conservative, please show them some understanding of early roots - you know, the colonial world that created their community."

"Yes, I understand the need to show precedents..."

"And since we rely almost entirely on the money and votes of a greying community, lets honor their legacy from WWII somehow...Can you do that?"

"Yes Sir" said Amanda. "It is always a good thing to remember the sacrifice of so many."

"Well, you have it then. Although somehow I suspect you already had a grasp of what it took to arrive at the modern picture. You know, it serves to show purpose in terms of garnering support..."

She nodded.

"Plus it deflects attention from me! As if I had some sort of agenda..."

London, 1621

At dockside, the heavy-mast sailing ship heaved-to with her cargo fully laden. Barely in her berth, her sun browned mariners hailed excitedly to the crowds.

Gathering below were carts, sacks, bails and lumber waiting to offload. Well strung carriages with passengers lay off to the side as owners, shipmasters and investors surveyed their ships in the bustle of action.

It was drizzling. The London Merchants, convening at the Inn for their Assembly, were smiling. This was clearly a changing world. Their world.

Agrarian subsistence traditions were being supplanted by mercantilism. Even the ladies, peering out from their dark bonnets held some excitement for the silk, sugar, cotton and ribbon that would fill the shops.

It was raw wood, crated china, tobacco, bales of cotton and spices that came heaving over the side in sacks and bundles, cargo in much abundance to fill warehouses of manufacture and redistribution.

Still, the notion of private ownership was something new to mercantilism: Private investors were outfitting ships for trade and expecting direct returns for their money!

Only a few, those in the distance watched fretfully, their cloaks concealing their loyalist and non-Puritan ways: England needed the money, aye. But these fruits of expansionism were bypassing the Crown unjustly. Their interests...

They traverse to the New World was not quick.

They anchored in the Caribbean, some people disembarking for freshness and water, and new fruit.

Those onboard understood the imperative: There would be precedence in settling the shores of America. The way was paved for them. Many had crossed before, like Cabot on his search for China, producing instead the Muscovy Company for London Merchants.

But now, what mattered was that the Directors of the *East India Company* were also for the *Virginia Company*.

They included John Eldered. Sir Thomas Smythe of the Muscovy company; Sir John Wolstenholme of Hudson Baffin; Sire Henry Spelman of Sir Walter Raleigh's Society of Antiquaries, and Henry Fleet, another merchant.

They had been provisioned for profiteering! Fur-bearing animals was the focus of trade in North America. Furs procured from the Indian native savage, yet equally vied by the Spaniard.

Precious metals for coin, and conquest of natives as laborers for harvesting raw materials was necessary for the Holy Roman Empire. Both would need settlements and territorial gain. And both would compete, using whatever liaisons they had with the Indian savage...

When Young William Claiborne left for Jamestown in October 1621, he had just escaped a massacre of all English settlers at James City by one Opechancanaugh.

**

The trip from Washington to the Eastern Shore of Maryland took them down US 50 by mid-morning. Except that it felt a little odd to be in the Jeep with the cage up, and no dogs. Amanda turned regretfully over her shoulder twice, knowing how much they enjoyed the farm on weekends.

But this was not a trip for them. Not that she did not enjoy the treat of travelling sans menagerie, but she missed having them in the back of the car, tails wagging, ears hanging out the window. And nothing was more enjoyable than watching their unbridled joy at the free runs across open field, or pointing for clay pigeons if Trevor were shooting. Of course, what she did not miss was their travel needs. Like a clean water bowl. Or dog bones. Or frequent stops for a patch of grass. Or a panting fit equal to a Boeing 747 when needing car windows down, and all human cargo shivering...

The Jeep felt roomy. Normally, baggage stowage was an issue - all of it stepped on; mud-stained and flaked with dog hair.

Trevor was chuckling. He knew exactly what she was thinking.

"What?" she giggled.

They did miss the dogs, and they laughed.

On the drive down, Harris their farmer had called to warn them about hunters still in the fields when they arrived. Something which did not phase Trevor at all, as long as they were all licensed to hunt; wore safety vests and handled their guns responsibly.

He had given his farmer hunting rights for the season, but he liked to know how much game was taken.

It was a Scottish tradition to hunt, he said, and he relished the sportsmanlike manner in which the Eastern-shoremen, as they liked to be called, conducted themselves in the field.

He also knew the Game Warden, Mr. Smith, and Trevor had made generous donations to the Department of Natural Resources for their good stewardship.

A call came in from Steve, a local waterman, asking for permission to walk their shoreline for artifacts. Today the tide was out and exposing much of the river bed. Artifacts left by colonists who settled the Bay in the 17th century. This permission Trevor gave freely, and invited them in for a beer when they were done. The collected bits and pieces however, had to be tagged and identified in the log book of the house. That was his rule.

So by the time Amanda unpacked and settled onto the porch wearing a oversized Oxford shirt and jeans with her glass of iced tea, she was already counting the hours of sunlight left.

Here, it setting sun bathed the grass lawns in orange hues, down to the waterfront where their boat was rafted to the dock in quiet shelter for the winter.

Water views stretched out on three sides, winter woods and geese crooning and chuntering on the water; shrill marsh toads bellowing from the shallows, and the evening closing around them.

Trevor came out to join her on the enclosed porch. She had snacks and fresh food out.

A buffet of cold cuts and condiments at a side board lay open for choice, and a wine bucket and fresh jam tarts that Carla had cooked lay on a colorful country dish glistening in the soft lighting of the glass porch.

From across the creek they must have fairly glowed in the darkness. Coffee, Amanda promised, would come later...

The thoughts that went through her mind began to swirl. By the time she told Trevor about the visit from the police, they were deeply engaged in a discussion about the deceased woman.

Trevor took the matter seriously, averting two calls on his cell to continue their evening conversation.

Amanda had nursed a feeling of general malaise about the whole affair. They talked. And as always, the natural beauty of the Eastern Shore of the Chesapeake Bay prevailed, and together, they turned in close to 11 pm.

Not until later that night, in the quiet of the wilderness did one thought come forward, with certainty. She sat up suddenly.

There was something amiss about that evening at the Gala: The woman whose hands were covered with wax paint was the same woman who had bumped into her when Amanda was leaning over to fix her shoe...

The mime, perhaps caught off balance because of his stilts, had leaned forward, and found the lady - instead of Amanda - to kiss and touch.

Was Amanda his intended target?

The thought was ridiculous. She put it from her mind, and settled back into bed to snuggle up against Trevor.

She slept fitfully. In the morning Amanda wasn't too pleased with the decision to go to the Diamonds.

She complained: If only he'd warned her.

For one thing, it was cold in the stern of the powerboat. For another, it was really too early in the year to find fish at the Diamonds! Not that she was an expert. But the Diamonds was a spot *way* out in the middle of the Chesapeake bay.

Nothing was going to avert Trevor.

They were pushing off the dock at 8.30 in the morning like all good fishermen should, and then out the creek to the open bay, rolling and pitching into the waves with a good Westerly blow...

Amanda was freezing.

Somehow, it didn't seem natural being out on the bay with March winds still blowing in April. The sky was overcast, and though weather could tame the bay in one Front, it was still winter as far as she was concerned – she, having been non-stop-busy for six-months-straight.

Trevor was having a good time at the steering wheel.

One thing about the Diamonds was that you could always find boats out there from the crack of dawn, he was saying.

Amanda looked away, gathering her heavy weather gear around her neck. God knows what they found there year round, being one of the deepest, rough seas-fishing holes in the Chesapeake Bay.

In summertime, it could be thrilling. Blue fish breaking and bass flirting with alewife was good sport for fishermen. But now?

Increasingly, Trevor was saying, stingrays were ravaging the bay. Chiefly because their only predator the shark, had decreased in population from overharvesting...

The bay was already stressed by human populations, he was saying, but along the shallows near the waterfront, where sea-grass must grow as nursery to many species, there was a serious deficiency. There, the shoals were agitated by powerful rays leaving columns of suspended sediment in the water: This blocked out the sunlight that sea-grass needed. The result was too much nitrogen. Added to a good spring-rain runoff from fields freshly fertilized, and you could kill a cow in the waters.

All Amanda could think of right now was a warm cup of coffee.

Why were they going fishing? Why didn't they just cozy-up into a lazy spring river, like the Choptank and fish for Shad as was the custom during the time of the dogwood/shad trees?

It wasn't long before she understood.

Trevor was playing around, and he had a rendezvous with another boat. The skipper was someone Amanda knew, James Lloyd.

They rafted, of sorts. That is, Lloyd's boat anchored behind and all of them huddled below decks, nursing coffee, soup and cheese puffs that Amanda had heated on the tiny galley stovetop.

"What we are getting from him is considerable..." Lloyd was telling Trevor.

"He was on his way up the food chain in Boston, impersonating as the Harvard point-of-contact, and thrashing around for leads..."

"What Bank was he looking at?" asked Trevor, taking notes.

"Atlantic Trade Bank. It held the offshore accounts in Ireland of South African wealth from diamonds, gold to illicit trade and tusks. It was enjoying the shelter Ireland provided, but with the meltdown in Ireland of its financial system, the rescuers were European Central Bankers probing for information. Information that was designed to elude them..."

"Did he have the records?"

"He hacked into the records. They were of Swiss origin. But following US banking investigations, they were moved by their owners in Ireland as offshore accounts. Staying well below the radar.."

"...and enjoying 12% corporate tax rates..." finished Trevor. "Who opened the accounts?"

"Surprise. It's not exactly clear at this point...Evidence of some activity in Ireland, but not all...It's bigger."

"Excuse me, Gentlemen" said Amanda, "I don't mean to interrupt, but may I ask who is watching the fish exactly?"

"We've caught him! He's underground, at my place" said Lloyd, grinning like a proud gangster.

Trevor turned to her. "It's a Safe-House... The man who appeared on our doorstep in Washington..."

"*What?..*" said Amanda, discovering their true agenda for this cold trip.

Trevor held out his hand to her. "Come!"

Then he turned to Lloyd. "Go on!"

"Better *us* than *they*" he said. "After all, he is British-born with Irish citizenship. We need to access him first with questioning. Once the FBI get him, we'll *never* see his data again..."

"Umm" said Trevor. Then, imagining another possible Assange, he added "Where was he going with his findings?"

"Not exactly sure. We've sheltered him and questioned him. He is forthcoming – if wary."

Trevor looked at Amanda. "The man that came to the house. He's not a threat. He's in danger...He's on the run. You've seen him!"

"Kendall?" she asked.

Trevor faced her. "He's got himself embroiled in...in political nuances between governments, if you will. This was a good way for Jim and I to meet without arousing any suspicions of a serious nature: *Lloyd* has a boat on the bay. *We* have a boat on the bay..." He paused. "Sorry, sweetheart. I should have alerted you. I didn't want to alarm you"

He pecked her with a kiss on the cheek.

"Me too?..." asked Lloyd offering his lips for a kiss.

"Thanks for telling me. I see it's important, and I'll reserve my questions 'till later..." she said.

She retreated to the rear of the boat. This was the last thing she expected. *What in the world was going on here?*

She looked out over the water, concerned. She had a fiduciary responsibility to the Senator...

What if this intelligence posed any conflict of interest? Her husband's position must come first, she knew.

She made a decision. No question. She would withdraw from the Senator's project.

Effective immediately!

She looked back at the them.

"What he found..." Lloyd was saying to Trevor "was a shelter for investments with an agenda: There was a trail of strategies for global acquisitions, encouraged by some NGOs; educational institutions, a religious group and a couple of other non-profits – one, a Financial Hedge fund known to the funding socialist agendas, here and in Europe. He had a contact at Harvard..."

"What is his disposition?" asked Trevor.

"He's cooperative. If we can keep him from the public eye and the American authorities just yet. He's nervous. He's a little unsure about whom he can trust. He's holding back some stuff, I'm sure of that..."

"My God" said Trevor, "I'm harboring a fugitive!"
"Shit!" hurled Amanda from the cabin seat. She was reading her text messages. Both men turned to her.

"Mr. Steve Williams wants us to join him and his booth party at the Caps Game downtown tomorrow. They're playing Boston Bruins!"
"No way!" said Lloyd. Clearly the logistics to travel the distance to Washington DC from the Chesapeake Bay, something that was not altogether impossible at high speeds, might give them away.
"He's keeping a check on his leash" added Lloyd.
They all looked at each other.
Clearly the Senator might know something?
With quick fingers and her lips parted over the words Amanda wrote "We're away for the weekend. Regrets!"
She looked at Trevor.
"What..?" she said. "Should I add *Ahoy*?"
"...So" said Lloyd "We have work to do. We need to keep him hidden."
"We'll have to move him around frequently. And we are being watched!"
"Right" said Trevor. "So let's get fishing in this damned cold weather..."
"I'll be in touch again soon" said Lloyd before casting off his cleated line, un-rafting. "I'm off to New York in the morning. I'm speaking with the FBI later this week..."
"Can we go home now?" asked Amanda, her lips blue.
"Here..." he said going below decks "I came equipped for...this moment" and he bit off a woolen glove from his hand to pour some of Scotland's best Whisky into a coffee from a thermos.
"Irish Coffee! Best collaborative drinks between two nations...*Cheers!*"

A flock of Canada geese flew over their boat squawking like sirens, an ice-cold bay under a grey sky with a menacing calm.

Her ears were ringing.

Chapter 4

Wales, 1942

In the dark, the ship that moved through the water was not at first definable. Her engines, old and somewhat overworked from several Atlantic crossings, told of her presence long before she came into sight. But it was a moonlit night, and the sea calm, without fog.

She ghosted into sight, a merchant marine cargo vessel and slowed to a halt at dockside, her diesels engines churning for bilge pumps seeping water out the stern.

Hawsers pulled her snug to the pier, and she was fastened hard by soft hemp bumpers, now fixed as a dark outline of the night.

Only later did two men emerge from the dock carrying a gang-plank aloft over their heads. Carefully they laid it down, resting it on sand bags, and it reached into an open black hole within the side hull of the ship, like a coal bunker.

Within minutes, the headlights of road diesels followed down the industrial lane of the dock: Three covered cargo trucks. They waited. Another lorry arrived, soldiers spilling out of the rear. They posted a watch, two up and two down, their military uniform and guns at the ready. The rest worked in stealth.

They loaded cargo. First boxes, large and small, then crates covered by steel straps and wrapped in burlap sackcloth, print marks and numbers painted along the sides. The soldiers worked fast, loading heavy cargo into the side of the ship in the darkness.

One Inspector at the gangplank counted boxes going into the hold, a Lieutenant to assist with a flashlight held over his papers. At each turn, one man followed the crates into the ship then came out, handing sheets of paper to the Inspectors.

The relay proceeded well into the night until the trucks were emptied and all inspections complete.

At the last count, the captain of the ship and one other were given copies of the sheets, and they talked. Then a final salute was made.

One truck unloaded four men who walked into the hold with the cargo, and the gangplank was removed, the ship's hull sealed.

The trucks left and the night air resonated with echoes until only the diesel engines of the ship murmured in the dark. Slowly, by quiet sailors unseen, the hawsers drew out and she pushed off.

The vessel left the harbor as quietly and efficiently as she came, no sign of her presence anywhere visible.

The night remained calm as dawn promised her light.

Less than an hour later, at pre-dawn, before the gates of the shipyard opened, Dockers began lining up near a small barrel-fire.

As the Main gates opened they chatted and guffawed their way into the warehouses and milling shops, many of them laborers skilled to refit, solder, rebind and untwist the metal of broken ships coming in for repair. England was at war, her docks in overtime to receive vessels carrying US supplies for the Allies.

Air-raid shelters were close, the shipyard was a target of the Luftwaffe whose bombs assailed them with some frequency, yet the Dockers kept coming.

One man had watched it all on this day.

As workers populated the shipyard, he disappeared into the stacks.

A millworker, he took his place in the mill shop. There, he honed with precision the edges of steel lathes and shaved wood planks for decking to within a millimeter of their required dimensions.

At the end of the workday, he left with everyone else.

Like many squatters along the coastal shoreline, he kept a boat beside his hut near the beach. Occasionally he used it for fishing. It had a small 5 horsepower Seagull engine. Easily, if he needed to, and with enough petrol, he could follow the craggy coastline to Point Fishguard and make the narrow crossing to Ireland.

Tonight, however, he would send his coded message.

* *

"Write!" admonished the King to his Secretary, his white-laced brocade sleeve waving in the air.

"Say...*say* to that whimpering fool touting the new world '*Doth the wool of thy cloth-trade not cover thee well?*'"

Silence.

Then he and Buckingham burst into laughing. It was too hilarious a situation: One of the Lords of England, with a patent for sending sheep's wool to Flanders for cloth-making, had written them informing them that the new world was just too cold to settle in!

They were fairly weeping with laughter, their silk stockings pleating beneath the skirt of their vestments. This was altogether *de Trop*...

"Nuh, nuh, nuh...Nay! *Nay!*" insisted the King "But write thee *'That you should take pleasure in the fleures de la jeunesse in the French that pass you in ships!..*" he howled.

"Truly? No sword for the Frenchman?" said the Earl of Buckingham with the King, now folding over in mirth, and a small glass fell from the King's hand with a crunch.

George Calvert, a *Gentleman Venturer* of the *Loyalist* Court having a generous Merchant-license to trade in cloth shipments, had warned the Crown of French cruisers patrolling the coast with such a force of warrior as to find it alarming....

"Wine! Wine! More wine!" coughed the King in merriment. It was too much for him, he announced.

"Nay! But tell him that his England's fortunes be safe...in our holds!" giggled the courtier, implying that Calvert keep his sword as sheathed from the cold as his privy in the weather of Newfoundland.

And this time the laughter was beyond control.

"A letter...shall we write him!" waved back the King finally, his feet unsteady and his voice thick as he weaved to his chambers for sleep.

"New World Indeed!"

**

Washington DC

Amanda walked the length of the mosaic floored terminal at Reagan Airport and climbed one tier to check in her baggage. She stopped at the Starbucks counter and ordered an iced-Caramal coffee with a small biscotti. It tasted good. And it calmed her nerves. She had fifteen minutes, and wanted to answer some messages.

One, to Barbara in New York who was in love and wanted Amanda to stop overnight at her apartment to talk.

"Again..?" texted back Amanda, with a possible "yes" for the night - but make if for next month, on their way up to RI for a sail.

Another text was from the office of Senator Steve Williams asking about her arrival in Boston: A limo would be waiting, and her stay at the Marriott downtown was confirmed. The meeting would be at 4.oo pm, followed by dinner with the Senator...

She had decided to resign. But clearly, he had no intention of letting her go. Should she disclose the affairs of her husband? No! That was not her determination to make. Besides, Trevor had continue with her work.

Actually, she had tried to explain herself to the Senator. *I feel I should withdraw on account of my husband's career and political position - which must come first in my life, Senator. Nor should I compromise anyone else's professional priorities...*

"Nonsense!" he had interposed. "You are no enemy of the State, Amanda. Anything your husband does is fine! I have every confidence in your integrity. Besides, there's nothing mysterious about what we're doing. It's all open for public discussion through my monthly newsletter to my constituents. So. Forget it!"

She was flattered of course, having just published an article for a Journal about Medieval History about anthropological aspects of markets in medieval England and how they worked.

Her material for the research was based on scholarly economic models, as well as her own original research found in the journals. But she was getting uncomfortable.

She opened her email.

She had messages from two scholars; one law school professor and several economic specialists. All of whom wanted to know in advance what the meeting would hold, even though they could not attend. She was greatly encouraged to keep at her work to open up markets, and she promised to keep them informed.

But just as she was about to close her cell connection she noticed a reply from Barbara already.

"He's a Brit! Later..."

> "ALL PASSENGERS BOARDING FOR BOSTON, FLIGHT 327, PLEASE CHECK IN AT GATE C"

She laced away all her belongings and prepared for the security check line. She took off her Button tab trench; her Lucie Ankle-wrap sandals; raffia double-handled satchel and placed them quickly in one tray. In another she put her laptop. That left her barefoot and walking through the screening device wearing her Boyfriend jeans; braided leather belt and a white Cherie shirt. She felt naked. Little loose for Washington standards, but comfortable for travel.

She gathered her stuff, texted Trevor, then turned off her cell.

The flight was uneventful, giving her time to prepare for the meeting ahead.

Chesapeake plantation settlement, she discovered, was a difficult business. So bitter were the years of settlements in the early American colonies of the 1630s that there was much hardship and lack.

Further, England was plunged into an impossible and brutal civil war by the actions of King Charles I.

It's effect roiled Europe, and King Charles was eventually condemned to public execution...

The costs had been high.

Amanda knew her history. But the supply of money was crucial to the understanding of a constitution conceived by the American colonies...

She read a scholarly article intently. It was an attachment from a trusted colleague in the academic world of economics and early history. "H" was how he signed his name. The article was drawn by him, long ago, he said. The citations, upon which this article was built, were published. The details included a Note written by John Winthrop himself, October of 1640 entered in his journal:

"The scarcity of money made a great change in all commerce. Merchants would sell no wares but for ready money, men could not pay their debts though they had enough [i.e. capital], prices of lands and cattle fell soon to the one half and less...

"This paper" said H in his e-mail "discusses the number of transactions made in the Chesapeake colonies without English money between 1631 and 1640 and shows that tobacco was used for money and as a standard of value. This premise supports a motive for independent activity and local self-sufficiency by Parliamentarians in the Chesapeake Bay.

This is significant to determine pre-agency and sovereignty of treasure up to, and even past the Revolution. This is important since the issue of debts owing to Imperial bankers following the Revolution were still inked on documents ungratified. So you do have to read what led up to the events that became precedents ...'

It may explain a lot. It may hide a lot. Only you can make that determination.

But dig carefully.

Amanda knew that long after the Protestant Reformation of Henry VIII when Catholics were purged and his daughter Queen Elizabeth ruled as Protestant Queen, the new young Crown of England - during the early colonial settlement era - was opposed to colonial independence and venturing. *Why?*

Because the new young king had turned Catholic again with his Catholic French-born wife!

The English court of King Charles I was now advised by Catholic Spaniards, themselves vying for the colonies as venture for their Holy Roman Empire.

In England, the king enforced non-compliance to his new regal authority through brutal Laudinian measures within the Carolinian movement.

Further, he was to stay colonial venture by preventing the circulation of English coinage in the colonies.

"Historians have generally referred to trade in terms of exchange and barter economies. But in the overwhelming number of transactions, it is clear that

between 1631 and 1640, tobacco can be said to have become the exclusive standard of value in the Chesapeake colony, often represented by receipts against future crops, and frequently supported by court findings for social punishment and public values..."

Amanda turned next to modern money and the magnitude of stock exchanges in order of their supremacy.

The New York Stock Exchange traced its origins to 1792. Known as the "curb market," brokers traded outdoors on the street New York City, and transactions were traded and recorded for business and finance. The Buttonwood Agreement, signed by the first 28 brokers and merchants, set in motion the NYSE's unwavering commitment to investors and issuers of money.

Framed by certain assumptions - laws of sovereign and independent ownership, such trading shaped financial holdings, this Amanda knew. These were the seeds of orderly trade in society since the beginning of time.

The American Exchange, or "Amex" as it was called, moved to the forefront of a modern world where economies were shaped by individuals exchanging assets over its counter for two centuries, all of them people freely competing in an open society as the basis of modern capitalism.

Recently, an historic event had occurred.

The NYSE Group and Euronext in 2007 marked a milestone for global financial markets. It brought together major marketplaces from Europe and America whose histories in trade was proudly touted as stretching back more than four centuries: The new combination was by far the largest of its kind, and the first to create a truly global marketplace group.

Thus by 2008, when the NYSE/Euronext welcomed the historic American Stock Exchange it became the world's largest and most liquid exchange group.

But something of greater interest appeared. A second market exchange. A *"Second Market,"* allowed buyers and sellers of *alternative* investments to access a robust market. It was designed to create an online investment identity; instant access to big data, comprehensive investor networks and transactions across a broad array of alternatives...

And it was a global success.

She read the explanations behind its mission: Historically, the world of alternative investments was opaque, illiquid and decentralized. *Second Market* brought significant market structure to these asset classes, and in the process, improved liquidity for sellers and enhanced opportunities for investors.

Further, she understood, the *Second Market* streamlined alternative investments by connecting buyers directly with sellers, providing world-class markets and operations with immediate expertise. *Second Market* brought together more than 50,000 individuals and institutions to close on billions of dollars in transactions. And most importantly, she noticed, there was in place a registered broker-dealer requirement for meeting the regulation compliance standards of financial trades, including FINRA, SIPC and MSRB.

There were questions. And she had work to do. Chiefly, in the area of liability and exposure to risk, especially in the cases of loses and failures.

It was in this area of finance that the Senator had shown particular interest. Here, she was to explore the roots of numerous transactions based both here and abroad. This was where he wanted her to search...

She was to deliver a Research Report and Analysis Review for examination.

Specifically, she was to list all the players; all trades, and all Big Data that showed metrics and financial performance. Particularly, she was to find, expose the owners and their worth...

Of course she understood her assignment.

She looked out the window. The leaves danced in the wind, and birds flew purposefully from one tree limb to another in full throated call to a mate somewhere.

The question she had was *Why?*

For what purpose?

She wondered at the irony of such a question. It had caused pain and suffering so many times in history when appropriated...

Money had clearly gone a full circle of understanding, especially coming from the tiny State of Rhode Island.

Anyway, that was not her task.

One Finch found its mate, and here, life would go on...

She returned to her Notes for the Senator

"The private banking sector issues bank deposits ("inside money") and the public sector issues coins, paper cash and bank reserves ("outside money"). Most payments involving private agents are transacted in bank deposits, and as such, the ins and outs of "inside money" are vital to understanding how the modern monetary system functions."

******

"Amanda, what worries me..." asked Luke Hambleton, Senior Senate Staff Officer "is the central economic model that allows for the normal operations of the apparatus. I mean, I get how you approach 'investors with a bona-fide ability' to show their general worth of something in terms of liabilities and assets...But it's not specific enough!"

"Umm" she said, her mouth full. He had insisted on meeting over a meal.

They were in the Lobby of the hotel having dinner. The "Meeting" with the Senator comprised of a "private dinner" with his Aide, evidently. And as stunning as Luke Hambleton was, Amanda was in no mood for socializing, let alone defending her proposal to one of the most grilling legal minds on the staff.

She held her ground. Amanda sipped some wine and looked at him. Table candlelight was giving his face the luminosity of a deeply etched monument, shadowy here, glowing there...

Then again, it was a solid question, thought Amanda. She would give it a straight answer. She put down her fork, and explained her research.

 "Umm. I see" he said, tapping the rim of his glass. "Like a calibrated balance sheet. So why hasn't anybody thought of this before?"

She smiled, the inquest over.

"Oh, I don't know Luke. Maybe there just wasn't any need for it before now..."

She popped a delicate mouthful of creamed onions into her mouth and began to cut a small wedge of beef Wellington...

"So here's what the Senator is most concerned about: Especially where you say that the private sector component of the monetary systems is at the heart of daily activity for market exchanges and economic progress...*What* at they trading in, exactly?"

Well not quite over, evidently.

She paused, looking up.

"Well. Things that must be paid and bought with precious resources. Assets for example, are cash..."

"Yes. Of course. Nothing changes!"

"Do they have value?"

He was testing her.

What he really wanted to know was the *Who*. Specifically, *who had the money...*

"Umm" he said. "What about exposure and risk? What regulation can an offshore-banker cite..."

He looked away, then added. "What about systemic risk, Amanda?"

She put down her fork. "This is basic free market capitalism. No global *systemically important* bank exposure requiring GSIBs or legal language protections!"

"Um" he said, following closely. "Any particular philosophy or political doctrinal position?"

Ah! She might have known...

"No. No political position. I leave that for the pundits and academics to figure out. I have no interest in supporting any particular political platform with *any* divergent philosophy..."

"But no GSIBs huh?" he persisted.

"No need. It's just a review of protections...that's all. "

He paused, looking down, and she started to wonder at his probing, her breath tightening.

Giving up any list of investors for any given day, on any given trade, at any given demographic was powerful data...It was a dangerous place to go.

More specifically, it was finger-pointing that, in the wrong hands, could be manipulated outside the safety bounds of free markets: Auctions, bids and market evaluations were trusted to be impartial, without prejudice or judgement...Guaranteed anonymity.

This was not her game to play. *Please, God!*

Amanda waited.

The next question totally surprised her.

"Your...err, husband? He has a bank does he not?"

"Yes."

"So, err...You have no other interest than helping the Senator drum up a business but for creating Jobs?"

She looked at him. "That's right."

"Nor...any other *intelligence* about hidden sources of capital undisclosed to the United States Government?"

As she collapsed into her bed that night, she knew they had been toying with her.

What was he getting at?

* *

April was waiting for her. Then all the dogs greeted her at the door.

Clara Carlos greeted her.

Trevor hugged; Barbara buzzed in with a message - and invite to a Wine Festival.

It was great to be back!

She enjoyed a cocktail hour with Trevor. They chatted and caught up on news...Nothing personal or too sensitive in nature. Just conversation and general affairs. The dogs shuffled about and cuddled, showing their bits and pieces and playful new toys.

"You're so... *spoiled!*" she admonished.

Amanda showered, unpacked and put on her sneakers. Downstairs she found Trevor reading the paper and she answered her messages.

She sat and regarded him closely. He was handsome for his age. A little grey at the temples, the brisk face with a reddish clan chin-beard, his hair wavy and cropped at the ears as he bend over to stroke the dogs. He was a natural... More than anything, Amanda loved his sea-blue eyes. When he looked at her intently, they could penetrate with intensity, as if sweeping her into his world of mystery with a devotion that was everlasting, it seemed. That was before...

"Signora..." called Carla from the kitchen door. "I go now. Good Bye!"

Amanda jumped up. "Yes. Thank you!"

Dinner was an hour away.

She walked the dogs, sampled Carla's superb salad and tacos, set up around the kitchen.

"Barbara called" Trevor said "We had a lovely chat for half an hour. Says she met someone...and wants you up there to help her shop for a new wardrobe."
Barely were the words out of his mouth and her cell rang. She picked up.
"Barbara! We were just talking about you..."
Trevor signaled: *Tell her I want to know the name of the chap she met...*
"Did you hear that?" laughed Amanda.
"Damned right I heard it. What I want to know is...how did some stranger show up at my door two days ago and say he *knew* you!" husked Barbara.
"What?..."
"Yeah! This guy shows up, and says he knew you.."
Amanda was processing the words, confused at the crossed signals.
"Barbara says he's *German*..." said Amanda.
"I don't know..." she said Barbara. "How to do you mean?"
"I mean, it's one thing to receive someone who says he knows my associate; it's quite another to arrive with my address *in his pocket*!"
"What?... I mean, I'll ask Trevor." said Amanda, walking from the room.
"And get this" continued Barbara. "He says he's in trouble and might be back...What's going on?"
Amanda froze. "I'll find out."
"Tell Trevor nothing. Or something. But I've got to get to the bottom of this first...Bye!"
Amanda put down the cell.
What just happened?

Dinner went well. They sat at their garden table in the terrazzo, a nook off the kitchen that resembled a greenhouse. There they ate Carla's repast of fresh salad; spiced savory chicken over rice, and a small serving of chocolate mousse followed by rich dark coffee.

Later that evening, Amanda found Trevor in his study, his head bent over his desk laptop, and the lights dimmed over his humming fax.

It was a full time job - this ministerial position, a political appointment of diplomacy requiring time-zone Faxes humming and producing unclassified information. All sensitive material would be viewed only on the secured premises of the Embassy, she knew.

Yet in his world, the sun never set on international incidents, sometimes requiring emergency official responses needed for one crisis or another. Even with a staff of responders at his office, it was enough to stress any man. Yet here he sat alone at his desk, coping with after-hours events that kept him away from Amanda.

And she felt alone.

Ever since their conflict at the Spring Gala, he had immersed himself in his work. It was easy to forget how sudden and painfully that scene had been, casting its shadow upon their relationship.

She approached, and while aware of her presence, he did not look up. Judging from the messages on his screen, it was clear that half his counterparts were women - all of them his equals in positions of authority, many representatives of constituencies; agencies or governments. And all of them celebrated personalities.

Yet here sat Trevor, not phased by any of them. He was at home. Amanda was his love, and he never pushed her.

She placed her hand on his shoulder, and he froze at the keyboard. Then he put his hand over hers and lifted his eyes only slightly.

"How are you doing..?" he said quietly.

She knew what he meant. He was enquiring about the heart, had there been healing sufficient to let him in? She leaned down. She kissed him on his neck.

He got up, switched off the lights. They sat in the deeply couched sofa of their front room with a drink. He listened.

For all that could be solved elsewhere, what mattered most was Amanda's progress with her project. He interjected suggestions, asked questions, and above all else, showed an interest in her abilities.

That night, he took her into her arms, and Amanda knew that for now, there was nowhere else she would rather be. She would trust again. The strain between them had gone.

Later that night, she crept downstairs, as she was wont to do, and she got some water. The true destination however, was her desk.

How did someone get Barbara's address unless they'd been in the house and gone through her desk?

As she reviewed her messages, she decided to turn on the kettle for coffee, and settle to her computer.

Clearly, work had been stacking up:

Lucy had checked in from the DC Council of Tourism. *Please could she write more on the article of the Monuments of the city...It would be a feature lead story?*

Amanda settled in at her desk, Trevor sleeping peacefully upstairs and the dogs undisturbed.

But as she researched her material, she looked up occasionally at the picture above her desk.

The Tower of Newport.
Always the sun was setting upon it, as if it had a story to tell, every night.
What a world that must have been, mused Amanda.
What secrets did it hold still?

**

It had been a long month of work for both Trevor and Amanda.

Amanda had sent off the Reports she promised to Luke. Several interviews with the SEC followed, and Federal Agencies had provided her all necessary materials for the Senator's Jobs Program Approvals.

Furthermore, the Senator had her sit through a few public and congressional meetings.

Finally, it came to an end. And this morning Amanda was excited.

She was out jogging with the dogs. She turned the corner and headed for the house, a run back which the animals immediately recognized with reckless abandon.

Satisfied that she had met all her objectives for the week, fresh plans were now populating the calendar: In a couple days, they were driving to New England. Next week was *Race Week*. Plus, the East Coast was ablaze and in bloom!

She spent the afternoon packing.

She and Clara had made arrangements for the care of the dogs, and Watson was in the yard with final suggestions about rearranging the landscaping of the estate.

Her cell hadn't stopped ringing though. Most of them left messages.

> *"Hey Amanda, this is Luke. Call me back first opportunity. I like your proposal..."*

> *"Hi Amanda, its me Barbara. So, what are you wearing when you come to New York?..."*

"Sweetheart, just calling..."

"Amanda.. It's Lucy. I Love your article. We go to print with it tomorrow. Can we talk? I want more...."

"Senator Williams calling for Amanda Wells. Please call back at your earliest convenience..."

And her email was full. She left her most important emails for later, and she activated her auto-response dial on her email responses. What couldn't wait a week, she thought.

She and Trevor had earned some time off.

With Clara dismissed early, and the sun bathing the city in oblique rays of bronze, a soft humid sheen glistened in the back garden as they packed the car for the upcoming trip...

Doubtless, more would be added before *Race Week.*

This evening, they would eat on the veranda an early barbeque, she decided.

She marinated Chicken in olive oil, lime, cilantro leaves, cumin, salt and pepper.

She combined tomatoes, chili and green onions to make a Salsa, and she heated a saucepan of boiling vinegar, sugar and sea salt; adding ginger, garlic, and dry spices before drizzling it over the tomato mixture.

"There!" she said with a deep sense of accomplishment.

She stood there and smiled at her work.

If only her life would allow more time for savoring...

Trevor found her there: He said he had just entered a Fine Bistro -complete with garden music and wine! He laced his arms around her, his lips nibbling at her ear.

"Prerequisite to all good cooking," she grinned.

In her finest apron, Amanda served grilled chicken garnished with avocadoes. They enjoyed their feast in large Indonesian chairs, and there, they sat together as the sun faded and the wind subdued into soft night whisperings.

Gradually, in the deepening torch-lit darkness, with Amanda producing freshly brewed coffee and dessert, they settled into conversation about the day's undercurrents.

"Why do I have the feeling that ...it's a halfhearted commitment by Steve suddenly?" she said.

"Because...he's unsure of how it will impact his community. And trusting your Congressional career to a concept for *improvements* - rather than stirring up doctrinal divides ..."

"No!" said Amanda emphatically. "He's an honest man. And what's to bicker about with political doctrine. It's an age old tradition for American politics."

"Well.." began Trevor, then he fell silent.

"What?.. " she insisted, snuggling up to him in the wide cane loveseat.

"It's about governance. You have to believe in something with a singleness of mind... A conviction worth risking everything for?"

She looked up at him "Go on."

"Chiefly, its because you have so many people depending on you to make the right decision." He looked down at her "Does that help to explain any qualms that he might have?"

She thought at moment. "No. It's not *qualms* he has for the greater good. Its prevarication about his personal risk, like..."

"Its sagacity, just and old word for caution."

Amanda thought about it a second. "Maybe" she said, rising to let the dogs in from the porch "I don't know how to explain it. He's deeply interested. Just a little non-committal, I should say...and there's more, I just know..."

"Since when do politicians show their hands without some tentative testing first?" laughed Trevor, following her into the kitchen with plates. He popped three ripe grapes into his mouth.

"Anyway" he chewed, "he's probably just busy and preoccupied with a lot of other things..."

"Umm" said Amanda, now thinking.

Later.

"So, to bed with us?" she angled softly.

"Right!" said Trevor, distracted by her proximity "But I'll...err, make some... enquiries about him? Maybe there are just... other competing... interests, like...In which case, you should be informed?"

"Like any working professional" she added, the suffragette, as ever so gently bit his lip.

"Umm..." he said.

Later that night Amanda thought through the progression.

Luke had said something about legal precedents. And Senator Williams was suddenly too busy...

What *changed?*

There was something about the New England legacy that had to resonate deeply within that region's past. Perhaps a history of something that happened, or as a precedent for trade and trafficking of goods. *What made them so skittish up there?*

And what about his interest in the present...What did he want from an analysis on financials – regional data and economic policy issues, maybe?

And what about the interest in the names of US investors...What was he implying?

She looked away and sighed. A little less suspicion, she heard herself say. Back to basics. The foundations.

So, beginning with land resources and proprietary ownership, the US Department of Interior regarded their resources jealously, perhaps?

This, she decided to explore. Why were they so fiercely *territorial*?

She was nudged. Not by Trevor who was sound asleep at her side. The dog. April was staring at her. Amanda got out of bed and cuddled with her. She slipped on her sneakers and went downstairs.

She switched on the light at her desk. Unfortunately, these nighttime visitations had become regular occurrence as her only way to keep abreast of the workload. She looked up.

There it loomed, that stone Tower facing her from the wall. It stood for something. Something that was surfacing in new ideas... old conventions...new *opportunities?*

Well, that depends on how you interpret the laws showing precedence, right?

That's how American law was written and interpreted. Either to be harnessed for the good. Or to be exposed.

Trouble is, she couldn't decide which.

Well, that's historians for you, she decided.

Another day, she would dig into her research. What happened in the events of the past...It sure as hell was defending something. Or hiding something?

What threatened people so?

She went back to bed and snuggled up to Trevor.

Treasure, as in territorial regions...

Then it occurred to her.

Each region protected their separate Treasuries.

**

Chapter 5

Trevor couldn't wait to get out of the city. He reviewed the agenda. *Last day*, he grinned.

His Administrative Assistant understood, approaching apologetically. She held up a folder.

An unscheduled visit from the Russian Embassy.

Eleven o'clock was the arranged time.

Of course he would agree to meet with them. That was expected...

He had a few hours to prepare. But not much. What were they up to now? And why the visit to him personally? An official matter? An issue?

Something new, evidently.

That's how these things worked. He waited.

As usual, the meeting went well. Up to a point.

The Russians had been Allies during WWII, and, regardless their bloody-minded socialist history; their flair for the dramatic and their god-awful weather, Russian affairs were never to be neglected.

Only today their accent was grating on Trevor, and so were the usual veiled innuendoes about revealing to the press etc. etc.

"Tea Gentlemen?" he said courteously, getting impatient.

The Russians grinned suddenly, cornflower eyes unmasking a cultural divide not so different from the British. *Of course they would have tea!* How else to share their compatriotic past...

All they wanted, Trevor knew, was diplomatic respect. They owned part of the globe that, if rich in resources remained largely under-developed. Their history as a state began when *Kievan Rus'* –hence *Russian,* united the East Slavic state and adopted Christianity from the Byzantine Empire in 988 A.D.

Rooted in a feudal world of serfdom subsistence, they had emerged as part of a European agrarian culture bound by a climate that neither Hitler, nor Napoleon nor even the Romans had survived in their quest to conquer Moscow as Empire.

The view from the large modern building on Mass Avenue was always bright and green.

Smoking or No-Smoking-in-America, Trevor lit up and offered them both cigarettes.

With tea at their elbow; smoke in the air and their knees crossed, they discussed matters in the office of the British Emissary in Washington DC that only the Soviets and the Brits could discuss as friends.

"So you met Ms. Ladevine DeBerle" asked Uri.

"De...Err...DeB...*Oh!*" squinted Trevor in recognition. "Yes! She was at the Gala last month. My wife and I were introduced to her by your Naval Attaché Mr. Gregor Vuoli" Trevor tipped his cigarette into the ashtray "A beautiful woman, I should add. She and Amanda got along very well."

They were both watching him. "Yes. We are sorry to tell you that she is presumed dead. Apparently a few days after the Gala, an intruder broke into her house and she was killed."

"Oh I am so sorry. What a terrible crime!"

"Absolutely!" said Uri, the spokesman for both of them. "An official police investigation is underway. She was not a member of our staff, just a friend of Gregor, a former minister here in Washington. We did not request diplomatic dispensation with this Enquiry."

"Enquiry?"

Uri continued "She has a brother who lives in Bethesda. He is supposed to be making all the arrangements for her. Gregor said he told the police she went out with a friend from New York. An engineer, visiting from Ireland. The police have been very good to keep us informed."

They both looked down, and sipped tea.

"I see. How very sad" said Trevor. He paused. "Your people are handling it very well indeed. Please let me know if we may be of any assistance..."

"They err...raised good money for the charity, yes?"

"Yes. The Museum Fundraising Gala Auction. It funds their operations here in Washington for the year. The Auction was highly successful, and people were most generous both with their donations of works of art, and in their bids to raise the funds."

"Gregor told us he bid on something. A...a...how do you say it... A snuff box?"

"Yes! That was beautiful. A silver snuff box - said to have been carried with Lewis and Clerk while they surveyed the US territories. It was a lovely object with some art on it!"

"Unfortunately, Gregor told us that he was outbid in five minutes, and could not afford to make a second offer!"

They chuckled.

"So you met the lovely Ladevine DeBerle?"

"Indeed. Please pass along our condolences to Gregor. Again, if there is anything we can help with… Amanda and I would be glad to do so."

"Thank you, thank you very much!" Uri paused "Do you remember if Ms. DeBerle…when she appeared at the Gala…if she was wearing a pendent? …How you say, extraordinary?"

"A pendent?"

"A …jewel"

Trevor uncrossed his legs and put out his cigarette.

"My dear man. As I'm sure you know, on a Fundraising Charity event in Washington, it is the one occasion that people open their vaults and display their finest adornments. The ballroom was literally glittering with jewels and private treasure!"

They smiled. And they both knew it was time to leave. They got up. Then Uri faced Trevor.

"This jewel, we believe is very similar to a jewel that belonged to the Romanov collections, and was last seen on the Queen on a visit in her youth to a family estate, Mr. MacDonnell?"

"Ah…" said Trevor, lowering his face to ponder the question. His throat tight, he was wanting for air.

"That event was indeed the source of much chagrin to that family, I do recall. But it was so long ago! The last war overtook us all did it not, Gentlemen?"

"Indeed. At such cost… Russia lost many good men."

"As did your allies…you will agree?"

"Of course. Of course!"

They were shuffling to leave, buttoning their costs. Then Uri turned. "I regret that so much of our gold shipments as payment for Lend-Lease supplies were sunk and lost by the German U boats."

"Sadly. A world long ago…" said Trevor, controlled.

"True. But a page of our history, nonetheless. The history of the Romanov treasure also remains our history. And it is most fortunate that the spies on our side of the war averted greater loss to the Atlantic sea of our gold shipments, although to this day, we do not know where it all is..."

"Umm"

"We were hoping, Mr. MacDonnell that you could find the treasure for us! You see, the jewel that Ms. DeBerle wore on her neck at that night, Gregor tells us more specifically, was one that came from a jewel collection of the Romanovs that disappeared in World War I."

"*World War I?* I had no idea..." said Trevor leading them to the door. "But how could that ever be...determined?"

"Very easy! The treasure is cited as collateral in one Bank Ledger of the failed Banks of Ireland now in receivership..."

"Oh?"

"The Swiss government informed us!"

* *

They left Friday night from Washington DC, both dogs in the rear of the Rover and their destination set for 'Aunt Amy's house in the Hamptons.' They planned to arrive sometime in the early hours of the morning, allowing for highway Rest Stops, and a bite to eat.

Amanda was excited.

She had anticipated the trip all month. There was nothing more beautiful, she told Trevor, than early summer days at the Hamptons.

Their itinerary also arranged for them to take a sailing cruise up Long Island Sound, mainly to deliver their boat *Tenacious* to Newport Rhode Island where it was registered to participate in the Annual offshore boat race to Bermuda. *Race Week*.

The Regatta was scheduled to begin Tuesday; and while neither Trevor nor Amanda had the time to participate in the racing event, they could at least enjoy the Start of the races and its many pre-start events...

Above all, it was known, Amanda was determined to wipe the etchings of anxiety off Trevor's brow. His work schedule had been brutal.

Being in constant communication with London, his calls began at dawn and did not stop until bedtime. What he would not cope with in the office on Massachusetts Avenue, he brought home. The Fax machine in their Study hummed with feeds all night long.

For those with social messages, it was known to better call Amanda on her cell.

It took two hundred miles of driving from the city, but gradually the calls tapered off.

On their final stop, they ordered coffee and took a moment to survey their status. There had been no business calls for over an hour, and, savoring the sea air as if it were their first breath of relaxation, they grinned with relief.

At the Hamptons they found Paul and Sarah at the beach house. Everyone else would be converging on the place later...

It thrilled Amanda no end that they could walk barefoot through frothy surf suds with Trevor.

Like kids again, she could introduce him to the world of her youth, never regretting the ups and downs of life or the transitions of growing up and losing parents... It was the place that, for them as a family culture, brought them together. Even as they worked hard and dedicated their lives to city places.

Saturday was spent with Aunt Amy tootling around Downtown. Shopping, lunching and chatting at the marketplace with friends and neighbors.

Then laughing with Trevor and Paul who joined them with two dogs in tow reeking of fish and saltwater marshes.

"*Saltwater marsh*...?" started Amanda. "Never mind..." She took the garden hose to them, which they loved and shook off. Then she hosed down Trevor.

It had been a beautiful day of sunshine, and as a faint suntan of redness appeared on Trevor's face, Amanda applied baby balm to his skin, and kissed his nose. Later that evening, just as daylight shortened its long shadows across the beaches, they strolled over to Paul's place for dinner. They lounged on the porch.

Not quite as Amanda had hoped, Trevor got a full dose of childhood frolics, storytelling and nasty-tricks laughter about her and the family... But she was glad to see that Trevor looked relaxed.

By next morning, he was eager to get going. There was a boat race to prepare for, he announced.

They had to drive back to New York City to Larchmont, and from there, the next morning, would set off to sea for Newport as a cruise.

In New York, Barbara, it was arranged, would drive back their Rover -left at the dock.

At Newport they would hand over the boat to their Skipper. The vessel was scheduled to compete in the *Newport to Bermuda Race*, and the Skipper would take the helm with his own crew - a team of young competitors accustomed to the rigors of offshore sailing.

Amanda didn't mind that the Skipper was coming aboard for their Cruise also. She knew that he needed to make early preparations to ready a boat for sea. This he would begin doing while underway, in the Sound. Plus, he was a friend of the family.

It did surprise Amanda however, that the Skipper called to inform them he was berthing one *other* passenger.

Not that it mattered, their boat was ample for several crew or passengers: The Master Cabin was up Forward for total privacy, its own shower and lounge quarters attached as a salon. But she was curious about the matter. He had asked to talk with Trevor.

"Who?" asked Amanda as they drove into the vessel's boatyard?

"Someone you know!" teased Trevor, now in the loop of things. Evidently he and the Skipper had talked at some length.

"OK. I give up!"

"Guess: A Naval Academy graduate...All-American champion of College Nationals in dinghy sailing in his senior year, a veteran Navy ..."

"Jim?"

"Yup!"

"...who flies jets?"

Trevor laughed "who flies jets......*and* space ships!"

"And space ships too!" she echoed.

They pulled into the boatyard.

Standing beside the skipper on the dock was a grey-bearded, bow-legged Jim Lloyd in jeans. One hand was holding a paint brush, the other a beer.

"Oh my God. Is he up for this race too?" she giggled.

"We'll see!" chuckled Trevor. "Hey...Jim! How you doing?"

The skipper's head turned, and Jim waved. All three of them were in conversation about a 'killer mission' – to win the race with this boat... Damned right there was work to do.

Within hours, it was Trevor with the bucket in his hand. Provisioning, safety and emergency checks brought back the memories of his own edarly Naval training, he told them. Before long Trevor was securing, stowing, preparing for the race like a pro.

He looked happy, thought Amanda, the boom box playing Reggae tunes off the stern transom.

Wearing only a 'very small bikini,' as Trevor put it, she plastered white sun-block on Trevor's nose, and she laughed.

Clearly, Trevor was having a great day at boat-side on a blazing hot day of the summer...

The plan was they would later all have dinner downtown with Barbara before bunking onboard for the night, and then push-off from the dock at first light.

It wasn't until later that afternoon that Amanda found Trevor below decks talking with Lloyd. She realized, in the confines of a boat, that they were never far from their work after all...

So all this was a premediated set up?

She did not mean to eavesdrop, but she could not help overhearing from the Galley where it was her chore to check the boat's freezer supplies.

"He said that in the second box of the Bank vault, he found an old Treatise. Something that was concealed as incriminating evidence in the early legal cases following the war. He said it described its very origins to the mid-19th century as the missions in Kenya and South Africa to dominate the local mines offering mineral collateral for Bank holdings using those assets..." offered Lloyd.

"He took images, and this is what it looked like..." continued Lloyd.

"Clearly, it was funded and fueled by wealth from old and new, as well as other occasional fascist organizations over the years, chiefly those concentrated in early mining venture overseas for rare ores and other exotic resources."

Amanda closed the galley door on them.

Trevor's voice could no longer be heard. But she was aware of the unauthorized material they were handling. She pulled from her duffle bag a long pink chemise, and if transparent, gave her covering over a scant swimsuit. She splashed water on her face, and tied back her hair.

She went topside and took it upon herself to survey the privacy of their dockage.   Then returned below to check outside the porthole.

She sat on the aft deck as if keeping watch. No "ears" listening to them - neither   above decks nor below. Sound on the water carried. There was always that danger of eves-dropping – an old ploy. Yet nobody was about. The skipper Tom, had been sent into town on an errand. They needed fresh sanding disks.

Amanda returned to the galley station. She made known her presence.

The doors to the engine room, across the gangway from where they sat, were wide open and two powerful diesel engines churned idly with mechanical humming to drown out most of the white noise. Clearly, nothing was getting recorded either by any hidden microphones.

"...The depositors were originally a group of early financiers.   Pundits and dictators   - usually found within the ranks of the military as defectors, or terrorists plotting various coups d'états..." Lloyd's voice went on.

"It was old world Fundamentalism using nefarious schemes to infiltrate Western wealth..."

Trevor was evidently listening.

"This movement had a shifting shape, even infiltrated into the Muslim Brotherhood, absorbing its ideology and doctrines for terror. We do know their infiltration tactics are old, even generational. Neither do they assume the sole trust of the Muslim brotherhood: They endorse social, economic, political issues too, including activists of any agenda. Environmentalists, open Media, Education unions, even the Liberal Arts are useful as a progressive transition to advance their socialist infiltrations."

"My God" said Trevor "He found their coffers in a Bank vault in the banks of Ireland...?"

"Not just the money, but the official Ledgers. It was originally deposited in Swiss Banks. But all moved to Ireland when banking opportunities opened up for large accounts and lower corporate taxes."

"So it's not the assets but the Ledgers that are incriminating evidence..."said Trevor.

"There is more. Here are the Records of repositories of treasure kept as *unmarked* catalogues."

Amanda came in offering bottled water. They each accepted and chugged. The cabin was hot.

"My God" muttered Trevor, his reading glasses on, water sweat-pimples across his forehead and brow which he tried rubbing dry with his painter's work-cloth.

"Here..." pointed Lloyd "...the exact content, weight and locations of gold bullion in repositories. Inventories of purloined Antiquities and objects in preservation, including much of the un-shown collections of the Hermitage taken down during WWII. These are their present locations..."

"London?" said Trevor.

"They were taken overseas for protection, hidden by various parties with the capacity to store them.... Other collections remain underground. See this list. And here are the assets and bonds of recent sales issued by Treasuries, Sovereign and private..."

Amanda came down. "Excuse me! Anyone want a sandwich from the galley?"

They looked up, and nodded, then Trevor began stowing all their materials and documents in the black leather briefcase.

"Excuse us sweetheart... We didn't mean to neglect you! I know you value your time offline..." said Trevor, looking at his watch. "But this is important..."

She smiled.

Trevor turned to Lloyd.

"Is there external intelligence to corroborate this?"

"He has this..." Lloyd said handing Trevor a large envelope, not minding Amana's presence.

"He stole it on the way out...Along with other banking information. Tax-shelters. There's a Data file and a hard-drive in there. Mainly lists, names, records and strategic accounts and filings to shelter profits by big corporations. Here, the magnetic security keys that open Ultra-secured boxes. This is...I don't know *what* this is."

"I can't imagine this makes him popular with corporations..."

"Or underground markets..." said Trevor.

"Precisely. They are trying several attempts to kill him. Before the IRS gets him, that is."

"I see."

"He needs protection, Trevor"

The cell phone rang. It was the skipper.

Amanda answered. "Hi Tom. What's up?"

Was there anything else needed for the boat while he was out?

"No thanks, Tom. We're fully provisioned. We're still swabbing and scrubbing the decks!" Then she added "join us all for dinner?...We're going out"

Jim and Trevor were finished, work rags still in their hands.

"Is Kendall working with you?" asked Trevor.

"Yes. He is fully cooperative, and he's handing over everything. He knows it might all end abruptly. And he wants protection to 'put his house in order" as he phrased it. How much time can you buy him?"

Trevor paused before responding.

"I'd need to get him to the UK, ideally. There are funds missing that we need to recover. He can stay at the Consulate for now. We want all this Intelligence *first!* Then, there is the issue of sorting co-mingling of accounts. Cross-check with Investments. Insurance fraud etc. etc. Euro-American. Asian. Japanese. Even German accounts still left over from the war...What *hasn't* he uncovered?"

Lloyd was holding a steady gaze. "He doesn't *want* to return. He's a liability in the UK"

"Then it's the Americans who must take him into their custody" said Trevor. "I'll broker some kind of a deal..."

"Right."

"You are *sure* he's safe?" pressed Trevor.

"Yes. Right under my nose. He doesn't know who I'm dealing with. But I need more time with him....And he wants to talk to *you*."

Trevor looked at him.

"Something about your Scottish heritage...not sure what"

"Alright" said Trevor getting up.

They were ready for another beer as the skipper inspected their work and approved. It was satisfying work, they laughed.

Tom declined the dinner invitation. There was plenty to do still before casting off at dawn, and plenty of food in the galley, he told them.

Trevor, Amanda and Lloyd left the boatyard for an evening in the city shortly after dusk.

"Not bad... for a sailor" said Trevor looking over his wife as she appeared on the gangway.

Beneath a stole, Amanda wore a dark-glimmering T shirt over designer jeans, her hair in a bun with a glitter pin, and in her hand a clutch bag that matched black leather perforated flats. She looked tanned; unadorned and artfully elegant for a dark summer night on the town.

"Thank you" she said, eyeing Trevor's yachtsman blazer and khakis - loaned from Tom who had insisted. *Sans the hat, at least...* They laughed.

To everyone's delight, Lloyd mounted an all-chrome Twin cam 103 engine Harley- Davidson. "Anyone for a ride?" he grinned.

"No thanks! We'll take the Taxi..."

Barbara was waiting for them downtown in New York City. And it was a shocker.

No surprise registered on Trevor's face when Barbara introduced them to her date. Only Amanda felt the twinge in her hand as Trevor squeezed unexpectedly.

"I'd like you to meet my friend" announced Barbara "Ian Steven Kendall"

He was wearing a leather jacket and a dark miner's hat.

"Nice to meet you..." they said, settling into a dark corner in the Pub for their dinner.

"Drinks anyone?" asked Trevor, searching up and around for service.

"Like I said..." Lloyd rasped to Trevor "*Right under my nose...*"

Amanda's cell phone pipped with a text message. Senator Williams.

"Meet you in RI" She showed the message to Trevor.

"Come on Guys! Let's have a wonderful evening..." belted Barbara.

**

At sometime before dawn, with all his passengers aboard and secured, the Skipper had deftly cast off the lines and set out to sea before light.

The vessel was well up the Sound by the time Amanda came topside for fresh air, and the boat was underway under full sail.
It had been a good night. Especially when returning from a night out in New York City to step aboard in the 'wee hours of the morning...definitely a little drunk,' as Trevor put it later that night, Amanda in his arms in the cabin.
It was a night of tenderness, the kind of lovemaking that framed their marriage with stolen moments when the children were asleep, or together on business travel trips. That is, before...

Wearing jeans under her life-vest, and with her legs crossed, she sat on the bow facing the wind, a galley cup of coffee in hand.
Her thoughts returned to the evening in town.
In a dark pub on the lower East side, where people wore black leather and bomber jackets, the words she heard last night from the man in the deepest corner made her spine chill...
From time to time, and with smoothing tones of jazz playing on a stage, Trevor drew her closer.
It helped. At one round, he pulled her up for a turn on the small dance floor.
"I'm sorry my darling" he whispered in her ear, his free arm waving at those watching from the bar. "...It's getting very close. But I have to take every advantage I

can... Lloyd promised there wouldn't be danger...But we've got to intercede before he goes undergound!"

Barbara, it seemed to Amanda, had no recognition. She was all eyes on the man talking.

He smoked, his eyes mostly down and his voice uneventful.

"...The financial framework and stock investment for these particular unregistered accounts, begin with aggressive hedge-fund tactics..." he said, his cigarette smoke rising like a veil from his hand on the table.

He puffed, mainly to pause. "...But after a period, to avoid detection, they slide into sedate endowment funds...

"Next, tentacles wrapped around the academic world, student loans, grants, medical research, business schools etc., where they are listed as donations. Gradually, they open up to insurance; banking and hedges against Sovereign defaults. Often they work on Fund Managers with a profile that suits their needs: Arrogant. A spender. A mouthy individual who touts success to goad others to excess across the landscape, making their own movements unremarkable."

The music stopped, and he shifted uncomfortably.

Then he talked.

Only once did Amanda ask a question.

"What sets them apart...Like, how are these *not* legitimate businesses and corporations?"

Kendall puffed demurely at his cigarette, smiled, ok with her question, then crushed his cigarette.

"That's how they begin. At least, to get into the infrastructure... But there's a second set of ledgers. So, yes. You are right... "

Trevor bought another round of drinks and put his arm around Amanda for reassurance.

It was getting late, dark and they were somewhere downtown New York.

Lloyd was unmoving, yet watching for potential intruders. Eavesdropping strangers, or others in the vicinity heard only diverted laughter. He had picked the right place for information."

"Go on!" nudged Barbara.

He did.

"...Once they have traction, there is no stopping the capital they can gather at the expense of small independents, usually by M&As. Mostly, they tout capitalism as their mantra. But pretty soon, they invoke other cocktails to justify an array of other acquisitions..." He paused, nervous. "I have their account numbers" he added simply. "They are...not small sums of money."

"They avoid labels and they network. Once the ball is rolling, and people start making money, they cannot be unmasked because they aroused no suspicion, left no trail, showed no outward collusion."

He looked down. Lloyd kept him going.

"There is a band, often legitimate bankers playing a dual agency role, they... communicate. Not terrorists, fundamentalists of anything..." He took a deep breath. "For twenty years now, they collaborate. It's as if they want to break-down conventional Western establishment, with money: They push and pull cash-flows; currency trading; influence of returns with deliberation and direction. They waiting for black swans... Their only footprint is found in offshore accounts. They are specific. They use code names."

"...hmm, tax paying?" mused Trevor.

"Of course not!" said Kendall.
Lloyd looked at Trevor, his eyes steady.
 "Who are these people?" Lloyd finally whispered.
Kendall smiled. He puffed, his gaze fixed.
 "Invisible. They have Exit plans. Strategy and finesse... looking for cracks in the infrastructure that allows them to feed into an agenda. They have infiltrated every conventional institution you can imagine with vulnerability, that point needed instant access/stoppage to cash. There are Accounts drawn to the US Fed, Central Banks; brokerage houses, investment banks. Sovereign funds. The Vatican. The..."
"The *Vat*...?" mouthed Barbara in disbelief.
"What is their *aim*?" asked Trevor, his finger gently raised for clarity.
Kendall stared at him.
Someone walked in.
Lloyd guffawed loudly "Alright Everybody. It's getting late you all... We are drunk!" he said, rising like a distracted fool. "Tomorrow is a big day! Let's all ...enjoy!" he looked directly at Kendall with a nod, the alarm given."
"Right!" they all shuffled.
They were outside in seconds, walking down a dark street.
The car was parked around the corner and out of sight. Lloyd's bike was across the street. He hopped on his bike, revved the engines and left in a storm of suddenness with Kendall on the rear seat.
Trevor and Amanda were in the car with Barbara pulling out the alley when two shots were fired.
They missed.
Kendall and his party had been spotted.
They had been identified.

Chapter 6

The Priest was puzzled at the letter in his hand. He pushed it away from his ink-blotter, got up from his desk and put on his boots. He walked out the Library door that lead to the Grounds.

They had let him stay as Elder Churchman. He was fit, and still strong. Over the years, all Church premises had become familiar to him and he knew every stone step, every gravesite, every tree and shrub that grew in on the ancient site.

He walked down the side of the open cloisters then out on the lawns West of the old Church. He stood, looking out to the horizon.

Beneath him the North Sea flailed at the craggy cliffs of Ireland. He scanned the open water as if he were scanning the history of time.

Since the Norman conquests, a Monastery had here stood as part of an ancient castle. Through medieval times - even through the Dissolving of the Monasteries by Henry VIII, here a solid church had stood.

Now as an old Parish Church, he could see beyond the cliffs and its ragged coastline.

The memories came flooding back.

It had been a long time ago since he received his first instructions. Yet here he stood, some twenty five years later, being asked to do what he did on those dark nights.

How was that possible?

He was young, strong and freshly ordained as a minister then...

How could he forget those nights?

It was always damp and windy, the ground soggy.

Digging grave sites in the Church cemetery for members of the congregation was not beyond his duties as a young Priest. That is, in the absence of an undertaker.

But three nights outside digging in the dark was hard and desperate work. He knew what the crates contained.

Gold and valuables from overseas must be protected, he was told. So he kept at it. This was war. This was for England.

He was to bury the basement stairwell to grade level, having sealed with brick and mortar the entrance at the bottom of the steps. He had filled the garden stairwell altogether with dirt.

On the other side of the entrance he had created a cave. There, the crates had been stacked, each with numbers and metal binding straps, all of them coated in oil cloth.

Sandbags were stacked to obscure them from view, then coal shoveled over the stockpile through coal-bunker doors, until only coal provision was visible. This, he had managed by himself.

Never revealing his secret caches, he had managed to fill to capacity the ancient Irish monastery with containers of gold – filling nooks, cellars, crevices and tunnels hidden deep within the stone structure, even graves were filled with crates and covered over.

For years shipments arrived which he must bury. And never once had he betrayed the secret.

Between the months of March 1917 -when the Czar abdicated and the Bolshevik Revolution unfolded, all that was taken from the Commissar of Finance, or from vaults of the Imperial Bank Building as gold reserves belonging to the Russian Imperial Monarchy had been systemically removed and shipped overseas.

Nobody knew. Not with any definitive certainty. Some leaks proved to be spectacular revelations and tales.

Mainly, in diplomatic communiques, it was said to be moving out of Russia. Ministers of foreign governments thought some of this treasure was used for war Reparations arranged by France at the Treaty of Versailles. Indeed some Russo-treasure had actually found its way to European banks and repositories. As shipping would allow, some went to the Bank of England in London.

Some came through North America, Canada. The sea route taken by trade vessels included Japanese cruisers sailing firstly from Vladivostok to Yokohama, and later from Yokohama to Vancouver.

Alternately, Russian bullion was loaded on steel railcars of the Canadian Pacific Railway and delivered to the Ottawa repositories of the Bank of England.

Occasionally, it had found its way to Ireland, only as diversion from prying eyes and enemy detection, and only where safe.

How it all began for the priest, he could hardly tell.

An elder parishioner, Mr. Breyer asking for a favor, it was…And never, over the years, had the Priest betrayed that trust.

That was during the First World War, the Great War, as some called it.

What puzzled him now was how such a request should be repeated after all these years. Mr. Breyer had long ago passed on. This was strange, indeed.

The message he just received differed little from the last time.

By special coded words he was given his instructions to unload the crates from the dock. Just like before, a ship would approach the tiny harbor. The ship would come in under cover of night, docking at the old pier at the base of the cliff, beneath the Monastery.

"*Extreme need*" the note said, in handwritten cursive on government-issued stationary.

He looked again across the sea. His lips moved in soft prayer. *My God. My God. What has happened now?*

Back at his desk, he reread the letter.

The inventory, he was informed, was not to be examined. The crates would all be numbered, their contents fully accounted and itemized.

* *

Amanda was horrified. She read her email. Why she opened it was the question. It was anonymous. Yet it cited her name and her case report.

> *"You are being toyed with. In 1913 when the Federal Reserve Act was passed - all land and possessions were hypothecated to the Federal Reserve Bank as collateral to a non-payable federal debt.*
>
> *H*

She sat there, and put her hand to her mouth.
How could this be? Who would know anything about any of this stuff? It had been Forwarded.
Someone had been tinkering at the other end of her email, or maybe at the Desk of her recipient?
H?
Some unauthorized spy?
Ridiculous.

In research analysis, it was one thing to tinker with employment figures, salary scales, commission for work – but statutory law was altogether strict about another area of specialty.
Old English Laws *did* survive the Constitution, and Rights *did* convey with certain deeds of title and proprietorship. Especially when coming from Treaties. The laws of an early territorial claim might have contained preexisting legacy rights that prevailed, or by Reissue of patents by the United States Government.

Unless, maybe, a clause or claim of prior preeminence had *already* been exploited and was being protected, regardless. How?

What was this?

A warning. A threat. A mistake...

She thought about it.

Perhaps she had misunderstood. Amanda thought about it. Her Reference citation was explicit:

"If the evidence is indisputable, then the laws that shelter them are also indisputable and still resonate as statutory precedent..."

Then it occurred to her. This Tower was built to overthrow the Crown a century and half before the Revolutionary War!

She dialed for the Senator.

"Rhode Island was a Proprietary State..." he said. He paused. "I see what you're getting at!"

"Shall I send you my Report Sir?"

"Amanda, this is terrific stuff. Can you develop such ideas into a working framework for a case?"

"Well, I have a call into the SEC for more information. There are lawyers doing pro-bono work... The idea is not to cause alarm, but to allow for some short term tax wavers to encourage the local economy. That's all."

"...but with huge potential for investors, I see!"

She grinned, if puzzled by his leap.

"Well done! Copy me with every step of your progress. Especially on how you want to quantify the assets..."

"Will do."

"See you tomorrow..."

**

England 1942.

Directive orders were clearly written.
HQ24 was an escort fleet of the Royal Admiralty deployed from Iceland. In the convoy was a Merchantman the *USS Idaho* carrying undisclosed cargo delivered from Russia.
Midway across the Atlantic, a US Convoy was to take over, and all ships ordered to proceed under full escort for United States territorial waters, just off the coast of Newfoundland.
The Skipper of the ship - requisitioned by the civilian Ministry of Shipping and Ministry of War Transport, knew they were in safe waters at last.
Code Name Operation POMPOUS was successfully delivered of her cargo across the open Atlantic.
 The US Convoy GM 22 was all but assured. Docked at Halifax Canada, they were now bound for New York, the final leg of the journey.
They hugged the coastline, remaining inside US territorial waters.
At New York they would be refitted for another delivery of Supply across the Atlantic for the Allies.
It happened in the dark.
It was dark, and silent where the U Boat surfaced, delivering two torpedoes into the portside aft-quarter of both Merchant ships, then it slipped noiselessly

below the surface and dove under the Convoy of all surface combatants.

Both Merchantmen suffered a hit. The first exploded immediately. The second released two white rockets to alert the Convoy of her hit as she lingered on the surface.

Briefly considered salvageable tugs came quickly alongside her stern. The Captain and a few hands went below to life up cargo for the salvage. But the wind came up, she sank suddenly.

 At a depth of 800 ft. off the coast of Maine, both ships were reported as having no survivors.

The Admiralty Board of Ottawa delivered a commendation for the Captain, citing his bravery in attempting to salvage his ship and valuable cargo. Especially since it became clear that the U boat had achieved its intended target without resistance; its precision and timing meticulously planned.

Both merchant ships had been singled out, without error, amid a Convoy of armed naval escort carriers. Neither vessel got a chance to deliver a single shot in retaliation. Both ships carried valuables across the Atlantic for shelter during the War.

Gold bullion.

* *

Chapter 7

As far as Todd was concerned, if there wasn't an IRS office in Connecticut there should be.

It was a great place to work. He had been up there occupying the Insurance Company offices of Hartford for two weeks, examining documents.

The previous White House had made a policy of tolerating no tax holiday for the more than $1 trillion held offshore in earnings by corporations. It made for political publicity.

Mercifully, things had changed.

To avoid taxes, hundreds of billions of dollars in profits attributed to overseas subsidiaries were to be repatriated: The official positions was that they should be paying a 35% tax rates when the money came home.

And their credentials should be examined closely.

Todd smiled.

Todd knew that Offshore, these moneys could enjoy 12% tax rates.

Oh Yeah!

The IRS was to consider the matter urgent. The crisis was not about tax-evasion. It was about the government's exposure to unmarked debt, to Liability and Assets unregistered.

Sovereign debt was also at stake.

There was the danger.

Publicly, money had to be collected from somewhere. Even if for asset enumeration purposes only.

Accountability was important in keeping tabs of expenses and obligations. From Military bases and other tangible net assets to things attainable and collectable, taxable or liable.

Information gathering was premium.

Todd knew that one way to find money was through insurance coverage. Since risk-aversion was a discipline for big business, insurance protection was bought a premium they paid in large ways. And it was all going offshore. Or at least, calling from multiple destinations - all of them eastward.

The worst offenders, decided Todd, were the Pharmaceuticals. They had special accounts sheltering enormous profits from the US Internal Revenue Service. Yet it was a fine line. So far, all American multinationals utilized legal ways to avoid paying taxes.

Traditionally, they brought home cash - tax free, and employed creative strategies for shelter. Even the names of the bank accounts were titillating. He looked down the list. They had boat names!

"The Killer B" account.

"The deadly D".

How about the "Sarah B" he chuckled. That sounded like a winner's boat name...

Bermuda was a boat destination where much was held in overseas accounts for offshore banking.

Todd looked over the Report submitted by the Securities and Exchange Commission related to official Business Filings.

The report had been published in various forms for public consumption. It had even made the Financial news:

> *Merck & Co. Inc.* the second largest drug-maker, had supposedly financed its acquisition of *Scherling-Plough Corp* with $9 billion from abroad without paying any US tax. This, the securities filings showed.

At the same time, neither was any of this a mystery, nor illegal. Todd felt he had to laugh.

> Then there was the drug-maker *Pfizer Inc.* bringing home $30 billion from offshore accounts for its acquisition of *Wyeth* while supposedly trying to avoid the disclosure of their profit.

"*What a country..*" muttered Todd. "No wonder the Government was going broke."

Here was another. It was posted in the newspaper.

> The *Switzerland and Delaware* disclosure of *Eli Lilly and Co.* - an Indianapolis-based pharmaceutical company had apparently set up vehicles for tax-free importation of foreign cash following a $6 billion purchase of *ImClone Systems* in 2008.

"What a country" he repeated, shaking his head.

He went outside for some air.

Still, he liked being in taxes. He was a smart sonofabitch. And it was a free country.

He liked the land of opportunity. It was a free market economy. Walking, he thought about it. Without it, there was danger, he knew.

Because if you stopped one man or company from making money, you stopped them all...

Only keep the laws!

They had arrived at mid afternoon, and their boat rafted up to the *"Matilda"* in the harbor just off Newport.

Tomorrow was the start of the big race to Bermuda. Tonight, if the Australians had their way, there would some real partying going on in the harbor, they laughed.

Racing Yachts had been anchoring all day and were already docking off the harbor with their hailing Burgees flying showing their different Ports of call.

It was colorful, and it was competitive. At their moorings in the setting sunlight, all yachts appeared harmless. But in the morning they would jolt alive with killer instincts and deadly strategy, everyone knew. It was serious business, a big event.

Tonight was dinner ashore and dancing on the lighted lawns of the Yacht Club.

Trevor was standing under a white tent which held the bar. He was collecting drinks for his party when the Senator found him.

"Too bad you're not competing tomorrow!" said Williams.

Trevor smiled. "It's back to Washington I'm afraid. But we had a great vacation *getting* here!"

They laughed.

"I'm clueless" added Trevor "But it's always fun with Amanda in charge. She's a great sailor!"

Williams agreed heartily, if a little too heartily, thought Trevor. Still, they were working together.

"I heard about your affair with the woman..."

"It was nothing" interrupted Trevor.

"Oh yes. Right. I meant your...err affiliation with the Russians?"

"Just routine business. Uneventful meetings" said Trevor, cutting off all interest to carry on.

The Senator moved on and Trevor threaded his way through the crowd.

"Hey Barton...!" yelled one excited voice across the bar.

"What's the bet I beat you tomorrow, Eh?"

"A Hundred Bucks!"

"Make it a Thousand you wus!"

"OK!"

With four drinks and the crowd thickening, Trevor raised his arms to move off to the side.

This was not the place for bankers tonight, he knew. Besides, he had other things on his mind.

He and Amanda had one more night onboard together before turned the vessel over to the skipper.

He sighed, nodding and chatting to various people on the lawn - *The Novice*, as he had called himself, had made a few acquaintances. One or two had shown interest in his profession and exchanged business cards.

He aimed for the Yacht Club waterfront. Most faces were totally unknown. A few celebrities, several CEOs, and only one couple he recognized, but that was it. However, there was one reoccurring head that peaked persistently in and out of his line of vision. Almost as if following him...

In this crowd, with the drinking and heady festivities, it could be coincidence, and he dismissed it entirely.

Besides, Trevor knew he must talk to Amanda about his plans. He had hesitated...She was so enjoying herself with old friends.

But Yes. He *must* talk to her...

A soft summer wind whistled through the rigging, and tunes of nighttime incantations drifted across the harbor as boats rocked gently on the water.

On this night before a day full of promise, Trevor felt more like a carefree sailor than a banker, and he realized the richness and fun that Amanda had brought to his life. He turned tenderly to his wife cradled in his arms...

They slept in the Forward cabin of their vessel.

When they talked, it was almost dawn, the harbor strangely quiet yet.

"Thank you.." he whispered in her ear. "I'm having so much fun up here with you!"

"I love you" she said simply.

 He told her how he enjoyed the party. It gave him bragging rights, he said, to have a sailor for a wife.

She looked at him soberly. "We have a long tradition in the family with our boats..."

"Oh yes?"

She propped up a pillow.

She and her cousins campaigned the family boat every year for this event. Since girlhood, she explained, when her parents used to take them out sailing. "Over the years, we've accumulated prowess and experience to compete a boat."

"...And money?" he added

"...and money!" she agreed. "It was much simpler then. But it was fun. Twice we've placed in the top three and had trophies..."

She smiled. "At every Thanksgiving Table – when the entire family gathered, first we said Grace, then we toasted for the next Trophy!"

The Skippers Meeting was scheduled for 9.00 AM on shore. It comprised of instructions. Race Rules; Start

Guns; Flag Signals; Committee Boats; Class Rules and Start schedules for class sequencing. After that, it was each boat for itself...

Finally, they cheered. *May the best boat win!*

It was a glorious morning, the wind picking up and the waves a gentle rise. Excitement was in the air.

The Newport to Bermuda Race Day was clearly underway as the town fairly rippled under increased blowing.

Boats at moorings pushed off one by one, and the sea took her vessels into her thrashing as they made their way offshore, beyond the Yacht Club seawall, followed by a fleet of Spectators to the Sailboat Start Line.

A flotilla of Media boat-engines circled, helicopters hovering, and Red ribbed zodiacs zipped around with high-powered lens and camera equipment for various News and Broadcasting Networks.

Slowly the vessels blossomed with sail unfurling, and Under full rigs, yachts of every color and insignia were a spectacle to behold.

The Morning Star, of Disney fame. Their own boat *Tenacious*, stood as a well known fixture of honorable mention. The *Endeavor*, of the Mid Atlantic Yacht Clubs. The *Courageous*, from the Hercules Foundation. The *Wayward Ho*, sponsored by Xerox. *El Fiego*, from Bolivia. The *Donnybrook*, from Ireland. The *Sarah A*, owned by Mr. Steve Williams. The *Liberty*, from the US Naval Academy.

Then came other classes. Some bigger, some smaller, each with their design registered handicap and ratings: The *Deadly Duo*. The *Swan*. The *Lazy Susan*. The *Killer A*. The *Killer B. Outbound.*

All the hotels were packed. From clear across the harbor the fleet could also be seen through binoculars. On one balcony facing the harbor, the boats were registered in a book. The man behind the binoculars knew each boat by name.
Finally, when they were all off, he turned away and retreated from the balcony of his Hotel.
Todd had what he needed.

The signal was given, and the official Start opened up a converging fleet of competitive yachts flying full colors and powering up to speed.
Few recalls, restarts, and tangles signaled a well-trained group of skippers deploying in waves of boats crossing the start line according to class of handicap regimens. They knew what they had to do, and what they were there for, each vessel to run at its full capacity.
The Spectator fleet of boats following travelled the few miles out the harbor, all Racers ahead in blustering wind and white-capped sea for a voyage across open water.
Over the horizon they peeled off, tacking into the wind for strategic advantage, technical skill and endurance.
Only those with sophisticated tracking devices could be followed on satellite navigational instrumentation. But in large part, the race ran silent for days, with only a few breaking radio silence and giving away their navigational positioning. Especially as the weather worsened.

Day and night, all the way to the finish line in Bermuda, the yachts tacked their way under sail-power across the ocean, manned with skippers and crew in heavy seas. It required skill, strategy, endurance and the will of survival. This year was not for beginners.

Alone at sea, aboard each vessel knew that only your own boat mattered - and only the navigator could analyze the vessel's tactical maneuvering; its stealth and night navigation.

Still, as a racing fleet, each boat represented the finest in maritime seaworthiness and technology - many representing software companies that designed their systems. One wrong decision could spell disaster, if not loss of life.

As a sport, it was a feat of the highest caliber for any corporate sponsor.

* *

The dock fell silent as the sky turned to a grey drizzle. Amanda stood very still, her heart heavy. She would return home alone.

"I have to go" had said Trevor, kissing the top of her head.

She was so disappointed she was in tears.

They had enjoyed a blissful few days together, and it had been a long night on their boat, loving, talking, and explaining.

But in the end, she understood.

It was always a fine line that he walked, he explained. Less a matter of crisis management than crossing the threshold of intervention, as he put it. And it was a judgment that only he could make...

He was leaving shortly after the Races, he said. Flying out of Boston for London directly ...due in part to news that was worrying.
Lloyd had called.
Kendall was an issue needing attention in London.

Amanda had insisted on driving him to the Airport.
"And the other?" she asked, referring to his reasons for returning to London so suddenly.
"Something on the radar with disturbing consequences" he responded.
She would never have guessed had he not gone through it with her earlier.
Trevor was on the Board of Governors of one of England's biggest banks. His family had held that post for several generations, and his responsibility in that capacity was one of responsibility, often demanding. Since it was a legacy position, it was not an impediment to his appointment as a Minister by the government. His loyalty was never questioned, and conflicts of interest never arose.
Yet, something had gone wrong. Terribly wrong, as his private secretary told him on the call from Scotland yesterday. There had been a run on currency.
He broke it down for Amanda in simple progression, not that she was entirely unfamiliar. But she was alarmed, and she wanted him to talk about it. Even if they were tired, drunk and excited - all at the same time.
They were alone, and to Amanda, Trevor could speak in trust and confidentiality.
The banks had used highly sophisticated computer modeling, he said...to follow financial transactions and trends. They had set up analytics that defined any

trend, even if barely recognizable. That was their first position of operating procedures.

 Their bank watched for any activity of acceleration, such as when the trend was reorganizing to show prevailing "bias" as they called it. After that, they searched for anomalies in anything that might be a threat, testing for a general equilibrium within an average statistical spread.

Following that, they called themselves to an Alarm Test -Stage Three Analysis. That is, they were testing for possible intervention - like, say, if pricing was showing a setback. Or if the government had to intervene for any reasons. If the equilibrium recalibrated to the norm over a period of short time, then they could assume that there was no crisis bubble. But if the bubble persisted then a Stage Four would be testing for market failure or endurance.

 By Test Stage Five, as Trevor called it, where the reality of the market could no longer sustain the exaggerated bubble, then they were on full alert for a bank crisis.

Amanda asked "What then?"

"Then a few carry on...but the norm is gone, and we are approaching a moment of critical failure - Stage Level Six - unless the trend suddenly finds reverse or tones down."

She looked at him, alarmed.

"By Stage Seven? We are in a crash mode"

 "So, how bad is it now?" she persisted.

"You don't want to know..." he said, kissing her. He closed his arms around her protectively. But she knew that he would have already informed Washington of his absence upcoming...

At least she had him for the start of the race...

**

An email had come in for Amanda.

She had long ago learned not to dismiss history as irrelevant to modern applications.

Like a doctor about to implement a blood transfusion, you'd better know the blood type. Many patients died without careful anthropological study ...usually policy makers dispensing wisdom found in traditional problems to embrace new technologies.

But this surprised her. It alluded to open warfare amongst internal factions at a critical time of development, and as legacy, would frame statuary law.

 "In terms of resources and division of labor in early community development, notice what happens to first-born sons (inheritors) of early planters (settlements) in the colony of Maryland where there was less social cohesive "accountability" for resources, money and missing persons...

Something strange happened in the late 1630s.

Those Chesapeake ties with Rhode Island have a lasting impact on trade and currency. It's one of those unsolved things that sits beneath us like a powder keg. It happened again, in 1913 Be careful. It remains concealed for a reason.

Best, "H"

PS: When Ben Franklin made King George cede sovereignty to the people of the colonies, the entire concept of "personal status" changed.

Revolutionary America gained Sovereignty with all rights to own land patents, and to strike a currency for their own financial system...

Amanda was already tampering with a highly sensitive financial system fraught with political liabilities. She had just one chance to get it right. And that chance was coming up soon. She was invited to support the Senator's presentation to a Senate Subcommittee for Financial Reform.

She had better be prepared to answer questions in his ear. They were testing laws of precedence needing to be changed.

At least, that's what he told her to prepare for.

*** ***

Washington DC, 1948

The Cabinet Minister was driven out of the White House gates and through the city after a visit with the President.
He spotted the large Department of Navy buildings on Constitution Avenue, and gave it a silent salute.
The Navy had come a long way!
Largely funded by Appropriation bills passed through Congress, it was developing a new fleet of submarine that would rule the seas. As the newly appointed Secretary of Commerce, he would help make it happen. President Roosevelt would have been proud.

Those days of agonizing over losses of US ships at sea were redolent with pain and frustration still.

How could he forget that meeting in the White House in June 1942. There stood Churchill, Hopkins and Roosevelt huddled in the White House to discuss a cross-channel invasion - later known as the D-Day Invasion. Who could have imagined such a thing?
The plan was to relieve pressure from Russia, their Ally, now fighting on the Eastern front...And suddenly news arrived that brought everything to a stop: Field Marshall Rommel had advanced the German *Afrika Korps* to Tobruk.
He reached for his pipe, it always served to calm his nerves, the memories still vivid.
The British were close to despair.

Europe had fallen.

Singapore had just fallen in the Pacific, now Tobruk in the Middle East? He never forgot Churchill's words: *"Defeat is one thing; disgrace is another."*

North Africa held some of the Empire's greatest caches of wealth, and Rommel just marched right up to Tobruk?

Only Roosevelt could save the day, it was said. Even as America remained divided.

Roosevelt gave a rousing pledge of support.

Thus it was that Churchill was able to return to London - not as a broken politician unable to mend the disillusion of the British people, but a hero with word of a massive consignment of military aid from America. The psychological effect alone of that promise - not the 300 or so tanks, changed the course of the war.

How could he forget...

Yet not long after the war ended, even as Marshall's plan was rebuilding Germany, he heard about a different turn of events.

It came to him on a bitter cold morning in Washington DC when President Truman called him in to say that their former Ally, Russia, was now the Adversary devouring Europe in a new "Cold War."

He would write a letter to Marshall, his old friend.

He would remind him of that moment - that blow they got when they heard about Tobruk. Not because of what followed, but because of the policy tactic that changed everything when Roosevelt spoke.

"Like the million rifles...the psychological effect" came as a promise to aid Europe to resist the Soviet Union...

Next week, he decided, Marshall would be delivering a Speech at Harvard University aimed at Europe:

They should resist the Soviet Union, even *without* military aid from America. This was *psychological* warfare!

Of course there was work to do.

He leaned forward and tapped the glass. "Bob. Take me directly home to Georgetown will you? I have work to do there!"

"Yes Sir."

**

Trevor had called from London.

Clearly, the case on the Extradition was heating up on both sides of the Atlantic.

European bankers wanted the detainee apprehended for fraud.

Here, the FBI was questioning Barbara about Kendall. Did Barbara know who he was? His whereabouts? When, and by whom was he last seen?

The names of Amanda and her husband had come up. According to Barbara's attorney, there were even questions about the Gala in which one elderly lady was damaged by grease paint.

Now Embassy staff were asking about Trevor. Where was he?

Amanda was wearing thin.

She kept her mind on her work at her desk.

She talked to the Senator during the day. Other calls she dismissed.

Later that afternoon, Amanda thanked Clara for her work in the house, and let her off early. She would take the dogs for a walk and fix dinner...

It took her mind off things. She ran with the dogs. The exertion felt refreshing and the dogs had a good frolic through Rock Creek Park Trails. Only once did she feel a need to pause and look behind her. But she saw no one.

The wintery daylight was closing quickly and the temperature dropping.

Arriving at the house she thanked Watson for his winterizing efforts Outdoors. He had come in today clear out the garage. He reported that the Garden gates in the outer perimeter were all closed "if the dogs want to be let out for a spell this evening..."

"Thanks Watson. That's most thoughtful of you. We may all have an early night!" she added.

Finally, with all the animals fed, she returned to her desk Mail and Messages - mostly to the kids with news, updates and schedules coming up for the family.

She was about to return to her work but decided instead to lay down.

Upstairs in a bedroom of deepening shadows from the window, she stretched out on the bed. She was fatigued, and she was worried. She missed Trevor.

Still, it felt good to be back home... Even if it had been a long day of questions and queries.

She had informed Clara - and everyone else - that Trevor was out for an indefinite period of time.

Then again, she told herself closing her eyes, that was the choice of life they had. At least they were safe here...

She wanted to get up. A headache and cold snuffed up her sinuses, but somehow she felt too weary. It was that change-of-the-seasons exhaustion when the body was less responsive to ideas of activity yet the mind restive. A few days *sans* pressure and quietness at home would do her the world of good, she decided.

In fact, after Wednesday, she would give Clara the rest of the week off. She would even cancel most of her own engagements for the week. She would coast for a few days, waiting for word from Trevor.

Bliss. Like a self-imposed Spring-Break..

 So much had happened - so fleeting was their getaway trip, yet so deeply entangled was the matter of Kendall that she was feeling anxious. Yes, it was dangerous. She was unsure which direction to take.

Sit still, Trevor had admonished.

She took a deep breath. She closed her eyes and sank heavily into a dreamless slumber.

She woke up still stretched out on her bed. It was 2.11 AM.

She realized that her fatigue was stress-induced. Anxiety about matters that put both Trevor and herself under scrutiny was one thing, but there was something else.

Perhaps it was Senator Williams and his agenda. The work was becoming onerous, if not without clear direction.

What was he up to?

He seemed...she wasn't sure. Like he was baiting her into ...*what?* There was something he was holding back.

What?

For one thing, why was he not responding to her emails? For another, she wasn't sure how this case was supposed to play out. He never really gave her a strategic plan. Just a "Go-Ahead."

What was his goal, exactly. Was he *watching* her?

The bigger picture was starting to take shape. Trevor, in his own world, was coming under review.

He had taken a huge risk offering shelter to someone who was officially "Wanted" by his host government. These things didn't sit well. Something was terribly wrong. Someone needs to talk to someone, she decided.

She felt like she was sitting in the middle of something. Should she go for a pre-dawn walk?

She searched for the dogs. They would look at her with such trusting eyes when they awoke.

She'd wait.

She picked up her morning coffee and saw the WSJ Newspaper come flying over the garden wall. It was delivered daily, and Clara usually picked it up when she came in, leaving it on the kitchen table for them.

 On occasion the newspaper went all day unopened - such was the crunch of activities that had crowded into their calendars.

This meeting. That meeting. Working as a volunteer suited her fine. But she noticed that it was no less demanding than a paying job! To say nothing of her own professional commitments that could not be neglected. Yet she managed it all and to a large degree enjoyed it all.

But this was different. She turned hastily to the newspaper and searched the pages. The news was uneventful. A story about Congressional wrangling. Magazine Fashion trends. Economic national debt and a few events upcoming for the city. One however, caught her attention.

> *"...The Federal Reserve's preferred price gauge, which was tied to consumer spending (stripped of food and energy costs) had climbed 0.5 percent annual pace. The Fed's longer term projection for inflation was a range of 1.6 percent to 2 percent. Rising oil and food costs may push up the prices of other goods and services."*

She sipped, eying her Notes.

> *"...The figures incorporate new, more comprehensive data from tax records and may*

> *help support the biggest part of the economy in coming months."*

She looked out the window. Two birds perched themselves on a bough, one chirping lustily, the other still. The garden promised bloom. She paused. It was an older plan planted years ago when plantings were unadorned and simpler. For a Tudor garden, it was ideal. Her thoughts strayed.

Then her eyes returned to the page before her. What balance sheet could be used to reconcile those figures, she wondered.

Either Congress wasn't watching, or the Fed was asleep at the wheel.

Or... the Report was *faulty?*

Was there some other issue that the Senator was wanting resolved? Some legal presupposition that framed an issue of modern currency, but bound by dated regulation?

Why did she get that feeling?

Of course, this was the United States. It was just the News, after all...

> *...*"Sales are improving in every region. They stand at near records in the developing world..." *Mike DeWalt, director of investor relations at Caterpillar said "...We've become somewhat more positive about economic growth in the developed economies of North America, Europe, and Japan."*

She felt uncomfortable.

There was something she couldn't quite fathom in his questions. Why was he so interested in the legal framework of financial operations and procedures?

She went upstairs to shower and dress, and she peeled away a Bandaid that covered a small scratch from the garden. When finished, she surveyed her appearance. There she stood, a mariner's deeply tanned if troubled face with generous eyes that smiled often, and hair that fell down her shoulders when not tightly woven in a knot behind her head. A linen blouse peered out from a short leather vest, and her long loose skirt flowed as freely as the dogs would require her to do when she took them out later. Then she heard them, and smiled.

Woof, woof.

Downstairs, she returned to work.

The Senator. *Where did he stand on all this?*

Should she talk with him?

She paused as a thought crossed her mind.

No. She should not.

He was watching her research, *testing ...*

*** ***

April got up, turned around again and settled at the bottom of the bed. Less than a year old, she was still a puppy. As a Springer spaniel, it had taken hours of training and outdoor exercise to get her to calm down. Her disposition, while sweet tempered, was easily excitable.

They had had a long and happy day together, all of them.

Sleepy-eyed as she was when Amanda let her out in the morning with the others, April was equally excited to get upstairs on the bed for the night.

 Dispensation from Trevor in his absence, said Amanda. April licked away at the hand that took her there. The whole bed!

April twirled, and twisted then wiggled on her back and over again. Rewarded all the while with belly rubbing, head patting and distracted stroking from Amanda, they relaxed well into the night until the books closed and the bedside light went out.

"Bed time and lights out!"

April was contented evidently, letting out mini snores and ruminating tremors as she slumbered. Amanda had to laugh. Then it wasn't long before Amanda herself fell into a deep sleep.

At first, the feeling was just one of disturbance, April licking her face.

"Uh!" groaned Amanda "April...*Go* back to sleep!" She pulled up the covers.

April did as she was told, turning round at the foot of the bed, than settled into a nest of bedding.

The next time April licked her face, Amanda was annoyed. So annoyed that she sat up, turned on the light and was about to utter some words of admonition when she realized the dog had left the bedroom.

It was two o'clock in the morning.

Amanda swanned down to the first floor. April was in the kitchen rummaging around with her bowl of food snacks.

Amanda had a furtive desire to settle the dog's needs and then get back to bed herself. It wasn't until she surveyed the kitchen and was halfway out to the front entrance that something made her pause suddenly.

Nothing in particular really. Except an awareness of something.

She froze. Had she thought defensively before coming down and thoughts about the dog...

She turned slowly.

She was standing there like a pillar of salt under a chandelier of Venetian glass fairly glowing in visibility. And there was April, poised like the hunting dog at the front door, a deep growl curdling in her throat.

"April..." began Amanda.

A car veered off, leaving little doubt as to its intentions. Amanda rushed to the window. Its headlights switched on only when it reached the end of the block to turn into Wisconsin Avenue; its chances of encountering a waiting police car in this city without headlights were not high. So he was leaving.

Thank God he fled!

She noted that the car was a sedan. Light colored. If she were right, tags that held some kind of red internal design. She would write it all on paper, she decided. Fresh in the morning with it all still in her mind. Security was not Amanda's strongest suit. Nor really, Trevor's. And while endless talks and discussions had taken place about their need to take precautions with gadgets and locks and silent dial numbers, the house was old. Period. Security was not part of its grandiose lifestyle. Institutional in décor, there were few valuables in it. It was the view of Amanda and Trevor that ostentatious consumption was unnecessary for those who had a meaningful life. Their wealth was elsewhere.

Vowing to take security measure more seriously, she went through every door and bolted it shut. The windows she latched shut. Drapes, she drew tight; screens and blinds, mainly to obscure visibility to any observer peeking into their open household. She'd install an Alarm system. She would turn it on at night. Starting tomorrow, she promised herself.

It's just that with three dogs and a restless scholar in the house, alarms were nasty little devices that could detonate like a land mine and scare everybody in the house with panic.

April was staring at her. She gathered her stuff in her arms and said "Good Girl!"

Much petting and licking followed. "Yes! You are a good girl! Defending your territory against intruders!"

She walked into the study, a warm library with walls lined by shelves, collections, bits, books and paintings of various eras.

In the far corner was a designated space for office functions. Computer, fax machine, laptops and head-gear for TV watching. Two leather armchairs and a comfortable oriental rug made it the most inviting room in the house at night.

It was Trevor's favorite room. Subdued lighting fixtures cast soft hues of blues, greens and yellow glows, turning the wall paintings into old friends, the Oriental rug into a parterre of wilderness grass.

Amanda yawned. What the hell, she thought. Some thief! She thought about making a cup of tea. No. She would resist the temptation to settle down at the computer and...

Nor the TV. She put down the device on the divan.

She froze.

Just like that.

Her mind was alert but cautious. She felt it. A presence.

Behind her.

How could she be so stupid?

She turned slowly. She would face her intruder.

Silent as a ghost, he stood there. Looking at her darkly from the doorway to the study.

Kendall.

*** ***

Chapter 8

The Diplomatic Consulate office in New York did not like getting unscheduled calls from the American Federal authorities.

Conflict resolution with the Americans was not their mission. Government to Government liaison was one thing. Extradition proceedings for sheltering a fugitive Felon was another.

"Hello Justice Oldertorpe" said the Charge D'Affairs. "How nice to receive your call!"

Less than 35 minutes after the call, the Consulate had sent a communique and was on the phone to the Embassy in Washington. A three-way call was directed through to London where it was 3 o clock in the morning GMT.

"...The FBI are...making enquiries again about a citizen who might have entered through New York. But somehow I got the distinct impression there was something else behind their questions. As if the matter had implications beyond what they were able to discuss..."

"Umm. Did they give any hints as to the timing of their enquiry, perhaps?" said Trevor.

"Not really. In fact they were briefed to confine their questions to the issue at hand. It was not just a compliance issue. It's a point of political enquiry... I'm certain of it."

"Right then. I'll make a few responses here with their Embassy in London."

In Washington, Chancellor Whittaker turned the Speaker phone off, he and Nancy had heard enough. To New York, he finished with a few words. "I'll let you know what's on their mind. There must be something else stirring the pot...Send me what you have and I'll work on it. Can you come down tomorrow? Right."

Whittaker turned off the device and turned to Nancy. "Send in Jack and Ed Benson will you please Nancy?"

Whittaker discussed the matter with his two Senior Staff members at the Visa Section. It was his duty to do so, as the Americans would expect.

However, Tim Whittaker knew exactly what was going on. Except that he wasn't certain about the timing. They were fishing, he knew it. So they had time...

The FBI were developing a case against a Diplomatic subject that had gone missing. What the legal terms of the case were however, was something he'd have to examine with care, and buy for time.

He walked down to the Rotunda where a reception was underway for the new Emissary to Australia. A sort of Welcome-to-Washington by the Diplomatic colony as a way of introducing their two staffs for potential collaboration and cooperation.

He checked on his car parked outside, first. It was up the hill from the Observatory where the Vice President of the United States held his residence. And he got out his cell phone.

"Trevor..." he said, leaving a message on his London home address. "Headwinds here in Washington...Suggest we wrap this up!"

Whittaker walked back to the Rotunda. He would call Fred Hopkins up at the State Department later today....

* * *

At the New Hartford offices of the Internal Revenue Service, new data was coming in from last year's tax filings. Plus a letter.

It was the Federal Government petition to the IRS to be careful of the disclosure of information about certain individuals that might be reviewed "for other matters related to finances..."

That meant potential changes in the tax and finance codes were being written up on K Street by lobbyists for Congress to authorize. Or so it would seem.

For Todd, this was nothing new. He knew the country had survived three difficult years, and the Surplus of $700+ Billion Congress appropriated to salvage the banking systems met with an urgent need to reform the banking system - let alone scramble for a way to pay for the damned bailouts. However, as in all political processes, these things were taking time.

"...Under the circumstances, given the plight of the nation and the rising unemployment, I would ask for discretion with public information about the tax returns of individuals who clearly stood at the upper ends of corporate leadership with large bonus."

It was an unusual letter thought Todd. And he had no problem with CEOs getting big bonuses. Such were the hazards and rewards of Free Enterprise, something known around the world as American exceptionalism. But to suppress information that had for years held public scrutiny was a little odd.
No. This was unusual. This was intelligence gathering. This was economic duress beginning to frighten leadership...
Anyway, what puzzled Todd was not that the CEOs were making a ton of money, but that the corporations that gave them bonuses had not reported the ton of money!
What were those numbers this year?
He'd have to check new systems of what was now called "Aggressive Accounting Methods."
My Ass!
More like University Business Schools calling it ways of thieving from the American government, he thought.
 Yeah, he thought.
Bring on the Reform!
But Congress, he knew, was a species all unto itself. The only clues came from the non-corporate returns filed by various Congressmen themselves. And that, he knew, was a finely orchestrated venture. Documented returns done by specialized lawyers, of course.
So, he turned to legitimate accounts of Corporations. There were none that he could see were doing anything wrong. The laws had been written years ago.
Besides, he liked American business. Bad enough getting competition from overseas...
Then it struck him. Perhaps American business liked the competition from overseas?

Certainly, the political flack was strong. Outsourcing. Jobs lost. Tariffs. Environmentalism. Protectionism. Offshore options for corporate tax havens...
The list was endless. But that was politics, he chuckled. Still, there was something about these corporations that just didn't sit well with him. If he could trace a few of these accounts?
Not that he should expect to find malfeasance. We had come a long way since Enron. Even he understood the new accounting rules that they worked by.
No. He'd stay within the parameters of the conventions of the American tax system. That's what he would do. Decision made, and it kept him busy all day.
He left the building still wondering what the call was from the FBI. He should call in the morning.
He took the Metro.
And then there was something else. Rarely did you see the lines merge between a CEO and a Congressman. Normally business involvements were safely separated in a Trust. That is, once a CEO left private enterprise and entered public office lest there be any tainting of his judgment for special or conflict of interest.
There had been exceptions, not the least a key Presidential candidate.
Several Senators, long retired from public office, were retained as Trustee of entities and even drawing income, but only in advisory roles.

* *

Washington DC

"Hello Amanda" he said quietly.

He stood there like a bird perched between light and dark, cautious, but steady.

"Kendall!" she said calmly.

"Please don't be alarmed. I'm sorry to be an intruder in your home..."

"You gave me a fright!"

His eyes looked away. "Trevor said that I ..." his hands trembled at his jacket collar "that I could come any time I needed..."

Amanda started to breathe again. What had just happened here?

She was about to remind him that she had a cell phone. That she had a front door...That creeping in was not ok.

He was struggling. "I'm sorry!" he said simply.

She glowered at him.

"Trevor said..." he repeated. He took a step back. "... If I needed someone where ... I didn't mean to alarm you! I wanted to sleep on the porch or something..." He turned to point behind him at the dog, "I didn't mean to enter the front door!"

He fumbled in his pocket. "Trevor gave me this key!" It was attached to a string. "It's the key to your front door. The dog...your dog saw me...and I came in ....I'm sorry!"

She knew the key. It was Trevor's. They rarely used it, and the door might have even been unbolted. But she said nothing.

"You don't know this of course, but at the beginning of the War, Ireland was allied with Germany, not England..." he said.

Amanda folded her arms, hardly the explanation she was looking for. It was a surprising thing to hear.

He proceeded. "Yes. Churchill finally turned over the Irish to align with the English, but many Irish were Spies for the Germans. They had the docks that sheltered German U boats to take to sea to sink Allied shipping crossing the Atlantic..." he paused.

She waited.

"Their sentiments, as you can imagine, had long been one of hate against the English!"

"Enough..." she said. "Better sit down, here! I'll make some tea..."

She needed to collect her thoughts.

He had some nerve, showing up here unannounced. She felt angry. Trevor and his damned Intelligence flotsam. She knew she should not to call the authorities.

Jesus what a mess!

She eyed him from the hallway. He was still sitting, clutching the collar of his jacket.

This man needed help. She sat down across from him. "Here, drink!" she said, offering herbal tea and a side cookie. "You were saying?"

He took the cup, ate the cookie and thanked her.

She smiled, waiting.

He got up and walked around to the side Buffet. He knew a good English tradition when he saw one. There was a tray of spirits, a decanter and glasses. Whiskey, Brandy, Port. It was all there, Trevor would insist upon it in his Study. There it would be offered, from man to man, as a measure of hospitality.

"May I?" he asked.

"Please do!" said Amanda.

Kendall poured his drink then walked to the window curtain and let down the blind. He drank.

"My dear" he said in a thick Irish brogue "You have no idea..." He took another swig.

April the dog lay at Amanda's feet and watched. Then she settled her head as the man returned to his seat.

"The Russians, your ally, were not your ally at that time. No! They were, and still operated like an Ally. But they were territorial Bolsheviks all along. And as far as we Irish were concerned, let them take England damned to hell...Is what we would have liked..."

"But they didn't" she said.

"No they didn't..." he repeated.

Amanda smiled briefly.

"The Americans of course, the greatest ally of all... carried the day!"

He took a swig. "I know what you're be thinking. The Americans. Right?"

She looked down.

"Well, let me tell you something. It was *my* father that persuaded them to back the English...He had cause, too, having aided them, big time, you see!"

He took a long swig.

"But there was a condition to that concession. One that would affect the end of the war partitions of Europe. Hence the difficulties of the Cold War..."

She waited.

"In a way that misrepresented the Irish contribution to the war effort as a friend! The deal was that they should still receive all concessions of an equal alley... Of course it would change the maps of Europe, and today, such divisions harbors deep resentment still..." He finished his drink. "Well, I've said quite enough!"

"How is that relevant today?"

"How? In ways of treasure, cultural treasure that would have deep and abiding ties with the past, stolen and parceled out..."

She took a minute to gather her thoughts. Both of them here alone in the Study, pondering the solution to his cache of information... *What would Trevor expect her to do?*

What was Kendall up to, she wondered.

"They want to kill me" He said simply.

She stared at him.

Amanda's cell buzzed with a message. It was Trevor, Texting a message from London.

"Err..."

"There's an Assassination team out to silence me!" he pressed.

She picked up her cell and checked the message. Kendall stepped outside into the hallway and sat to wait.

She replied that an unexpected storm arrived on the porch during the night.

It was a code.

Would he know anything?

Considering the time difference between Washington and London, he might not receive this message until later. Surprisingly, he texted back immediately.

"It's Alright. The storm will pass... "

"OK" she replied.

She walked back out, finding Kendall still sitting out in the hallway.

April, heeled, was staring at him.

"Are you in need of money?" she said, her voice level.

His head was down. She approached him cautiously. He had dozed off.

She hesitated, uncertain. Was he stable? Delusional? A threat?
She looked at her watch. Clara would be in a few hours.
She was alone in the house.
Alright then. She knew what to do.
Then again, they might find her dead with her throat slit...
Her rational thinking returned, and she had a plan to set up.

There were routines in this household. Lighting up the kitchen quarters early was one of them: Trevor always left by 7.00 a.m. when working ...
At the rear sections of the ground floor, in the manner of 19th century architecture, accommodations were made for waitstaff. A modest bedroom, clean - close to the kitchens, with furnishings and bathroom attached. Amanda occasionally put a dog in those Housekeeping quarters and closed the door to separate them from the fray.
Or, she would use the space for projects, especially for ironing shirts or a dress since it was warm, cozy and close to the laundry facilities.
Clara used the rooms frequently...
 She decided to put Kendall there for the night. He needed rest, a place that was safe. That much she knew.
But how not to alert observers – those surveilling the movements in the house, watching from outside?
If Kendall was on the run, his pursuers should see no house-lights switching on in the upstairs guest bedrooms that might indicate a visitor in her household.
"Come with me" she whispered, awaking him.
April paced beside her.

Amanda went into the kitchen, and asked him to stand in the shadow of the doorway, her finger to her lips. She flipped on the culinary lights and she turned the Coffee-maker on. She put a slice of bread in the toaster and moved about the kitchen with normal calm.

Nothing unusual there.

The Housekeeper's bedroom, now illuminated by the kitchen lights, offered the privacy and shelter that Amanda needed to guide Kendall down the hallway. She pointed, he nodded and entered the bathroom, closing the door behind him. She pulled out extra blankets.

Ten minutes later she knocked softly on the door, ajar, the lighting still dim, and she placed a small tray of thermos tea, buttered toast, muffins, marmalade and cheese wedges on the bedroom credenza. She moved to the laundry room, pulled down some towels and shirts from Trevor's stack of ironing items, and lay them on the seat.

April never left her side.

She closed the bedroom door, then walked down the hallway to shut the door to the apartment. Ostensibly, it could remain shut all day. She made coffee in the kitchen, then returned to the Study and emailed Trevor.

She moved to the window. It was still dark, she knew, except for a street lamp whose light could penetrate the windows and illuminate the house - including the apartment, sufficient to offer ambient nighttime lighting. No one watching could tell if the apartment quarters were occupied or not.

Trevor would be proud of her, she decided.

Amanda went upstairs before dawn.

How long she dozed she could not tell. She showered, dressed and snoozed intermittently on her bedroom chaise-long until well after sunrise. A respectable hour, for Washington DC, that is.

April never left her side and received well deserved head strokes for her protection.

It was still early when Amanda called off Carla for the day with a message: With Trevor out of town, there was little to do and no need to come in today. Besides, this was Friday. Please to enjoy the weekend!

Amanda was staying home, regardless, and had no plans for entertaining.

This was good timing.

Normally, Trevor's way of keeping in touch with key personnel from other Washington delegations was to entertain on weekends - something that would send Clara to the Fish market on Main Street, then to *Dean and Delucca* on M Street for provisions before managing two sous-chefs for the dinner party.

Sometimes Amanda wondered if she were running a Weekend Restaurant business. This would always make Clara laugh. Clara could handle anything. And she always saw to adding more staff when needed for a smooth operation.

Otherwise, for Amanda and Trevor, it was only close friends who were invited to their retreat on the Chesapeake Bay...

Amanda took a deep breath.

Staying home for work in the Study was actually Amanda's idea of a great opportunity to get things accomplished. She looked forward to it. Especially now, having Senator Williams' demands nipping at her heels.

He wanted a full report on how to set up a new fund for New Englanders. He wanted his own Fund to participate. He wanted new participants, contributors from other Funds...

Plus, he was making his case in Congress on something strange and untested, a new tax haven for investors!

Surely he had accountants?

Her mind paused.

And now she had Kendall in the house.

On her Notes she quickly scribbled some thoughts. She needed to consult with a few more parties that Barbara had recommended for her final report. Financial analysists, economists, attorneys... even as she was waiting on the SEC to approve the idea.

April was waiting for her.

She checked her watch. *He* was still sleeping, clearly. In fact, he'd need a full weekend of shelter. He was in bad shape, she realized. She went to the window.

She forced her mind back to work.

She'd close up on the historical record: She'd check the email once more from her source.

**

Amanda picked up her phone and dialed.

"Simone" she said "what do you know about post WWII treasure that disappeared after the war?"

"The story is long, so we don't know exactly the details. But there is a lot of speculation that Russia had no idea what the meaning was to Supply herself for a long and protected European war!"

"They expected what, then?"

"Their troops, when returning from the front, did not have enough provision to get home. They had to forage - if not steal from fellow American allies. It was a mess. That's because they had no idea about provisioning an Army with the kind of production and stock that should feed, Arm, dress and shelter offensive battle lines, much less conduct an air or naval war – This they were unable to do. They had bought provisions and tanks from the Americans and promised to pay for it in gold. They had men ill-equipped in the field as troops...Their attrition rate was high."

"Roosevelt had been preparing for war, though..." said Amanda.

"Perhaps. But Russia was in a terrible state at the time. Many claim they should never have been given equal status as a major Ally, considering the cost of supply and provision by the other Allies. And as you know, it was Churchill's big concern that Russia was still a socialist state, her public dissemination embracing an economic doctrine that *opposed* free market capitalism!"

"I see"

"After it was all over, at the Yalta Conference, that they were given rights of territorial conquest on a European map is yet still being contested... Treasure of course, was there for the looting."

Amanda listened.

"Churchill managed to stem their demands somewhat, but Roosevelt wanted his United Nations as his legacy to ensure a lasting peace..."

"Unlike the League of Nations after the First World War."

"Right. But what Russia got were huge concessions to proselytize communism, especially as a major role player in the United Nations...It's a diplomatic history for Foreign Affairs scholars!"

"What treasure did they have?"

"Well, let's just say, they *didn't* have! Much of the Russian treasure just went missing. To this day, we have no clue what happened to it. If it turns up, I shall know."

"So, it's less about material wealth as it is the winning of hearts and minds for Socialists?"

"Oh yeah! Until Regan ended the Cold War."

* *

It was noon when Kendall appeared. If not pink and rested, at least shaven and clean.

Again he stood at the entrance of the Study, April having bounded in and made all the necessary announcements.

"Good Morning!" said Amanda looking up from her desk.

"...I'm sorry" he said again by way of apology for his night intrusion. "I was..." he cast about "*desperate.*" His eyes said the rest.

"No worries!" she chimed, determined to make him relax "I've food in the fridge and dogs to walk. So, make yourself at home!"

He nodded.

"Do you always work so hard at your desk all the time?" he asked.

"If you mean why aren't I cavorting with friends at the local pub, then yes. I work a lot!" she grinned.

"I know. I know. There are two types of people on earth - those that are Irish, and those that wish they were!" She got a weak smile.

She must keep this man alive. He was on the edge of his endurance, she realized.

She walked up to him and looked at him closely "Kendall, Trevor told me it was alright for you to be here. You are to trust us!"

"Right!" he said with a lame look.

"... Please eat with me in the kitchen! Then you're welcome to hang out in the front rooms. There are the newspapers, a library of books, magazines, music, games, DVDs, an off-line laptop, any paperwork you need at that guest table over there...Here, the TV for some Washington sports entertainment and news...In the kitchen is tea, coffee...snacks. I'll make dinner at 6 pm. Is that alright?"

"You've been most kind" he said, peering at the windows.

"Don't worry. I've closed all the lower-level shutters, except for the living room and dinning rooms. That might provoke suspicion. Otherwise, the house is secure. Get all the rest you can while you're here..."

"Thanks!" he said.

That gave him the weekend.

April watched him, then she sat down and yawned.

He did eat. And then he retreated to sleep for another six hours, the door to his bedroom left slightly ajar, perhaps nudged open by the dogs.

Amanda spent the day at the computer.

Later, she walked the dogs. Finally she found herself setting up a roast turkey for an informal dinner.

"Has the storm passed?" texted Trevor.

"Not yet..." She replied.

"You'll be alright" he answered. "Be patient."

He reappeared for dinner.

"Mashed potatoes, sweet potatoes, greens, gravy and rolls, followed by ice-cream and cake" she said, a smile on her face.

They talked.

Chiefly, about they talked about general observations and nothing in particular.

New York, he said, he particularly liked. Then there was Barbara...He liked her very much.

Twice he paused to reiterate his appreciation for Trevor's hospitality.

Only once did she see pallor return to his face and eyes darken with sudden fear. Especially when the doorbell rang and April gushed forward.
 It was the neighbor, asking if she might spray paint their side of their common-fence at the tool shed.
"Just being neighborly..." said the woman, waving.

By the time they finished dinner, Amanda noticed a little freshness coming back to his face.
"Here!" she said, finding him in the Study watching the news after dinner. He accepted the glass of brandy.
 She sat down across from him "It must be tough on you just now..." she started.
He turned off the volume.
"You must be feeling like you're a fugitive." she continued.
"I *am* a fugitive!" he said. "The FBI want me. The Counter-Intelligence of half-a-dozen nations want me...I'm not sure how much more of this I can do!" he said, taking a deep swallow of brandy.
She waited.
"Trevor wants to keep me hidden from Extradition. It's not something he can expect for much longer." He paused. "I am happy to hand him everything I know... before they get their hands on me. That's why I came..." he looked down. "It's like living as a street dog..."
"I understand. I'm sorry Kendall. I don't know the full extent of what is going on. But if it's important to Trevor, you have my full support and cooperation. Is there anything I can do for you?"
"You've done enough. I do need to get lost again" he said, looking up. "I can't expose Trevor to any further risk. He can't be found harboring a fugitive. So, if you don't mind, I will give *you* all my information..."

He hesitated. "I don't mean to impose...It's just that I can't count on much more time before they hand me to the authorities. "

"Yes"

April was staring at them, then sat again. He patted the dog's head.

"Sure?"

"Yes!"

"Ok then... Let's get started." He got up.

April went instantly to Amanda's side. Her hand went out to relax the dog.

"I have here a complete Dossier of the names of the owners of the Swiss Bank accounts that were issued within the period *prior* to the new laws..." he said, unzipping his backpack.

"Did Barbara give you a hand with all this...?"

"Her backpack!" he pointed, with a grin. "Plus computer time to record everything...Here!"

Two hours later, with printed copies in hand and documents spread out in every direction, Amanda looked up.

"Can I ask you one question?"

"Sure."

"Why are you doing this?"

He straightened up slowly, then looked down.

"I was educated at the London School of Economics. I came home to Ireland and was offered a job that gave me dignity. An income that allowed my family to spread its wings for the first time in several generations. England gave me that opportunity. So I wish to give back. Ireland is done. My parents are safe. And debt free!" He smiled.

Amanda nodded.

"...But everyone else is *not*!" he added. "Far from it. Here. See this!"

More lists, names, documents, accounts, email traffic and corporate brokerage accounts.

"My biggest fear..."he said "is that large funds soak up these accounts - capital that belongs to individuals - in one precipitous collapse. It will take down with it unsuspecting savers; small enterprise expense accounts, and many others. It will devalue currency and hyper-inflate the cost of living in an Emergency move that could induce bleeding sovereignty funds, or government treasuries with large deficits, to scarf up troves of hidden assets without-a-name! Especially if it were orchestrated as a *planned event* by key interests."

"Wait..." interrupted Amanda. "Just a moment...Did you say a *planned event*? How can a planned event be an Emergency? What are you saying here?"

He got up. Walked to the window as if waiting for someone. Then he returned to his seat, his thoughts reordered and his blue eyes ice cold.

He looked at her gravely. "I saw your Notes - your Senator...I'm sorry" he said calmly. His hand was up. Amanda looked at him, shocked.

"I couldn't help seeing your Final Report on your computer! Please...Excuse me!" he said apologetically.

She sat back. This was a man who lived in computers, she realized. He could probably read digits on a screen from the next room.

She took a breath.

"No" she said. "That's ok... No mystery!" she placed her hands on her lap. "Just a small- enterprise opportunity for a Fund in New England..."

"Who are you working for?" he asked.

She looked at him and noticed the scowl on his face
"Why?"
"Senator Williams. Is that ... *Steve* Benton Williams?"
Then he stepped back, hesitant.
"Yes. Why?"
" Well. Its just that. He's... on the list!"
"*What list*?"
"This list...corporate investors, a Fund wanting to know about who has money to spend, invest and ...who is accessible for tapping as collateral to purchase a non-payable federal debt fund!"
"*What*?"
"Have you sent him anything yet?" he asked
"No! Yes! Well I'm about to.. Everyone with an interest in...Wait. What are you saying?"
"Don't sent him anything!"
"Now hold on, Kendall. Trevor never objected to my efforts...He's a recognized..."
"No. Trevor wouldn't know! It's not public yet." He put down his handful of files and walked over to her. But there will be a run on his banks...He will be ideally positioned to accept seized accounts like this one..."
There was fear in his eyes again.
"Remember... I'm releasing confidential Bank information: These are tax-evading, offshore accounts and identity shelters for God's sake! These are government-wanted details. They represent billions - if not trillions of the world's circulating money. Unaccounted for. Untaxed. Hidden from legitimate accounting principles! "
"Just a minute Kendall. I have a hard time believing all this..."
"That's because you don't know..."

"*What?* That the Senator is doing something helpful to his community...?"

"That he's on the take! He's a receptacle for all those with assets...Yes! He's using you! It's what he's going to Congress for...An Emergency bank receptacle"

"Now hold on just a minute..." began Amanda, getting frustrated.

The front door bell rang. It was already dark at 5.00 PM.

He froze.

Amanda pointed to the bedroom. He disappeared. She gathered generally the papers, then answered the door.

April moved to the front door without growl.

Outside was a white delivery van. "*Where Flowers Bloom for You!*"

"Mrs. MacDonnell?" said the courier.

He held a delivery of a prodigious bouquet of flowers.

"Thank you!" she said, receiving them with a big smile.

She signed the receipt and closed the door behind him.

Kendall reappeared in the hallway.

The blooms were beautiful. Spring blossoms. Colors of flecked tulips; yellow roses and Lady's Lace in a lavish display of deep red Dutch tulips. They filled her arms. She nuzzled at Daffodils, Carnation.

"Oh how lovely!" she uttered, finding no card.

"Trevor!" she knew, and placed them on the side table of the Entry hall.

Then she saw a card that was tucked deep within the stems.

"*For the Queen of night-research*" It was signed "*Ted*"

She looked up, puzzled.

"That's Senator Williams!"

Kendall took two steps forward and suddenly his fingers closed over his lips for silence.

He fairly whisked them off her and marched into the kitchen where he placed the basket of blooms on the table with a plonk.

Then again, another good plonk. And another...

She was about to say something when he asked again for silence, backed her off, and ran his fingers over the blossoms. He squeezed. They were silky to the touch, sturdy and strong blooms, enough to sustain a good fingering. But hardly dignified...

Amanda was about to say something when he froze, his fingers tight on one bloom. He pulled.

Out came a small metal stem with a round head.

He placed it on the counter.

They stared. This was no biological creation.

Then another. Even a third.

He walked to open kitchen drawers and eventually found a roll of tin- foil wrapping paper. He placed all three listening devices in the tin foil and threw them outside the kitchen door, keeping his head low. He dimmed the lights.

He turned to her "Now do you believe me?"

This was too much. She cupped her mouth and stepped back in disbelief, her eyes moist. *Oh God.*

Where are you Trevor when I need you?

They stood in silence, April staring with doleful eyes, the computer in a dark brooding hum. The minutes passing.

Finally he spoke. "I've got to go!"

He moved with stealth and was gathering his stuff to load into his knapsack.

"Wait!" she said, confused like a mother hen losing a chick.

He looked back at her. "Look. Your place is probably being watched by now. They suspect Trevor is giving me cover. Please be careful!"

He walked back into the bedroom, collected a few items, then wrapped an Ombre scarf around his neck and prepared to leave.

She stood there, mesmerized, feeling helpless.

He paused.

"Thank you luv!" he said in sociable Irish fashion, planting a kiss on her check "Don't let the dogs lose after me!"

And he was gone - slipping out the rear kitchen door.

She stood there, wondering if he was either still on the rear porch, or if she should have done more...

Just gone. Just like that.

Her thoughts started to swirl, her eyes watering.

Hurt, annoyance. Confusion. She couldn't decide which...

She must have sat there in dark contemplation with her thoughts for a long time. The Study was silent.

Finally she got up.

With new determination she went through the house with the eye of a manic wiping away evidence - All evidence of a, of a guest, intruder, fugitive, *whatever*...

She was furious.

All gone.

He never came, she decided.

Those damned flowers...

* *

Chapter 9

A winter storm shut down the city, if not half the East Coast. The Federal Government was closed and one mid-Atlantic region declared a state of national emergency.

Fred Truitt lived on Capital Hill at a newly built luxury apartment building where most congressional staffers stayed. He worked at the Department of State.

Just a few blocks from the Houses of Congress, where a re-developed zone of Washington DC's Southwest district had been planned, a Renaissance project was abandoned. Its financing was tied up by Central Bank *Easy Money* policy following the Bank-Bailout failures. The old district had been leveled, and though some units were occupied by new-construction pre-sales, much of it remained vacant.

Still, some Federal Buildings had been completed, and nearby, the old Navy Yard was now seeing total refurbishment.

Federal workers emerging from Underground Stations that debouched into the new office buildings ebbed and flowed in a tide of daily commuting.

Fred was short, middle aged and a New Yorker who found himself isolated in a building of gregarious political Interns. He mixed, finding them chatting about Congressional bills; appropriations and policy budgets.

But he was alone, it seemed. He did the dusty digging of enforcing forgotten foreign policy, such as it was, and commuting to the Department of State.

He lived a private life, sometimes celebrating the weekend with a pack of beer in his apartment on the twelfth floor. Most weekends, he flew home to New York.

Still, his building never rested. It was in constant circulation by residents moving through the Fitness room, coffee alcove, sports lounge, business center, Concierge quarters or Conference rooms.

Downstairs was a private movie theater, pool deck, underground parking Garages, mail rooms, ATMs and lounge Foyers. It served as a vast underground city.

Only those cars with Automated Remote Access keys could enter the building when the garage doors opened. Few used it.

From here you could access underground transportation to Reagan National Airport and fly out of the city. From here you could flow throughout the city itself by Metro. And since parking in the city was a generally difficult, most residents left their cars parked underground.

The building served as a vast underground city, regardless the weather.

Snow fell gradually at first, softly covering the ornate Houses of Congress as they debated - some locked in anguished disputes over policy; bills, blame and financial melt-downs. It was a ritual. After hours, such remonstrance by congressmen was done before an empty House for the benefit of a video-production to be circulated amongst their constituents back home. Today, most staff was planning to leave early, snow beginning to thicken on the streets. By mid-day, the city was rendered inhospitable to traffic, and Federal workers dismissed.

With a blizzard now draping over the nation's capital, all legislative sessions were adjourned, and debating on the Floor of the House was ended.

By nightfall, the National Guard were called in to shuttle Essential personnel and staff to their building - where their paperwork continued...

Fred saw this in his building. And it gave him some comfort.

His week had spanned the globe. Today, reports and troubles erupted everywhere. His desk had been cluttered with notes, Memos, cultural disturbances and political messages. Some might require military interventions, others extra inside observations, and some portended economic ramifications. It was a mess. When the call came in from the British consulate and Diplomatic staff, it was like an invitation to a Spa.

They had dinner at the *Café Delux*, he and Whittaker, a favorite place for many, if now the only place open.

The conversation was cheerful and general for most of the meal. What came out later, trudging out to the dark government-tagged SUV and standing in the night snow, was of more value to Whittaker.

"It's not that they don't take your word for it, it's just that there seems to be an end-game in play at the Justice Department. They want the Extradition papers *signed* and the man *delivered*. We know he is being sheltered for what he knows..." said Fred.

"Good God!" said Whittaker. "Why don't we just collaborate on the Intelligence that he might have garnered?"

"We should" said Fred.

"But...?" said Whittaker "...something is holding him back from coming forward. Is there something we're missing?"

Fred looked down. There were times he preferred not to take sides. The Brits were Friends.

He opened the door to the waiting vehicle, snow now dotting his scarf and hat. He was about to step in.

"You may wish to ask *your* Emissary about that..." said Fred. "We know he has him...But I appreciate your overture."

Fred climbed into the rear seat and rolled down the window "Good night Wit. And thanks for dinner!"

"I'll call you from New York" said Whittaker. "We need to make arrangements..."

Fred returned to his building and made a call.

* *

Amanda missed Trevor.

She was tired of travelling to Boston, and increasingly weary of Steve Williams' demands. Or rather, his nuanced position of making *her* life his business!

This was supposed to be a bona fide effort to create Jobs.
Unless...?

She paused.

Nah!

She had met with several analysts, including those from the Business and Laws schools of Harvard and Boston College. They were all about optimization, paradigms and profit centers...Their credentials were ample, and she had incorporated their suggestions into her Final Report, complete with credits, specialization and citations.

But honestly, she felt tired of it all.

She stayed at her hotel and lingered by the heated pool, her mind considering the finishing touches.

She dressed and after a meal, returned to her room reading data, business reports and analytical findings. A stroll downtown before evening was her only planned outing. And she missed Trevor.

There was something about the Brits, she decided. They were sincere. And they held the identities and accounts of people as human beings. Not digits, units and profit-points as the Americans did.

Why? Did they hold to a higher standard? For a small nation of people with a long history of Empire and conquest, they remained intrinsically human, perhaps rooted in moral bearings for individuals over globalist strategic agendas...

Was Trevor unique? She knew she loved him, regardless their difficulties.

She was gazing down a street where the sun painted a pink Boston dusk, city lights just coming to life. She stopped at an Irish pub.

Amanda ordered the Shepherd's pie and beer – for *'those dark hours of life, where only a warm Irish heart glows'* added the waiter.

Two karaoke songs later and she was ready to leave. Her thought flew to the night when they had gathered for a long night at Pub downtown New York City...Without Trevor at her side, she didn't feel she belonged here, she sighed.

Her phone vibrated. She picked up.

"Good news!" belted Barbara, calling from New York. "Your idea is getting traction with a lot of support from private investors and account managers. They want to help you set this up with a one-time donation!"

"Really?" asked Amanda.

"Yes!" said Barbara. "You're doing a *great* job! I'm going to set up a fundraising event for your Jobs-training program. Next month. Bye!"

Amanda sighed with relief.

Thank God for good friends, she thought.

She thrust the phone down her raincoat pocket.

It vibrated again. Amanda was walking past a set of townhouses, almost to the hotel when she dug in and pulled it out.

Last call, she decided. Trevor!

"This is your lover, my darling!"

"Hey..." she burst out, "I Sooooooo miss you!"

"Good" he said, business like, "it's the way I like my women!"

"you egotist!" she giggled.

"...panting at the dock for my return..."

"You're flirting with danger here I hope you know..." she admonished.

"Oh yes! I know. And there is nothing I want more than to be flirting with you ..."

She closed her eyes, leaning against a wrought iron balustrade to a townhouse. "God, I miss you!" she said.

"I'm doing my best..." he said "to get back as soon as possible. I have all these important things to do, but all I want is you in my arms! I want you....right there where I can see your eyes and kiss your face...and ravish you!" he rasped in her ear.

She blushed suddenly. "*This* girl has her price, you know!"

"Oh?"

"Yes. Like flowers. And wine. And viol...Speaking of flowers. Did you know Mr. Steve Williams sent me flowers?"

"I'm not surprised. The lecher has his eyes on you!"

"And of course...your friend was in town, you know"

Trevor did not respond.

His silence, she knew, was deliberate. It was a clear indication not to proceed in that direction on a cell phone. Later then.

"Anyway. What time is it over there?..." she asked.

"Late. Or early. I don't know. And I want to whisper sweet words to the lady of my life..."

"Umm"

"How's your project coming along?" he asked.

"Oh!" she sighed "Slow. But *getting* there. Barbara has a long list of parties interested in supporting the concept. But I just can't get him to commit to anything, like..." her voice trailed. "He's not *embracing* the plan..."

"That's alright darling. As long as he isn't embracing you, I'm satisfied..."

She laughed.

"We do have an Event next month in New York. We might explore some advantages to satisfy questions...Its being arranged by Barbara" she said.

"I'm delighted. Any news on the progress of the boat?"

Funnily, the question surprised her. She hadn't thought about it. And nothing would have given her more enjoyment. She looked up at the gathering night sky, smiling.

"Offshore somewhere. About mid-way I should imagine..."

"Their Marker fell off the radar...I can't follow their progress online. Just wondering why..." he said.

"I'll call the monitoring committee and check."

"Right"

"Oh my darling..." she groaned. "I so want you home!"

"I miss you too Sweetie. I shall call you again tomorrow..."

She walked on.

He wanted to know about the boat.

How was it performing on the Newport to Bermuda race? That was strange. They were all being tracked on satellite with designated global positioning markers.

Tenacious had no Marker?

Was he telling her something? A warning perhaps?

She would check in the morning. Yes, she decided.

Still, Amanda was walking on a cloud. The doorman to the hotel could well have been from Mars, or the street made of gold... To hear Trevor's voice was everything, today.

Amanda did not notice that she had been followed.

**

Below decks the Captain laid back on his bunk, his topside deck Watch just completed.

He opened his laptop casually and grinned.

The boat was moving at nine-to-twelve knots average. As far as he knew, no competitor was in sight at this position of the race. That meant they were winners.

Once arrived at the dock in Bermuda, he would be met by a Resident Agent willing to berth the boat and take over the management of all affairs.

So the trip was a success... All he needed was to arrive in one piece. The vessel was solid, if with a large *plonk* sound in the engine room whenever they tacked the boat. But being under sail presented no problem to an engine not running.

What he cherished most was the data on his laptop.

Not the schematics; sailing data-points, charts, markers and tracking devices being monitored and calculated of each contender in the race...

Rather, the data-sheets of the accounts, names and banks that provided the content of the offshore accounts he was lodging in Bermuda.

The columns were impressive.

From the ranges of 2-to-4 US million dollars, the list was prodigious. Hedge Accounts. Each with serial numbers, passwords, entry codes and transfer information.

In the 3-to-9 US million dollar range, the names became recognizable with institutions and banks.

Over 30 US billion and the receipts showed Sovereign entities.

At another column the assets changed.

Over 100 US million and global entities dominated, including, surprisingly, non-profit institutions of social and political recognitions. Like Harvard. And the World Bank. The Vatican, and some other unique foundations.

From the US alone...

He flipped back to another spreadsheet...

The skipper of *Outbound* was his only threat. A mean-spirited man with a quiet cachet of accounts himself: But nothing like this load. Not like this. No!

These programs had just been put on *Tenacious* the night before she sailed, the laptop sealed and placed in the Chart Room without anyone suspecting a thing.

Information, clearly, ported from a source in Europe.

A source perhaps under government custody, he assumed.

But not before these accounts were removed. And all tax-free... to remain beyond detection no less.

Wow! What a prize.

What amused him though, where the names of the Accounts.

The Sarah A.

Susie B. Sentinal.

Kill'em Hoss.

The *Susan Constance* Account - now that one was huge...

Would there be one named the *Mayflower*, he chuckled.

Perhaps that had been the name of the first in a long sequence of accounting years ago? *Joke.*

Anyway, one thing was clear. With electronic data, the files and paperwork did not need to be warehoused for safekeeping. That was the best thing about all this. It could all be printed up once it got there, and *Voila*, instant Offshore-Account!

How the hell it got onboard, he wasn't entirely sure. But there it was...

And if he were not such an able sailor as well as a manager of a large funds, he would not be here, invited on this trip for a boat delivery to the tropics.

No question about it.

The numbers were impressive!

Only, what was it all doing aboard *this* boat?

* *

Something had been puzzling Todd all these days. And now it came to him.

It was the suffixes to the account numbers. They were different suddenly. Especially on the larger accounts. Suffixes to accounts not just held in US Banks, but on government accounts.

Some accounts even had Alphabetical tags, and were simple to identify:

IT, Italy.

K, England.

E, Spain.

R, France.

W, Swiss.

Damn, he should have been a cryptographer!

**

Amanda finally got to sleep. Still in a reverie about her accomplishments and the assurances of the man she loved, it took hours to settle her mind.
Percolating to the surface of her thoughts came all the quaint moments of the day. Like the funny remarks in those long-winded reports that cited Boston as the first city of 'colonial ventures'
Or, the Irish coffee she had at the pub.
Or the fun in Trevor's voice.
Come to think of it, she liked Boston! A lot.
Even the splashing kids at the poolside the day before. If all the seniors around here were as polite as the one seated beside her at the hotel Spa pool, then this was a city to celebrate... He was a wonderful gentleman!
He reminded her, funnily, of the actor Gene Hackman with his thinning hair, pot belly and bespeckled gaze of hesitant intensity.
Todd was his name, he said.

* *

The *Outbound* crossed the finish line in First Place at the Newport to Bermuda Yachting Race.

When it came in from a long windward tack to cross the finish line first, the cannon went off on the Committee Boat to celebrate the winner.

She was sleek, strong and a wide-beamed 44-footer, stem to stern, one of the highest classes of the One-design boats, a big-boat competition vessel on the water. Her sail spread power was enormous.

Everyone was interested in her performance as a vessel. The hull was closely tied to the RC44 class of boats, savvy skippers from around the world holding titles in a variety of competitions and notoriety. One thing was known. She represented big money.

Normally, the logistics of delivery, repairs and provisions were managed. Boats were designed for owners with a set of crew who enjoyed the thrill and lifestyle of competitive racing. The management team would have unlimited expenses. And all accounts were paid onshore.

Bermuda was one of their venues where traditionally, the win was a hard fought sailboat race. Hence it was the fastest, sleekest and the most advanced cutting-edge technology that mattered...

All Handicaps were fastidiously examined. If a boat that was quick upwind and capable of 8 or 9 knots in 12 knot breeze, but perhaps tricked out with a keel's trailing-edge trim able to better point, then the odds of a win increased.

Yet, if it had for its class a masthead asymmetric spinnaker on an articulating pole that enabled up to 17 knots downwind in 20 knots of breeze, that that had advantages.

This was high tech competition – mainly for high tech sponsors wanting visibility, if not national recognition and marketability in sophisticated industries.

The logos and banners said it all. Team shirts. Sails. Hats. Gear. It was big business, and it boosted recreational boating industry.

Still, the prevailing hallmark to winning this celebrated race was usually reserved for the boat most able to handle speed in all kinds of Atlantic sea conditions with a fearless crew and strategic execution. After all, it was the race of risk-taking...

Tenacious finished with a respectable ranking, somewhere about one third down the fleet. For her class, she ranked first.

 Not bad for a 50 ft boat of older construction. And she was not one of the most expensive or even well capitalized boats by comparison. He budget posted at one million dollars from dock to campaign, all total. And, family managed.

Tenacious was nowhere near the cutting edge. But she was a classic beauty. Her hull was sleek, her lines elegant and her sails bright and full on the horizon. She was a photographer's star.

And here she came. She was a boat that arrived where she was supposed to arrive. And left from where she was supposed to leave. She held the tacit title of *Flag Ship*. No race was done, or even begun, without *Tenacious* in the mix.. Such was the venerated reputation that had followed her over the years...

Neither was the crew exceptional.

Boat hands registered for boat deliveries, and usually coming *not* from brokerage yacht houses, but from college trained youth and fun-loving sailors with competitive backgrounds in sailing as Junior sailing champions. Even if long summers and the lack of serious jobs marked their career, some were still earning a living on board to get through the student year...

The race day was complete once *Tenacious* came to anchor, and ceremonial events followed at the prestigious Bermuda Yacht Club where its famous burgee flew high atop its flagpole.

The owner of *Outbound* was present with the win at the Trophy Presentation ceremonies.

He was well known as the CEO of a Hedge Fund having made his own fortune on a Merger and Acquisitions that gave him half ownership of a regional wireless company.

It was known to a few how he achieved his gains. His corporate acquisition lasted eighteen months before the capital dried up and it applied for refinancing. When quickly sold off, his name was known and attached to its profit-takings.

The buying company was strategically set up in advance, and the margin of profit was already leveraged out long before it arrived at the moment of sale - or showed any profits to any government entity. Its destiny was early anticipated by a Business Plan spreadsheet two years ago, and, painted in soft grey coloring, the numbers of profit were not fully matured or even materialized. Just a banking venture indicated on an accounting system showing *Assets* and *Liabilities* as projections.

Neither was the business important nor the brains of its originator cited: It was a formula for the cycling of monies, including insurance, debt service, fees, advertising and marketing and a small Foundation to be spun off.

The Brand Name, office spaces, sign posts, Logo and the tour on the big boards was paid for. Even a Franchise business, manned by underpaid 23-year-olds out of college was planned out.

Tony Sandoros was one amongst many of the CEOs.

He was a big man with a blond complexion that turned wiry and ginger in the sun or weather. He did have a blazer, but clearly the Bermuda shorts and T shirt beneath it showed he had been at sea. And he loved the image. It lionized him amongst aggressive investors and CEOs.

Following the Yacht Club's Presentation in which happy winners walked off in earnest, the rest would gather on his mega-yacht.

It was moored just off the harbor.

There, Sandoros had a gathering of cohorts who sponsored yachts in the race. They were the officers of brand names known well in the world of business venture.

Many on board his Yacht represented larger Assets.

Listed as Holding companies, they managed corporate accounts, trusts and offshore subsidiaries. Exempt from home taxation, they all held accounts in the banks of Bermuda. If one day an enterprising tax plan at home might encourage the repatriation of funds back home, then they might consider...

But then again, there was little accountability and oversight out here. It was better this way.

To be invited on board the Sandoros boat – was an exalted privilege.

A shaded party of cocktails and food aboard the stern of his yacht was more than an inebriated extravaganza where the rich and famous gathered, it was a scoring of the highest accolade in discrete circles...

Some faces seen on the stern of the boat were rarely imaged in the media. Usually they hung in private office walls, framed and signed.

Today, the waiters served food from a menu feast served on white tables around the rail of the midsection deck space. Prepared below-decks in a luxurious galley, food came from everywhere in cold storage refrigeration.

It was an International event of exotic foods: Two chefs from different continents offered Mexican chipotle and yellow fin tuna roll; pan-roasted Chilean sea bass and black garlic mojo scallops. To show Italy, they served capesante on display upon roasted sea scallops and merluzzo made of pan seared cod, guance with braised veal cheeks and sautéed spinach.

Dessert ran the gamut from Belgian chocolate cake to New York cheesecake. With it, a barista served every conceivable coffee off silver-plate, yacht-monogrammed.

Along the top-masts of the yacht, ights and music marked the white hull. Into the night and from a distance, it reflected against blue tropical waters.

* *

Chapter 10

The FFG US Navy class Frigate stood off.
The vessel had a nasty sting at sea if angered and a deadly force if needed. There was little on the water that she could not out-maneuver or neutralize. Her electronic eyes were advanced and penetrating.
What the Lt. Commander saw through his binoculars was nothing unusual on the horizon. Except for the sighting on the Radar at 2.00 a.m.
He would wait.
Once a surface combatant, the mothballed fleet of relatively young ships had been recently modernized and reactivated as Fast Patrol Ships
Re-outfitted in dry-dock and modernized, her engine and propulsion equipment had been boosted for high speed chase. Habitability equipment, electrical and combat systems were versatile and refitted for lighter utility. Her Helicopters, upgraded and able for flexible adaptation at sea were newly deployable at high speeds and altitude.
Supported by a special ops team whose background was rarely advertised, the Lt. Commander of the Frigate knew his priorities.
He was observing.

Aboard the party boat, only one man, up in the pilot's house, was on watch. He must have been prevailed upon to be allowing some guests to stay onboard, thought the Lt Commander at the bridge of the Frigate, his binoculars against his forehead.

The yacht's "house-guests" were still variously slumbering off their party. Disembarking from the vessel would be their mandatory protocol since in all probability the vessel might be preparing to sail from her anchorage.

Mr. Sandoros was known to keep a tight ship, and his Captain was certainly ordered to usher everyone off in a timely fashion, in the manner of a recluse host.

Being a former Navy man, he was always in command. He had a drug- free - and germ-free ship, he claimed. As far as he was concerned, life was too full to indulge in side dalliances. One was to be always alert. Always on station.

And for good reason.

Below decks was a cargo to be shipped. Bermuda was the overnight pick-up point, and the Gulf of Mexico his rendezvous, off Costa Rica. The party, clearly, had been a good diversion. Nobody noticed the stowing of crates during the night.

The Frigate was spotted by the Captain of the Yacht through his binoculars. Not much bigger than a coast guard cutter, it remained afar, and definitively not a vessel with designated markings. She lay low to the waterline, and could be lost in the haze of the sunlight.

A wild knocking at the cabin door of the bridge reverberated across the pilot house. It was from a Forward deck door that was kept routinely closed for security reasons - as per maritime regulations, and for general sea conditions.

He was flustered, the young ships waiter who appeared, his shirt stained red. "It's... Mr. Sandoros, Sir."

"What of it?"

"We have a situation. He is dead...Last night he asked for breakfast and coffee to be delivered to his cabin at dawn. We knocked, and when we asked for instructions for the day's menu and meals, he did not respond. We found him on the floor of his cabin. Dead."

If there was one thing the Captain knew above all else, was to report to the authorities all that could not be solved on a ship.

He picked up the receiver and dialed for radio frequencies reserved for emergencies. This required police work, he knew.

Bad for yachts with guests still onboard - all of them under his protection. Especially since they were people answerable for the safekeeping of billions in wealth and assets, individuals who were rarely separated from their laptops. Yet their cabins were empty.

By the time he picked up his binoculars again, the Frigate had moved.

* *

Amanda had to complete her report for the Senator. He was getting restless. Williams was pretty persistent with his demands.

Barbara called.

"Does it matter to you..." asked Amanda "where your money comes from, if you accept it? I'm just asking a hypothetical question."

"You bet" said Barbara after a moment's reflection.

Amanda paused. What was Barbara implying?

If there was suspicion about intention on the part of the Senator, as Barbara suggested, then she had to be corrected, thought Amanda.

On the other hand, was he hiding something?

If so, she just couldn't see it.

Was he afraid that she might discover something?

What was it?

The Senator was an honest man, she felt certain.

On the other matter, Barbara was right. Everybody had a right to earn a living in true and honest ways. It was part of his assumed role in society. He wasn't a commodity; a horse to bet on, or a money- laundering conduit.

Of course it mattered...

Then why was the Senator insisting that she disregard the lower tax brackets as job seekers, and focus only on those enterprises deserving investment venture capital? Plus, he wanted to know who in New England they all were. By name, by size, by bank account...

It would appear that he was engaged in a pretty targeted campaign, as if filtering specific parties.

It was a long day.

That evening, Trevor called her.

She talked. He laughed.
Still, he reminded her to keep her eye on the prize.
"Keep at it" he told her. It was a good and worthy cause, job opportunities...
Amanda kept her underlying suspicions to herself.
Nor did Trevor mention the unscheduled appearance of Kendall at the house.
Clearly, it was all behind them.
"I'll be back shortly" he promised.

Washington was humid at this time of year.
Amanda was getting busy at the house. Carla and the dogs took up much of her time. Especially April, who never left her side. She seemed fretful, nipping at the others and barking at everything.
Trevor did not return to Washington DC.
His affairs overseas were taking longer than he thought. Three weeks had turned into a month.
She offered to fly over to London to join him.
He told her that even if she did, he was immersed in issues of commerce in Brussels, having to do with worldwide ramifications. He was most concerned, he said, with things that seemed to threaten the very sovereignty of the nation, let alone defend its position diplomatically. He had meetings with key people, he told her, some leaving him little time to himself.
But at one point, he asked her if she felt that she was in danger.
Of course not, she had replied.
He remained vacant on many other favorite issues that they shared, and to Amanda, he seemed preoccupied.

"It's for your own good" he actually said to her on another occasion.

What was?

She let it go.

Yet increasingly, she felt that she was being watched, his calls monitored.

She thought about it.

No. Actually. Barbara was right.

The Senator was *probing* for information...

He was afraid of something.

Deathly afraid, she decided.

* *

Hans Lugge felt the tremor in his hotel room. It was just after midnight. He was watching a late show on TV.

He got up from his bed and opened the drapes of the window. He took a step back.

Less than thirty meters away from the fifth floor of his harbor-side hotel in Hamburg Germany, he was looking into the lighted cabins of a ship moving.

She passed like a large building - upper decks and passenger quarters, compartments, railing and lifeboats, gliding through Hamburg and out into the open sea. She was *The Queen Mary*.

He closed the curtains. Too close for comfort. Then he laughed. Talk about ships moving in the night!

He opened the curtains again.

Still, she was glorious vessel, topmost amongst cruise ships. She was a classic. Elegant, strongly built and silent. That's how aficionados referred to her. But her displacement capacity could send tremors through any medium at such proximity. And it vibrated the walls of the hotel along the wharf.

That such a bulk could pass in the night without much detection was an tribute to her silent running and complex construction.

For Hans Lugge, such a moment was a treat. An unexpected child's surprise for a grown man.

He was in town for the weekend.

A German Beer-fest in Hamburg. Plus the football game heralded all day with celebrity Rock Bands on wheeled platforms, and a citizenry rally that kept the police on edge.

Hamburg was a lovely German city.

Such as it was, he was also on mission. He was to meet a friend ostensibly. Downtown.

The American in town was on an Inspection Certification Survey project for a ship in dock at the Bloom & Voss Shipyard.

Actually, he was a defense contractor from Washington DC. He was often in the area for joint ship-building ventures and contracts.

More specifically, Hans Lugge was to meet with Special Agent Vaughn, an IT Specialist with the US Government.

Lugge had alerted the Americans. They would meet downtown. In Hamburg. After the football game.

Lugge was accustomed to reviewing large dumps of data on his screens. As a cybersecurity expert, he had just about seen it all, and watched the hackers market, track, steal and take each other out. Most were in it for the money. And recently, while the Americans had improved their counter-cyber defenses, there were huge holes for fringe lunatics to pass through. And even *he* didn't know as much as some...

But here was one account that had caught his attention, himself a hacker living in Frankfurt.

Not that he held any political allegiance, but something was disturbing... even to him.

It involved information flowing neither in nor out of the United States. But rather, within the IRS and Banking communities of the United States. A huge amount of money was shifting around.

"Like watching a school of fish all swimming in one direction" he said to Vaughn. Either fleeing, or following. He could not decide which, he told him.

Agent Vaughn waited. He was a good listener.

Until he saw the bigger fish, Vaught thought it was all going into one entity. Bermuda. And it involved the suffix codes of military defense budgets, but without cyber protections. "How could that be?" said Lugge, his eyes bulging.

Vaugh took it all in.

Lugge went on to explain that there were some things that mattered in life. And the sacrifices of his parents, his grandparents and those who fought for values on the battlefields of Europe deserved better than the mercy of hackers half way around the world, and half his age, taking in large amounts of cash...

He promised that he could have for Vaughn all the suffix codes, the lists, and the accounts. He would pull them off his computer, print them up, and hand them over. They could meet again downtown tomorrow, for coffee.

The next day, Vaughn found him at his table in a Café, holding in one hand an image of the *Queen Mary*. He was just sitting there.

Dead.
There was no briefcase at his side.

* *

This was the big day. Finally it arrived.

Amanda was wearing a dark blue Lauren suit, her hair pulled back in auburn waves that shone as cameras flashed.

Media power cables was rigged everywhere, photographers pressing. They were sprawled on the floor, around the perimeter of the Chamber, under the bench of seated Senators, at the foot of her own platform. She looked around and felt alone at the Witness table. A jug of water was before her, a courtesy for the delivery of a testifying statement.

This was news of some interest in Washington DC.

Here the local press would be recording every word. Especially as key sound bites could be discussed on radio talk shows and aired by pundits, pollsters broadcasting television nightly news feeds.

The business community would be interested, many of them worldwide investors, big and small were beginning to take notice of the Hearings in Congress. The Senator had posted a Press Release the day before. As the final minutes approached and the Chamber settled down, Amanda was buzzed by noisy Nikons – some cameras as close to her as they could get, or to her belongings and her briefcase stacked beside her chair. She looked around.

Somewhere seated behind her was an assistant staffer, and an Attorney. They were the team.

Where was the Senator?

It was a little unnerving because in the end, she was alone at the microphone, with unblinking feeds grasping every legitimate opportunity to nuance the information of the Senator's Responses about a new revelation and its potential use as political capital.

She looked behind her and across the Chamber. At the door two officers stood, members from the office of the Sargent at Arms of the US Congress.

But no Senator Williams arriving?

She felt as if she were buying time for him, and as the mikes cleared for business at the Senate Hearing bench, his appearance was anticipated.

Then oddly, the bright flashing and the noise fell away from her consciousness, and her nervousness steadied, almost leaving her in shock as she recalled the warning from Kendall himself.

She realized then that this was no accident.

She was to take the fall for something. Or someone. She was sitting there, all trussed up like a sacrificial lamb about to become the victim of a nasty turn...

Where was the Senator?

The decision was made.

The panel would question her.

She smiled professionally.

Then something strange occurred. It stopped everything.

The lights went out.

What was happening?

One Sergeant at Arms of the Chamber called out. Everyone was rattling, their equipment collapsing as many sank to the floor in self -preservation. There was dust everywhere and the room was dark.

It took a few moment, but order was restored when the lights came up. Malfunctioning power plant, someone said.

But it was a security breach, and according to standard procedures, all Hearings proceedings were quickly adjourned. Like all other government buildings in the city, these were standing emergency drills.

Emergency Procedures took over. Security had taken over. Everything was amber.

She was swooped along by Escorts and ushered down the hallways, along with the rest of the panel. She was offered a place on a golf cart train as it descended deep into the belly of the Nation's Capital.

The underground tunnels and private underground railways connected the main Capitol building to Congressional office buildings aboveground.

But damned if she knew which was which underground. She felt disoriented. This Subterranean complex was vast.

* * *

Chapter 11

Trevor was in Scotland. He made the conference call to London and New York, speaking with his counter-parts in the UK Home Office, and with Attorneys representing the FBI on the same line.

Others were also listening.

"If we take 'harboring a fugitive' off the table..."

Trevor's eyes rolled at the sound of that old saw again.

"...Or 'obstruction of justice' and interdiction with Extradition proceedings....Then we might have something going here. Is that it, Mr. MacDonnell?" asked the Americans

"Yes" said Trevor decisively.

He had already consulted with his authorities. The London Exchange and Royal Bank of Scotland were in full Agreement.

What took so long was working with the Americans. Getting past the Department of State was not easy since they were behaving as if they held supreme authority over all matters international.

"It's a case of concern for all of us..." said Trevor gently.

"Alright then. Can we ask for a Guarantee that ALL information related to US Banking and Accounting will be on that list?"

"You can have that Guarantee" he affirmed.

"May we see the data in print?"

"You may" Trevor paused, then added. "I shall be returning to Washington in the next couple of days. I will be in New York for an Economic Round-Table for Ireland's Chamber of Commerce Conference. I'll send you by secure pouch advance copies of my itinerary, and we can draw up our Agreements. Is that suitable?"

"It is Mr. MacDonnell" A pause followed, clearly a few words were exchanged on the other end.

"We hope to have your party in readiness to testify before a Grand Jury to support his allegations?"

"He is ready" agreed Trevor.

Bill Todd from the IRS and James Whittaker from the Diplomatic Consulate in New York were both listening. Theirs had been a long journey to this point. And both were assured of a resolution.

Still, Trevor was not happy with the exchange.

He did not mind giving the Americans the information they needed, but he did mind very much not having an assurance that Kendall would be safe in their custody. Evidently, there was some question as to his disposition.

As long as Kendall could provide banking information regarding outside interests, then handing over the rest of the banking information to the Americans was fine. It was dated stuff, many entities having long gone out of business. It was their decision, Kendall knew this.

He sighed.

Evidently, they believed that Kendall had not handed over everything. What Trevor wanted to prevent was damage to Kendall himself, a diplomatic subject. He needed more time with Kendall.

So, the deal was struck: Respect for the subject/submission of all information to the Americans.
Next, Trevor would call Amanda.
He would try again later.
She had not responded for two days.

**

Outside the Capital's street-level Entrance of the main building, a man on the sidewalk stood to observe. He was walking a dog, cigarette in his left hand. Behind him a water spout and monument disgorged into a landscaped fountain. It was a corner park on Capital Hill.
This exit, he knew, was where staff appeared from inside the underground subway to the Senate Office Building.
He knew very well what had happened inside the buildings to the electrical grid. He had done his job.
He was Asian, perhaps Chinese. Clean, short and his hair line receding slightly, his face clear of expression.
The dog was muzzled and had been in the park for over an hour.
The man was waiting to verify with visual evidence all parties coming out.
The dog was thirsty, clearly. Dried saliva and foam were falling from the sides of its mouth.
The man stubbed out his cigarette with his foot, and the dog stooped to sniff at it. The man's foot came up and hit the dog in the eye. The dog squealed out and was jerked at the neck by the leash sharply.
Amanda emerged, and the dog recognized her.
The dog was April.

He picked up the dog and threw it inside and slammed shut the van doors.

**

Security beneath the city was as tight as security above ground. The Nation's Capital was a network through which few could penetrate.

Airspace was routinely flown by choppers, planes and rescue aircraft.

Traffic was re-routed; entrance gates guarded by sniffing dogs and Federal buildings insulated by screening, barriers and security guards.

Everywhere, there were frustrations, if not by staff then by visitors as well.

The city remained inundated by tourists milling about Museums at the Smithsonian Mall. Parks, fountains and restaurants filled with sightseers. Teenagers poured out of buses in a daze. Unsuspecting visitors from every corner of the globe saw it as nothing less than vacation time.

The Park Police, in quiet discipline, indulged pedestrians at the traffic lights, if often slowing traffic to a crawl - or even having to shut down access to the city altogether. This condition could be annoying to local residents who enjoyed perambulating in their city – joggers down a pretty street, a river run or Rock Creek Park where they took children or pets.

Still, even with a fresh set of uniformed police Avengers standing at every street corner, the city was a hospitable and popular place.

But nothing went unnoticed. Especially on Capitol Hill. Subterranean streets spanned miles. They had been trenched long ago when digging out canals for transportation barges through rock, sand, rivers and marsh. More recently, the subway system ranked amongst the best in the world.

City underground passageways, a honeycomb of intersecting tunnels, were monitored with lazar-detection security beams and sensitive devices recording every move and tremor.

Amanda had lost her bearings. Or so it seemed.

She was still underground beneath the Capital Congress, she knew. Her train-golf carts motored slowly through the tunnels.

The subways opened up before her. They turned corners and entered subterranean passages reminiscent of WWII bunker living.

At junctions, they stopped and disembarked. Attended by police in special uniforms, this was standard operating drill procedures for Congressional members when under assault.

Ahead, she heard police patrols running - in combat boots, like a drumbeat... Were they on a drill too, she wondered? What was their task?

Her motor train was clearly independently powered and kept them all moving down the tunnels. Few spoke.

"Oh My God..." said one woman in front of her.

"When are we getting out of here..." said another.

Amanda saw the building signs flash by...

They were moving westwards: The *Jefferson Building.* the *Madison Building.* The *Library of Congress.* The *Cannon Office Building. Longworth House. Rayburn House.*

By Bartholdi Park she knew where she was. She was at the US Botanic Garden, located at the south lower side of the House of Congress.

Her group were going on into an underground parking garage where a special Security van would take them out of town, evidently. That was the procedure, at least...

She wanted to get out.

She took her chance when the train of golf carts slowed down. She slipped off and pressed against the wall in the shadows. She was fairly ignored, and the train moved on.

She walked out. Simple as that.

She moved through the US Botanic Garden and came out at the Conservatory Exterior beneath a neoclassical limestone structure resembling the arches of Versailles.

That's when April had recognized her.

Amanda yelled out "April!"

But that van was turning off the overhead ramp into the Interstate I-295. It could bypass the city in minutes and be in Virginia, easily.

Amanda walked in the bright sunlight, bewildered by all that had occurred. Out in the open everything looked normal. No panic. No distress. She was ignored, and she never felt more alone, if not lost...

What had happened?

Was this an accident?

A coincidence, at best? A threat? And then... what was April doing in the hands of a strange man? Yes, surely that was April, she was certain. Why the muzzle? What did it all mean...

She was thirsty. Did she even have her bag with her...

She stood, collecting her thoughts.

What was going on, she wondered. She was unaccustomed to being so disoriented, let alone out of control...

One car hit the horn. She looked up.

Kendall.

He tucked the car into a spot reserved for Visitors and ran over to her, dodging traffic.

"What are... you doing here?" she asked

He grabbed her elbow and led her through the Botanical Gardens, emerging from the *Jungle* and *Orchid* bays, striding across the *Desert* displays and out to the National Garden Fountain.

"Wait!" she said.

She was holding on to her cell, about to call Trevor. He took it from her and slipped it into the water fountain. He turned nervously.

"My phone! Kendall. What are you ..."

"Come on. You need protection. You are being tracked..."

"Capitol Hill is the most secure place on earth" she managed, breathless now from the pace he kept.

"Actually it is! But you were diverted at the last minute from the Congress to the Office of the Architect's office where you not?"

"So?"

"Did you not see that work crew working underground outside the building on the corner of Independence Avenue and South Capital Street?

They walked.

He marched her North across the great vista of the Nation's Capital, crossing the Smithsonian Mall on 1st Street.

"I don't know. There were so many people about..."

"Exactly! So one thing is certain. Somebody does not *want* you doing any more talking..."

"What, what are you...saying?"

He led her to the side street and into the Fine Arts Museum. She dutifully opened her bag for inspection by Entrance security guards. Big smile.

"That's ridiculous!" she managed.

"Yep!"

"What... *Why?*...Wait!"

He nodded, both of them descending wide granite steps inside the Gallery and proceeding through wide hallways that showed a street-level fountain percolating water from above and down to their level in a subterranean waterfall behind glass. It created a shimmering prism of daylight, hiding those seated below in a coffee bar.

Finally they sat and he ordered two cappuccinos.

She was puffing, glad to pause. She sank deeper into her seat behind an Art-deco potted plant and collapsed her gear onto the chair to her left.

He looked at her solemnly. "I am sorry about your cell phone. I shall apologize to Trevor and explain everything...Please forgive me?"

She was tired and angry. "Not really Kendall. I mean, this is a bit much...You just happen to be there when the lights go out, so to speak...?"

He wasn't listening. He looked around, checking for prying eyes.

He leaned over, reached for her laptop and unzipped the pocket of her bag.

"What are you doing?" she asked.

He switched it on, and raised his finger subtly. "Again. I apologize. But there is something I must do..." he said, punching in a few keys "May I access your computer desktop?"

She stared at him, annoyed as hell. But in deference to his ties to Trevor, she acquiesced.

"*Tenacious* - our boat. Password. *3816*" she added when he looked up.

He pulled out a stick from his pocket and inserted it into the computer.

"The lazar detectors are down, following the exodus from your building. Benefit for the Media, really. We are free to roam underground. Down here, there is no connectivity. There is no server signal underground" he said casually. He put his hands on his lap.

He was transferring data.

"Be sure you don't go online after this entry. This is material that should not be opened. Show it only to Trevor. And be careful..."

"What is all this?

It was all over in a two minutes.

"We need to keep you safe. You opened a can of worms, and...well my darling" he said in his Irish brogue "You have made yourself a liability" he smiled. "Like me!"

The Cappuccinos drained, they waked.

She was still angry. "I want to call Trevor."

"You must!" he said.

They moved through the Exhibition halls, and up to the main entrance level of the Museum.

He turned left into the Gallery of Portraits, passing some of the greatest works of art in the Nation's Capital Art Gallery. She followed him into arched Atriums and across the Afternoon Tea colonnades, then down the Busts and Statues of famous artists, century by century, starting with the 17th.

She was getting frustrated. They walked, he was talking, smiling, talking.
She eyed the guards standing at every corner of every century of artwork.
Finally, they reached the Pennsylvania Street entrance. It was sunny and windy outside. He hailed a cab.
She was about to speak.
"Go home!" he said. "I shall join you in an hour there, if I may... to collect some things that Trevor has... I do need to retrieve my vehicle before it's towed."
She had forgotten about his vehicle left by the Capital. A cab pulled over. He opened the door.
She opened her mouth to speak.
"Don't let that computer out of your sight!" he said.
He was gone before she could say a word. She was frustrated beyond measure.
Traffic was snarled. The cab took longer than usual to arrive at her street off Wisconsin Avenue. She sat back, a breeze coming through the window and onto her face. *What was he talking about?*
She had asked him to explain himself...
"Right" he had said when marching her through the museum "Know this. Senator Williams wants your project killed. No, don't look at me. Just relax, and smile. You were an aggravation to the bigger picture. And Better-the-Enemy-you-know than the Enemy..."
"You're crazy!" she snarled, stopping him.
He grinned suddenly "No. I'm just *Wanted*. Watch out, for Trevor's sake!"
"Does Trevor know this..." she demanded to know.
He grinned again, saying nothing.
Of course Trevor knew!
Kendall cited a few names and companies for her...
"*What* corporations? *What* are you saying? And *Why*?"

"Your ...Senator wants the government to bungle it all." he said through clenched teeth.

She nearly stumbled. He forced her forward like a marching Foreman, he even smiled at a guard.

"What?"

"He has scandals to rock the White House and most of Congress!"

"What? Are you...mad? What are you implying?"

"They want total banking dominion. And I mean Dominion. That's what I discovered in the flow of moneys."

The cab took forever to get her home. Down, and around the Lincoln Memorial. Under the Kennedy. Up Water Street to the Mosque. Up Massachusetts. Then Up Wisconsin...

God, the man was slow.

She got to the house in Chevy Chase. One of the dogs came bounding out to her. Carla showed her face, waving from the kitchen.

"Ms Amanda! Oh! Ms Amanda!" she said.

"Hello Carla. You're working hard tonight?" she said looking for April.

"Yes... My sister, her husband and family they all staying with me for a vacation. We a big family! I happy to watch the dogs this weekend, I check in from time to time, yes?"

"Yes!" said Amanda. "Where is April?"

"She go with Signor Watson to Embassy for to stay to wait for Mr. Trevor. I say it ok?"

"April?" repeated Amanda.

"Issa April... She wait for you always here at the door. No eat. No sleep. She wait...Mr Watson, he say he take her out...She go with him..."

Amanda looked around. Then ran upstairs, changed, and went for a jog. Perhaps April was out on a walk.

Why was April with Watson their Gardner?

Had she been mistaken? She paused to call Watson.

A car came to halt at her side.

Kendall. There was no time to lose, he told her.

"I've lost my dog!" she said simply, her eyes empty.

The sun filtered through the trees, leaves dancing in the wind to riot shadows all over his vehicle. He was talking to her through his window, his face drawn but sincere. More like bravado, actually. He was clearly stressed, if smiling at her.

She stood there, unmoved.

He looked down, turned off the engine, then faced her calmly.

"Look. I've given Trevor everything I could. What I had were the Accounts that bought distressed mortgages from banks using offshore money. They were brokered by Investment bankers. Some were big banks with proprietary trading license to transact...Do you recall?"

Amanda closed her eyes.

She had just heard it all at the Hearing.

Kendall got out of the car, and he paused.

"This is worse" said Kendall, his hairline moist with perspiration.

"Buyers, I mean big buyers, are the holders of American government debt. Chiefly assets bought by the government to relieve distressed banks. Some are foreign governments hoarding American and European property assets. There are billions worth. Including major foreign sovereign countries who bought the debt. They make the mortgage crisis in the US look like pocket change! .."

He paused. "Trevor has bargained for my Extradition in exchange for the data. But now, you are a liability." He looked at her. "Your dog...if he is taken, is a message of intimidation. You've been under observation for a while..."

She stepped back, her hands flew to her face and she wanted him to stop all this. *April?*

This was too close.

"This is Intelligence. You have it all on your laptop..."

He did not need to say it. *He could be next, after April...*

"...Hoarding the US dollar in order to make the Fed print more paper...It's driving up the price of commodity ownership...." he looked down and paused in frustration. "Do you understand what I'm implying here? Its manipulation of American stability in the extreme!"

Amanda looked up and took in a deep breath. She knew what she had to do.

She turned into the house through the garden. He followed.

Kendall walked into the study and started packing things away. The materials he had given Trevor were strewn across the desk. He pulled over his backpack and leaned it up against the desk.

She peered at him from the kitchen, preparing a snack.

"I'm sorry..." he said. "I don't mean to burden you with all this...I don't want Trevor to be found with all this..."

He gazed up at the ceiling as if seeing the situation from a different perspective. "It's enough to scare the hell out of me..."

Then he sat down on the coffee table, his head bend.

She offered him a bottle of water.

"Thank you!"

"Food?"

"Sandwich to go...if you don't mind" He got up and proceeded with his packing. "May I use your facilities, please?"

She nodded.

Before leaving he stood there, moving his head from side to side as if something needed to be completed. Some resolution within his head had made him pause.

She nodded.

"...I can tell you this now. They don't like your little attestation for the Senator's effort to make jobs. It exposes too many sponsors. It's a threat because it offers the names of the investors behind the lenders of both small and large trading in your region."

She must have looked baffled.

"That's a SEC requirement right? That includes those...how shall I say it.... tampering with American interests? They are in conflict. And they plan to challenge American interests - from offshore if necessary. But certainly without *repatriating* their profits for taxes. Even if they change the tax code."

"Williams is a public servant serving his State in the House of Congress" insisted Amanda.

"More. He's a chief investor!"

"Trevor wants me to inform you of the truth. Senator Williams has set you up for a failure. He's not expecting any Approval for this proposed legislation. Not at all. In fact, it's a ruse to get you to provide critical information for him and his cohorts..."

"I don't think you understand..." she began

"He wants to pan the horizon for anyone with accounts, credit and discretionary spending..."

Amanda put down her cup of coffee. "The truth. He commissioned this Research for intelligence?"

He looked at her and started laughing. "Hell. He doesn't even like legitimate and well capitalized small business operations!"

"Stop this Kendall..." she insisted "You're finding conspiracy villains in ..."

"I'm sorry to disappoint Amanda. What do you think you were being bugged for....with flowers....in your own home? He's about to turn evidence on Trevor!"

Her hand flew to her face.

He continued "He ain't no friend of the people. Amanda, he's exploited you and is out to enrich himself with a fee to himself of enormous amounts...!"

"Does Trevor know this?" she interrupted.

"Not all of it. But he is being followed. As are you! You need to get him out of the country. As we say in Ireland There's nary good ending to this one..."

"He just got here!"

He paused.

"Are you *sure*...How certain are you?" she asked quietly.

"His name is on my Accounts in Switzerland, Amanda. You should be informed like any professional should be."

A car drove by the house slowly, pausing, its lights dim but clear in the dimming daylight. The clouds gathered for weather outside. Kendall's car was still out there, parked across the street.

 "There is much more to this than you know. I do know this: Someone will be the Scapegoat" he faced her. "And you, Amanda, are in the vanguard of a flying flock of game birds... So watch out!"

She peered at him. *Trevor trusted this man.*

Trevor had promised Amanda that she should be informed. "Like any professional should be." His words, exact.

Those were the words just used by Kendall. How would he know that those were the exact words used by Trevor to her...? Clearly, they had spoken.

She turned to him squarely.

"Right then. Time to go!"

He went out, turned on the engine and pulled away towards Wisconsin Avenue.

Seconds later, she heard a police siren.

Of all the people to be trusting, thought Amanda. She knew enough not to be a standing liability to Trevor, if they came asking about Kendall. Right now the thing to do was to be gone from the house.

Carla - and Watson – would know what to do for the dogs.

Oh, my sweet... April!

She picked up her bag, briefcase, and keys. She tossed everything into her canvas tote.

She flew down the basement steps and into the garage. She backed the Land Rover out the rear, and she drove off, uneventfully, down a side lane from the house.

In her briefcase at her side was the laptop into which Kendall had installed his information.

In the rear view mirror, two cars pulled up to the house.

At least it was not in the house, the data.

The house would surely be searched. No question. If only to find her Hearing notes and documents for the Senator.

By now, she was clearly the enemy.

* *

Chapter 12

Amanda entered the Rayburn Office building from the Independence Avenue steps. The granite steps were wide and stately, part of a new design. They were grand for Congress.

An Amendment introduced by the Speaker of the House, Sam Rayburn, in 1955 proposed construction of a third House office building. It allowed for the building to be designed by the Philadelphia architect chosen for his simplified, classical structure that harmonized with the Capitol Congress using white marble over a steel framed structure.

Amanda let herself in with her pass card hanging from her neck. Not officially an employee but a member of a Congressional Committee nonetheless, she was entitled. With such a pass, she could enter the halls of Congress from any entrance or parking lot at will. It was coded for privileged personnel.

She was nervous. She had never used it before.

Until now, her team would assemble and enter as a group through the D Street Entrance. It allowed for an informal gathering in advance of the meeting, all of them arriving upstairs on the second floor of Starbucks on Independence Avenue where, coffee in hand, they sat in the cloistered lounge of dark leather chairs around a roaring fire to consult and share notes.

It was a culture of working professionals on the Hill while serving on the staffs of Congress.

Still, men kept their careers short here.

Capitol Hill, its wide and tree-lined streets of neo-gothic townhouses were affordable only to lobbyists and associations. This Hill had seen the nation grow over the centuries, if with its share of turmoil like the unrest of African Americans like ML King who in the 1970s marched and burned down parts of the city in protest against the white race.

Otherwise, Capital Hill was quiet, even slow with lumbering buses and congested traffic moving in humid, sweltering summers.

Today, Amanda entered unaccompanied.

Security guards were careful, as always, focused and armed to the hilt when making an inspection of persons and items entering the building. They knew her. She was one amongst many they recognized.

Once cleared, she knew the routine.

Still, being shy about her person, such close scrutiny made her perspire, and that condition led her straight to the bathrooms for refreshing.

She was in, at least. What was legitimate and open to her before, was now shrouded and hidden because of intelligence...

She knew the Senator's office hours, all his appointments and those of staff.

Ground-level state hallways were large and flanked by granite stairways. Four stories above grade, the building also had two basements and three levels of underground garage space...

It had taken years to build. Once completed, one hundred and seventy Congressmen from the House of Representatives were here accommodated in three-room suites with modern amenities and domestic comforts.

Below them were housed spaces for nine committee quarters, including various needs for general staff like a cafeteria; book station of the Library of Congress; medical facilities; communication centers; postal office; gym and media rooms for press and television.

Beneath the building a subway tunnel with two rail cars connected it to the main building to the Capital and pedestrian hallways joined it to the Congressional Longworth Building next door.

Amanda walked past two iconic marble status - one, the Spirit of Justice, the other, the Majesty of Law. She passed a procession of eight marble rhytons drinking knowledge from horn chimeras, and finally, the oil portrait of Sam Rayburn followed by a marble relief and a six foot bronze statue of his person.

Amanda pushed the elevator button, smiling at a few staffers walking by, and made her way along the second floor to the Committee Room where she normally assisted the Senator. His place was designated as a sitting member of the Committee for Labor and Management.

She walked on, as she had done so many times before. One by one, she passed the doors of various Congressmen marked by plaques, all of them closed for the weekend. Only some remained open for lingering staffers, doubtless cleaning up a week's work, especially if their Representative had sponsored legislation offered on the House Floor - their long months invested in the crafting of language for proposed amendments to the US Constitution was always a source of pride, leaving a massive clean-up.

For Amanda, these were familiar surroundings. Her own weeks of work for the Senator had been rewarded if not saluted as an achievement worthy of presentation.

But the Hearing had been difficult from the start.

And now the mood in Congress was somber following news of fraud, scandal and revelation from financial intelligence... A sense of suspicion hung in the air at every turn.

Then again, that was the nature of work on the Hill. It was the public duty of this Assembly to weigh the merits of proposals, the good, the bad, and all in between.

The Senator, no longer an elected official and without a vote, had been invited to serve on this Committee by the presiding Representative from New England. He, in turn, had trusted Amanda to produce a viable bill for him.

Amanda had felt awed by the burden of such responsibility. Here, at least, the trust of her team had currency and value. It was a place of thought, sincerity and fairness, if not always easy to attain. It was collegian.

The matter pressed her on. She had strange feelings of being a betrayer, sneaking about. But there was a reason.

The Senator had, in his locked cabinets, reports that he consulted periodically. Why had he so suddenly changed his thinking on the very issue he was called to advance? This, she had to discover.

She turned into the Chamber and stopped. Just as she thought...

The cabinet was open, or rather, still opened from the day's activities. Open for a final inspection by the floor staff on duty – an officer whose job it was to walk through the rooms and seal the cabinets each evening. This had not yet occurred.

Most offices kept their confidential papers in their small office vault. Otherwise, routine paperwork on this floor warranted little supervision since it was considered safe on these premises when surrounded by like-minded Representatives. Or... about to be entered in the public record anyway.

The Senator, Amanda knew, did not have use of the vault safe. He neither had permission to use the vault as a non-official member, nor did he remember the combination, as he often said. He simply kept his papers in his briefcase. Or he took them home in his briefcase.

"I'm too old for this kind of high tech stuff... Hell, I can't even negotiate a cell phone with all those teeny-tiny digits and letters to punch out! Give me an answering machine and a real phone any day" he laughed.

His Answering Machine was always lighting up, Amanda knew, and his Fax always in feed. She was the one who had to sort through the messages. They came in from all over, just as if he were in office as a full-sitting Senator.

In fact, one message was still coming in from Harvard thanking him for his generous donation to the University.

She stood there.

She remembered the voice from another message that she heard, just last week.

How nice, what a generous man.

Amanda went through his folders.

There was little of interest, or anything that she was not already aware of, having written most of his report herself. But for one envelope. Here was something different, tucked inside a file.

For one thing, it was classified and stamped DOD. Clearly delivered by Special Courier from the Pentagon, it came from the Office of Intelligence, signed in by a staffer, unopened yet by the Senator. This belonged in a secure vault, surely?

She opened it. After all, she served on his staff.

What was surprising was the list of Ledger Accounts. They had been transmitted - picked up from various sources, they showed source origination and were Classified. No continuous leads. No point of contact.

One page was circled in yellow.

The Senator was to view US Citizens investing in Ireland.

Down the list her eye roamed, account owners cited by their corporate headquarters; their date of origin and their amounts. One column was circled with the words: IRS reviewing...

The names were small; the dollar amounts large. Millions. Millions, flowing daily.

Why was this important to him?

Then it struck her.

These were tax-evading accounts.

Whatever he had intended to stem, or harness, for his State had been turned on its head: The IRS wanted them for tax evasion and repatriation. These people had petitioned for exemption from penalties!

There was no way he would access these funds for his project if they were already targeted for confiscation by the government. Since no legislation could be passed without a way to fund it, his proposal to tap these resources was useless.

He was backing the wrong horse, whatever his intentions! No wonder his enthusiasm for the project had waned. The Intelligence Report was for him to see. Not only had the numbers and accounts been leaked, but they were being used by the United States for political reasons.

She was surprised. He could have explained things to her. Instead he sent her up to fight his battle without informing her...

She flushed with feelings of resentment. No. Wait. Perhaps she had...*misunderstood?*

She checked her watch. She'd been in here too long.

Her eye caught a familiar name.

On another page, the names of individuals whose accounts had been targeted came from a different source. The source was without origin. It was only a sampling.

It listed the Senator's name.

A line was struck thought it.

The next sheet was a duplicate, cleaner. His name had been omitted. Again the source of the transmission without identification.

Something had happened here. If the senator himself had been piling money into offshore accounts, then this was what? A warning? An advance Intelligence Report?

No way to hide behind large corporations or lie. Here the names of accounts had been revealed to include his own!

This data came from untraceable links about who sent it, or where it came from. The work, evidently, of an Internet world - darkly transmitting untraceable links...? The kind of world in which only specialists trained in cyber-software could understand..?

She knew the source.

She put the files away, closed the cabinet and walked out of the office.

"Amanda!" yelled Peter Klinton, an African American Intern from Arkansas. "How are you doing?" he came along side. "Still working late for the Senator?"

She smiled. "Our Hearing did not go well..."

"Oh, the blackout, right?" he pointed up with a grin.

"Sort of..." she laughed. "More like an issue of cold reception!"

"Don't worry about it. Happens all the time...We're having a drink at the Coastline later. Join us! " He gave her a wave, and disappeared.

Amanda left the floor, her heart beating furiously within her chest.

She knew very well she was on Close Circuit TV. But she was there legitimately. No problem.

She took a deep breath and walked calmly.

Not only had she discovered a Senator untrue to his philosophy because of his own financial mess, but because people - like Peter would become disillusioned.

What a shame, she thought.

She walked down the granite steps of the Rayburn Office building and out into the sunlight.

At least she understood now why he had failed to support her program, a program he pushed on her until he could no longer show his face, that is.

But what was his next move?

* *

Amanda made herself some tea and sat in her Study. Tomorrow, Trevor was coming home. She was delighted, of course. And there had been some odds and ends that she and Carla had arranged.

But that evening, she felt alone, cold. She walked to the window. She remembered Ian Kendall on his last visit here – him and his stupid little car parked across the street. Her thoughts wandered.

It must have been hell for him, falling upon all that data. Then he lifted the information, left the country and hid it from the authorities...

Normally, in today's world, few would stir over just another cyber heist. Most of it was done by hackers. But no. His data was different. It was incriminating. It was embarrassing. It was *old money!* Much of it reversing assumptions of ownership and wealth since WW II.

How could she forget that evening? Sitting right here in the Study, he opened his heart to her. He told her why he did it.

"My boy. He's graduating..." he had explained, his voice soft.

Chiefly, he was talking to himself. "What difference does it make?" he said. "Is this a tribunal or a campaign that must be won at all costs?"

"Neither. It is the truth, Ian. That's all" said Amanda. "The truth."

"Does it matter so much to you?"

"Yes."

That's when he opened up. He sat down. "My son is graduating from Harvard. And I wanted to be here!"

"Harvard?"

"Yes. And why not? A good Irish Catholic in Boston...He got admitted, and six years of study brought him to his Comprehensive Exams before graduating, right? So he's graduating, and I wanted him to know how proud I am of him!"

Amanda sat down beside him to listen.

"But things did not go so well for him. The body of peers reviewing his work did not like his position, they said."

"What position?"

"That the Marshall Plan - that's the topic of his thesis - did not allow for the Irish to redeem themselves fully after the war..."

"That was a long time ago" she said.

He looked at her and nodded. "They were allies of the Germans. What's that go to do with anything now?" he looked at her. "My son, he claimed that some...of the Irish were *not* working for the Germans. They were aiding the British!"

"They asked him that?" said Amanda.

"In his position paper, he held that the Irish got no favors from the Marshall Plan. He asserted that they had made a contribution to the war..."

Kendall wavered.

Amanda spoke. "They disbelieved him?"

"They did. And he said he could prove it..."

"What do you mean, *prove it*...?"

"He cited the case of someone listing the Russian gold destined for America as collateral for loans. He suggested that the gold was buried in Ireland so as not to be sunk by the Germans, the cargo was never loaded! The perpetrator was no Spy for the Irish. He was aiding the British! My son thought he warranted an...award. "

"Why should that affect his dissertation?"

"They said the man was a thief, if so. They are denying him his graduation. Too controversial, they said. You see, the Irish were actually never really forgiven for their alliance with the Germans. Even the Catholic Church turned their back..."

"And you ...blame their decision?"

"They are an academic institution with an agenda! They have a reputation to uphold if they want money for their endowments that remain amongst the largest holdings in the world...One of the largest on record in Ireland..."

Amanda let herself sit down in the seat at her knees.

"Now wait a minute, Ian. We all have moments of frustration with our Professors! I know a few I'd like to throttle quite cheerfully. But really, this is Harvard you're talking about. Show some respect for our academic institutions of higher learning!"

He glowered at her. "They were on the list of accounts!"

"I still don't get...how all this relates to the Senator or have relevance..."

"In the bank records, the Russian gold was used as guarantee collateral for some of the biggest loans on record for the re-building of Europe after the war. And America made the loans." He paused.

"TOR programs of these bank accounts show this..."

"TOR...?"

"They are sort of unauthorized conduits, without links, and untraceable. They are broken and discrete sources of code that transmit data without showing who or where they came from. The government will get this data, no question."

She was glaring at him.

"I stole them. *I am the cyber-thief!*"

"My dear man" said Amanda softly "That is theft, breach of confidential information of the worst kind. Do you realize this? Let alone the illegal handling of sensitive documents with names and accounts from banks, you're ...you're..."

He put up his hand "I know. I am aware. But it's been going on for too long..."

"For a price, you mean. You stole this data to sell it?"

"No. Honestly. That was not the intent. It just happened this way with... my son."

"What has this to do with the Senator's name on this...this ...mysterious list?"

"He is on the Board of Regents at Harvard. I showed him the list of people who had diverted money to offshore accounts. He saw his name. I told him his name would be removed if he persuaded them to consider their decision about my son's graduation."

Amanda was stunned. "Did he agree?"

"Yes. Plus he made a $100,000 donation to the school."

"That's corruption, amongst other things..."

"This way my son graduates!"

He turned away. "You see, we should know. The boy's grandfather, my father, was the priest who buried the gold..."

It took her a while to absorb.

Should she... call Trevor? Should she ...*what*?

Her thoughts swirled, let alone her own actions of seeking answers by examining office paperwork! Was it wrong of her to try to seek answers for herself? Should she have been prying...?

In his correspondence, was there a reason that brought her Hearing to a dismal session? *Where had she gone wrong?*

Yes, she would not forget that day that Kendall was here...What a tortured man he must be, and she felt sad.

The sun was setting and long shadows touched the rail of her garden. She missed April, and her hand went to her mouth to bite back a sigh.

Upstairs, alone, she opened her bag and retrieved the document. It was a sheet from the Intelligence Report. A sheet giving the reliability of the information. It was a dossier.

His history was well documented.

Born and raised in Ireland, the son of a Minister, he had been trained as a software engineer and earned his degree at the London School of Economics before employment at the Bank of Laguaerny.

Chiefly, his responsibility was to watch for cyber-security. He managed bank interests, client codes and investment accounts.

That, plus the fact that his son was at Harvard University now entering his dissertation for review by the University faculty.

Amandas thoughts were in turmoil.

Tomorrow she was going to New York. She'd be meeting Trevor there, first.

They would talk. Perhaps he could advise her.

Amanda Wells looked down at the list before her.

Well into the night, the bedside table lamp cast its long and secretive illumination over the words.

How to explain the realities of a world that was desperate, destructive and without prospects? Who would have thought that Great Britain and its British Empire had been brought to her knees? *Any by whom?*

What reasons embroiled Europe in a second world war?
More importantly, how to reconcile the past with the present dilemma?
On the one hand, a Senator was blackmailing for information about financial dealings; on the other hand a cash of treasure intended to pay for the war was hijacked and used for other purposes...How to explain this, let alone assign blame and prosecute for malfeasance?
What came first, the mission, the means or the men?
She put down the papers and looked up.
The stone Tower on the wall was still up there. The first Tower-Keep of the new world intended for treasure; conquest and defense. She wondered at the sacrifice of wars.
To what end all those battles? Based on moral freedom and private property? It came down to the *greater need...*

The wind howled outside, or was it a branch beating against the wood siding of the house?
She closed her eyes.
What of real history? What of individuals were ever making choices for themselves? What of wars?
...Even Max de Robespierre, himself a champion of the French Revolution declared *"Terror is nothing more than speedy, severe and inflexible justice; it is thus a consequence of the general principle of democracy, applied to the most pressing needs of the patrie"*
How bloody convenient!
She switched off the light, her window shutters shuddering in the wind.

She lay there. The thoughts of those actions, so many years ago surrounded her. How could it all have been possible?

Who would have thought that the British Empire and all its majestic might could have been brought to such desperate measures?

She could only imagine. A slow creep, probably, a social movement that spread through society at the turn of the century; a century of such sweeping innovation, discovery and social benefits that it changed the world forever with new industry, wider labor prospects, and new opportunities for modern commerce.

But it had its darker side.

Even before the first war, WWI, the pressures of growing populations and industrial centralization left smaller nations damaged by an economic slump - the Great Depression of the 1930s. Especially those nations who had come to depend on trade between big nations using industrial goods.

As large economies contracted, seeds of destruction spread across Europe to ignite two world wars...

And here was Ian Kendall about to reopen old wounds and old assumptions.

* *

There were times when Trevor would have liked his job to be easier.

As it was, he was scheduled to meet with senior council in New York on matters long ago buried. Mike Booker his assistant, was with him.

"I don't get their interest..." said Mike

"They're fishing. That's all. They're in the business of drumming up investor interest" said Trevor. "So, ready?"

"Yes Sir!"

"Then let's go up and satisfy their questions"

They entered the glass doors to one of the biggest Trade and Investment Firms in New York, The Ruthamond Federated Capital Bank.

They shook hands all round and took seats at the conference table. If Trevor was right, they were soliciting for potential business. Clearly, it was a very large interest they were after. Unfortunately, the treasure they wanted to invest and manage was sheer speculation.

Trevor could have laughed. Except that it was no laughing matter. He should have been attended here by historians, not lawyers sniffing at potential profits.

As it was, Erick Brickman greeted them, Chief Financial Manager of Foreign Accounts.

They finished their first round of discussion, and, two coffee's later, Trevor sat back finally and pulled down his vest.

"Gentlemen. I understand the idea. But I rather think we're overreaching ourselves. The moneys owed to the United States by the United Kingdom for Lend Lease supplies during WWII have been paid in full. There is no outstanding asset that needs investing or management by your Firm."

"We heard that considerable portions of that treasure promised were presumed lost. Now if it is found, it is available for investment.."

"Well you heard wrongly. There is nothing to consider. All obligations have been fulfilled. Period."

"The Russians have asked us to discover what happened to their shipment of gold sent over to America from England for their Lend Lease supplies." Mike rolled his eyes.

"We wanted to give you the courtesy of explaining, just in case you could shed light on the matter, what happened to it. These are not exactly small sums of money."

Trevor might have expressed his impatience, if not his disdain. But he was, above all, a diplomat.

"The Russians, as you well know, were Allies at the time. President Roosevelt and Churchill relied on Stalin for Russia's burden of fighting in WWII. The Americans were to be paid for their supplies sent to Russia. These were war-time agreements made under the Powers of War Act.

Further, it was well documented that many of the Allied ships crossing the Atlantic were sunk by U-boat action. It was a time of war. We have all moved on. Today, we are all the beneficiaries of peace, thanks to those sacrifices. Germany is a viable economy, their citizens peaceable and industrious, and they are a valued contributor to the global economy..."

"What of Ireland's role?"

"Ireland did what she had to do!" admonished Trevor.

"Yet Ireland has enjoyed a financial bail-out?"

"She has recovered. And she responded with the only options available. She appealed for European help, and has now rehabilitated herself to full financial health. She and her people are upstanding members of the European community" said Trevor.

"...That's funny..." giggled a junior man at the end of the table flipping down his pencil. "How's about the IRA?"

Trevor faced them squarely.

"As a British Minister, I should inform you that we see Ireland as a nation with a long and venerated history and a people with much to offer the world, even as we went through periods of difficulty, differences, or financial stress."

"Yes. Yes, yes..." waived Brickman "But it has come to our attention that there may be investment opportunities of Russian wealth previously lodged in England at the time of the war. If it were discovered to ...to...have been...well... not lost at sea?"

Trevor had heard enough.

"Look. Gentlemen, I fail to see the benefit of casting about for stuff long ago settled. To the penny, all debts owning the United States have been paid in full. If there was any deficit outstanding - whether previously lodged in England or sunk by U-boat, it has been repaid in compliance with all official Agreements. Again, all accounts are closed and satisfied."

"Well then..." said Eric Brickman extending his hand "You have more than explained things for us. We have no further queries..."

Trevor was already standing, Mike Booker at his side closing the briefcase.

"That's Wall Street for you!" said Mike in the elevator.

"True. But they have nothing on us in London..." said Trevor preparing to dial out from his cell once they hit the bottom floor.

"I'm having dinner with Amanda tonight. Care to join us?"

"No Sir. I'm going out to a fine Irish Pub for a drink!"

"I don't blame you!"

"What were *they* after...anyway?"

"I'm not exactly sure. But if they're right, somebody owes the British government a hell of a lot of money..." He pressed *Call*.

* *

Trevor and she had made plans.

Amanda was reading on the train up to New York. There were matters to examine with the events of WWII. It was background information for a Deposition which Kendall had asked her to draw up.

Not only had the socialist movement of World War I swept through Europe and left its mark on American society, but the world was now mapped on a global scale of commerce.

By 1942, the developments that followed the Japanese bombing of Pearl Harbor unfolded swiftly. One week later, America officially declared war. Troops were mobilizing with the full concurrence of the United States Congress.

Almost simultaneously, Great Britain declared war on Japan. Within days, Hitler declared war on the United States.

Off Malaysia, Japanese aircraft flying from Saigon bombed the *HMS Repulse* and the battleship *HMS Prince of Wales* - the ship on which the British Prime Minister Churchill and President Roosevelt had just rendezvoused. Both ships were sunk.

Russia had been just invaded by Germany, her former ally.

Communist as Russia was, she made secret arrangement with Churchill and Roosevelt to combat Germany, and she became a powerful member of the Allied Commands in Europe during WWII.

As a result, America would provision Russian Armies fighting on multiple fronts. Russia would pay for her provisions, and differences amongst them would be resolved after the war.

Germany, meanwhile, was out to dominate Europe. With Japan, it would dominate the world.

Gold that once belonged to the Czars - long ago overthrown in Russia by socialist revolutionaries, was kept in vaults at London. This was because the Czar family had been related to British Royalty, sending all their treasure and Crown jewels for safekeeping to England during their overthrow.

In London, the world was in turmoil, and not all could see the motives of conquest.

There was such suffering, discontent and loss. There was disaffection with the government, the Army, the factions amongst class. Only the leadership stayed in the City of London. Air raids were common and deadly in London. The German Luftwaffe Air forces dropped bombs nightly on British ports, cities...

The affairs of Parliament were in disarray. A maelstrom of criticism surrounded the British Prime Minister's Government, the military was failing.

In North Africa, the British Army lost almost half the territory gained - almost three hundred miles to Gazala.

German Field Marshal Rommel was receiving massive deliveries of tank reinforcements and using them to drive the British Army back into the open desert, south of Tobruk.

At sea, all shipping supplies from America were being sunk. The United States was divided under Roosevelt.

In Asia, Japan had advanced so rapidly after Pearl Harbor that Singapore fell by mid-February.

There was turmoil and government collapse. Lord Beaverbrook, *Minister of Supply* was shifted to *Minister of War Production*. Sir Andrew Duncan took his place and Lt Col Moore Brabason stood as *Minister of Aircraft Production*. A Col. Llwellyn was named President of the *Board of Trade*. But barely five days later, Beaverbrook resigned from the War Cabinet. Churchill's Government resigned.

Still, in the new War Cabinet, Churchill was to proceed as Prime Minister...

Spies were everywhere present. Those in key positions feared intelligence leaks, infiltrations, conflicting war sentiments in all quarters, from Washington to London.

Roosevelt needed to be paid for the Arms he was sending to Europe. Congress was insisting...

In that climate, it was German U boats waiting for plunder. Gold payment was targeted for sinking, as had been others carrying payments to America for *Lend Lease*. This, as strategy, would impair the United States and set back the Allies in some measure.

And where were the Irish in this mess?

The Irish had backed Germany. At least, until persuaded to cease and desist by the British. But it took two years to do so. They were, in the meantime, spying for the Germans who kept U Boat naval stations there.

Thus it was that shipments of gold, as payment by the Russians scheduled to cross the Atlantic to the United States, was never loaded.

This Kendall had said.

And he asserted it not by an Irish spy, but as an Irish friend of the Allies who diverted the cargo, filling the holds with sacks of sand instead, and hiding the real cargo of gold on land, at night, in a graveyard, so that it would not be sunk. * *

Amanda would have to explain the full extent of Ian's visit to the house. This, she knew.

If Trevor was to cover for the man, then he should know everything. She made notes as she recalled the events of the evening.

"I'll give you a full explanation" Ian had said before leaving. "I'll be sending Trevor the full lists and details of which accounts were cited using the Russian gold as collateral. In fact, I shall be delivering to him all the information gathered from the Irish Banks regarding the security breach in cyber-security."

She had earned his trust, she knew.

Trevor's negotiations were key to his survival. But it was her that Kendall trusted.

"You have much, already. But to you, through him, I shall forward a letter signaled by this symbol, the Celtic Cross. It will be the location of where the collateral is, or rather the shipment of Russian gold was buried for safekeeping during WWII. That is where it was hidden..."

Then he added something else. She'd have to talk to Trevor about it. But she promised, anyway.

"There is one other thing. If there is a letter sent to the British Embassy for me, could you be the one to accept it and keep it for me? I petitioned Harvard to agree to my son's scholarship and graduation. Will you do that for me Mrs. MacDonnell? I rely on your husband's integrity as an Emissary to see to these requests as I place myself at his disposal?"

She nodded at him.

"Lord knows, it's not the first time an Irishman has placed himself at the mercy of the British!"

And that's when he left, recalled Amanda. Except that she said one more thing. The words surged up from nowhere, except that in her heart, she saw a wounded man. Amanda remembered saying one more thing to him.

"Ian... I am sorry for your difficulties..."

He had tipped his forehead with his knuckle, an old fashioned gesture of acknowledgement. Then he left.

Before leaving, Amanda had left messages for Trevor. Not explicitly, that is, but enough to inform him that there was information he needed to know about.

He was on travel, of course, and on such occasions his secretary handled all his calls and monitored his communications. She was always helpful, discrete and friendly. Amanda liked her a lot. Still, there were some things best left alone, even between a husband and wife only. That is, until the healing was complete, and then perhaps she could give him her heart in full. Trust had a way of being shy.

That's when she put down her pencil, her task done.

She was on the way to New York. They would meet, she and Trevor.

There was more she did not write. Nor would she bring it up. Like the call she got recently.

The landscape moved rapidly outside the train window. The sky a pink dusk as the sun set on a blowy cloud-driven landscape.

It was totally unexpected. It completely took her by surprise. Even as she answered in a business-like manner.

"Mrs. MacDonnell?" said the brusque voice, foreign. "I wish to speak with Mr. MacDonnell. I am Antoine DeBerle"

"Yes Mr. DeBerle, how can I help you?"

There was no immediate response. She listened closely.

"You do not recognize the name, then?"

"Please excuse me Mr. DeBerle..." she paused "my husband is the one with better recall than I, is there a message for him?"

Again, a longish delay. "I am the brother of the Ladevine DeBerle? You both met my sister...at the Gala in Washington?"

"Of course! How could I forget such a lovely woman?"

"Please tell you husband that I have been to the police about the woman found dead. It is not the body of my sister...They are mistaken!"

"I see." She said.

"I do not understand. I just received a message, I think it is from my sister. She is in Bermuda, I believe...Please tell Mr. MacDonnell that I communicated to him this information, yes?"

"Of course I will..."

He was gone.

That night of the call, she thought about the events that lay before her.

How could she forget the night of the Gala?

One detail prevailed above all others, and it remained elusive until she switched on the bedside lamp and collected her thoughts on a page in her note book, a habit formed during her University days.

There was something that came up when Kendall was at the house.

Kendall knew something...It was something outside the events of the Russian gold. Even outside the conflict with Harvard.

It was the recognition of the jewel. Yes, he knew something about the stolen necklace and tiara considered lost on the premises of Trevor's home in Scotland, those many years ago! How could that possibly be?

Had she touched on something when she suggested that there was a spy? A spy of what, exactly?

A Spy.

So if a spy was involved, then that suggested the whole affair was planned, but for what cause? In whose interests?

If was an intrigue related to the Royal family, what? A spy *within* the royal family?

Surely not.

Thank God she was an American! It was Trevor's domain, and surely there would be an explanation.

Still, the question of the jewel itself finding its way on the neck of a Russian woman at a Gala was also his explanation to make...

Anyway, she and Trevor were meeting now. He was returning to Washington with her, and he would resume his duties, he told her.

But she felt cold.

* *

Chapter 13

Amanda called Watson their Groundskeeper and left a message. Where was he? Why hadn't he called her? What news of April?

If she was looking for answers, she was disappointed.

He apologized.

Someone had misled him about the dog.

She fretted.

The household was not back to normal without April. Amanda couldn't reconcile the loss. There were no credible leads. No resolution.

She was beside herself. Was there no end in sight? She would talk with Trevor, she decided.

Now!

She burst into Trevor's office before his secretary could stop her...

"Trevor! It's been too long. April is gone, and we still have no leads. I'm now certain something terrible has happened to her...I expect you to do more!"

He looked up.

She did not see them at first.

He was in conference with members from the Chinese Embassy. Amanda startled them.

He introduced her. His wife, he said, with a smile of remorseless pride. "Come to wish me a happy day!" he laughed.

"Oh" said Amanda "I'm sorry!"

They smiled politely.

She smiled politely.

The meeting was over, and she waited outside.

Trevor came out and led her through the Embassy, his touch light at her elbow, if tight with resolve.

He was not pleased.

Smiling at the staff, nodding to his colleagues, and joking with security as they walked through the building, he walked her out to where the car was parked behind the Chancery.

Today he had driven the Ford. It was parked behind the Embassy.

He only once glanced up at the security cameras that monitored all critical pathways of the Embassy in quiet electronic wheezing of relentless duty.

Their exit was uneventful.

He walked to the Land Rover which she had driven. Noticing her gear on the rear seat, he climbed into the driver's seat. "Keys?"

There was no mistaking the look on his face. He was annoyed as hell.

"Look, I'm sorry Trevor... I didn't mean to come barging in like that..."

"Is Carla dismissed for the weekend?" he said, his jaw tight.

"No. She's coming over periodically across the weekend. Her family is visiting her and she wants to..."

"The dogs?" he asked with quiet tenacity as he waved at a pedestrian before crossing Massachusetts Avenue.

"They'll be fine. Only *April*...Oh God! Why?"

"Because we're going for a trip!"

"What?" she said, touching the dash "Where?"

"Philadelphia!" he said, looking into his rear view mirror to spot any followers.

"You are being *followed*?" she asked apprehensively.

"Yes!"

"God!"

"Explain!" she insisted. "April..."

"I'm trying to get to the Authorities with some information..."

Now she was getting mad.

"I should think so!" she blurted, noticing his temperature rise with traffic. He threaded mercilessly out New York Avenue and onto US 50.

"What...*what* is going on with us Trevor?..."

"You'll see!" he admonished, clearly fighting to stay calm.

By the time they were on Interstate 95, he was pressing hard on the accelerator, his eye on the rear view mirror. At Route 32, where the road took a small bend, he veered off suddenly, leaving the highway at a sudden angle that put them on Interstate 83, Northbound.

"Trevor?" she squealed, knowing the tenacity of the Maryland State Trooper patrols. His speed was unnerving her, and the Jeep was less than steady.

Traffic 83 Northbound was slow. First NSA, then Fort Meade were disgorging employees at close of business. The Parkway lanes went from fast to slow, and the ramps added volume bound for Baltimore – their drivers Texting messages.

She gasped at his reckless weaving and lack of road courtesies.

She reached for her throat zipper and opened up for air, her Under Armour vest clinging tightly. She was still in jogging clothes. The Jeep lurched and Trevor hit the horn on a driver.

From a casual trip to the Embassy, albeit a foolish spontaneous reaction - into a breakneck dash up to Philadelphia? *What was going on?* The tension in the car was palpable.

Finally she spoke. "Yes thank you..." she said sarcastically " I had a wonderful Hearing on the Hill..."

He swerved and she was bounced.

"I know you did!" said Trevor, his foot firmly on the accelerator again.

He turned off for Pennsylvania Avenue to a lesser road, finally slowing down for the grade of pavement and congestion.

"Wouldn't a phone call do for you?" she asked, annoyed at his tenacity to get to Philadelphia without so much as an explanation.

He opened his mouth to speak. But as he looked into his rear-view mirror, he burst on the speed again and charged.

"You'll get us both *killed!*" she cried.

"That's the intent of the people behind me" he said, his voice angry."

"Who?"

"Them!" he indicated.

"Who is 'them' exactly?"

"I'll explain. They want to stop me from reaching my destination. At all costs"

"Who?"

"The people you...err... interrupted in my office!"

"*What?*"

"A delegation from the Chinese Embassy. Supposedly, new arrivals to Washington. They came to object to our position on their human rights issues. Something they wished for us to withdraw, they said. Issues of banking and finance..."

"Wooha!"

"You have no idea the reports that are coming in" said Trevor "They are especially targeting activists in China. Especially those of Western faiths. Mostly, they go missing. Many are tortured..."

"By whom?"

"Well, let me put it this way. Just before you made your appearance, they told me they liked your style. In Congress! They have very long arms and even longer memories..."

"But how...?"

"They were threatening us. These are not your sane minds in China who have enjoyed immeasurable expansion and profit with the West. These are a different group of Asian finance bands..."

Amanda put her hands up to her face. "Why?"

"They have come to Washington to negotiate new terms on the debt they hold. It's not pretty. They are fearful. Nor will they be rewarded. In any event, you interrupted their ...veiled threat when you barged into the office!"

Amanda looked out the window, shamefaced.

They drove in silence.

Then she smiled.

"Hope they have a sense of humor.."

"I would hope they have any sense, period. They mean business, and they don't want 'Reformist Uprisings' as they put it, within their borders. Evidently what you are doing is of some interest to them..."

“Why?”

“I’m not sure. Unless…Unless there is something else going on?” he faded. “Anyway, they are using GPS to track us. They especially said they don’t want us going to meeting with a team in Philadelphia from the Federal Government…”

“That’s something relating to Kendall isn’t it.?”

“Yes. It’s a set-up we arranged for New York, initially. But they were particularly focused on *you*” said Trevor. They drove in silence, her thoughts a jumble.

“Oh My God…*April*?”

He turned to her and said nothing.

She let the landscape slip by. She hated the city now. She hated all that she saw.

Amanda looked at Trevor carefully, his profile strong and full of intensity, their convictions…

A principled British gentleman, she once called him. But seeing him driving like a fiend down a country route he was unfamiliar with…he was focused on survival! This was a different Trevor. Perhaps she didn’t know him at all, she wondered.

She spoke calmly. “Kendall did say that I should check my mail on my laptop…Who are we meeting with in Philadelphia by the way?”

“A group called Global Tax Management and Repatriation Systems.”

She waited.

“I’m holding information for the Internal Revenue Service they would rather I didn’t disclose!”

Amanda shut her eyes. The last thing she wanted was another lengthy explanation.

She knew enough to understand flight. And she was getting tired of this intrigue…

Finally Trevor turned into a Farm warehouse just outside Kennett Square, and parked the Land Rover behind the Garage.

The sun was setting on Pennsylvania, her vast crop fields a yellow horizon of stubble and stalks, now harvested.

It was quiet. They saw a red pick-up truck outside the entrance. The owner was just closing up.

They walked casually and crossed the lane to an open street. A small restaurant across the street was there positioned for truck drivers engaged in long-haul deliveries. They found a table, sat and ate dinner quietly.

By the time they returned, the pick-up had disappeared. And instead of returning to the highway, Trevor headed further down the Farm lane.

They waited, a cold and lame sun set behind the heavy shouldered mountains of Pennsylvania.

Finally he edged behind an abandoned barn with cupola vents and small night lights.

The stink was awful, Amanda wanted to wretch.

"In here..." he said, pressing open a wooden door that presented a small concrete enclave, fans blowing air up the stacks.

The stench became almost unbearable.

She held her nose. "Oh God!" she said "I think I can't breath...!"

"Here" he said, finding a cleared floor. It had tile, it was swept and tidy. He brought in her gear and a Jeep travel spread of rough pile, left from his last hunting trip for his duck-blind.

She was gasping, almost gagging.

"Manure?"

"Mushrooms" he said, tucking her in behind a concrete milk well.

She glowered at him.

"Theft of muck is hardly worth protecting in this rural area. They thrive in the dark, and it's...good manure. Open up!" he said, nodding to her laptop.

"What?"

"Can you go online?"

She would have like to level a few invectives at him. Instead she said "I should. In these mountains of Pennsylvania and at this altitude. Depends if there's a tower nearby...Why? To signal for help?"

"No. To see what you've got. It's all on your laptop..."

"What is?"

"What I must hand over to the Internal Revenue Service tomorrow! Those thugs may be waiting for me in Philadelphia. If we ever...get there alive!"

"This is it? *Here?*"

"I saw you had your Laptop in the back of the Jeep when you came. Why go home where they'd be observing...?" he said.

"Kendall...did he tell you about this?" she asked.

"No. They did! Clearly, they know this data is in our possession. And they are tracking us...I didn't have it, so it must have been with you!"

"Look at this!" he said. "This company is a US multinational and has purchased another unit promising to pay the parent a large amount of cash in this Note Agreement. But since both are American - there is no tax bill for the parent under the US Law!"

She was tiring. And she was cold.

Trevor was oblivious.

"Then, citing certain tax laws, the newly converted foreign subsidiary can access the multinational's existing offshore cash by borrowing from a foreign sister unit, according to the SEC Filings....In this case the amount is for $356 Billion. And 40 Billion over here...And here...And Oh my God" he said finally, these numbers are boggling."

Amanda was curious now. She looked over his shoulder. "Here's one from Kendall" she said "He says to watch the alphabetical names. Like Bs, Ds. Etc. This one is the Killer F Account. Look at these staggering numbers!"

"I don't like what this is suggesting..." muttered Trevor "I don't like this one bit!"

"What?"

"They plan to make a run on our currencies with a competing currency!"

Amanda recalled Kendall's words. Trevor went on reading.

"Who?" she asked.

"The Debt Holders"

"What does that mean?"

"This is the proof! Kendall. He's been tracking their interest in currency exchanges. If the US dollar is no longer the world's reserve...Then how about being paid in Boston for work with foreign currency...subverting tax obligtions."

"That's like subverting the laws of a Government by... Can they do that?" she asked.

Trevor wasn't listening. He was reading off his electronic device. "They're buying out entire banks here, redirecting their reserves and altering their reporting... Three, four and six at a time with these offshore accounts!"

Amanda looked at him. But for the stink, it was almost funny...out here in the middle of nowhere hiding beneath a blanket.

"Who needs guns when you can take a country hostage by subverting its Treasury?" muttered Trevor.

"Oh..."

He looked into her troubled eyes. "Come on. Cuddle up! Let's get some sleep. Tomorrow we definitely get to Philadelphia."

Trevor actually slept. But not before he sat upright and said something.

"No. These people are not Chinese either! Their Embassy never laid eyes on them. They just introduced them to the Washington colony as fellows...No! They aren't even Friendlies. The Chinese Delegation never heard of them! They wanted *us to shed some light...*"

He stopped talking.

Thank God she wore her outdoor gear, she thought. It was cold.

* *

The man that found them had a beard that glowed in the dark. Holding a lantern, he stood there - a very large grey beard. And he wore a panama hat.

The lantern wavered. Over his left arm was draped a shotgun.

Amish.

He wasn't too pleased, but he wasn't surprised either.

By sunrise, Trevor explained himself. Within half an hour the man brought them warm milk, egg sandwiches and bacon.

He would take them up the road in his buggy, he said. And there was a car at his cousin's Enoch, if it aided the cause of the nation, he said. It would get them to Philadelphia.

The Land Rover could stay in the barn, he said.

"Now Go!" he admonished, pointing a bony finger.

Trevor thanked the Amish farmer, and they walked towards the car.

That's when she heard the sound. It was a distant, muffled bark – somewhere captured inside a car perhaps.

Amanda froze. "April?" she called.

A van camouflaged against the background coloring of the opposite granite building started up, the engine pulling out.

"Hey!" yelled Amanda.

She ran towards it, her arms flapping and her legs stumbling "April!"

The dog war barking.

Amanda turned in a desperate appeal to Trevor. "It's April in that car!"

Trevor turned on his heels and ran to the farmer, grabbed his shotgun and aimed at the car. The car's wheels lost traction as it accelerated.

The Amish rifle fired like a Scottish blunderbuss, delivering a blast that exploded like cannon. Trevor reloaded, and aimed at the car. The car halted.
Suddenly the rear door opened, and an animal was tossed out with such force that it rolled several times.
"April!" screamed Amanda.
The dog was dazed, attempting to gain balance, but faltered.
"April!" yelled Amanda.
The dog recognized the voice, and then lurched forward. Shedding grit and sand with a good shake, Amanda and April joined in a heap of dust, their reunion a tangle of unbridled joy.
The car took off and Trevor let it go.

Trevor made his call. One hour later, they were in Philadelphia.
On the top floor of the Hyatt Regency Hotel, not far from Philadelphia International Airport, April was sleeping soundly on the floor, dog food and a water-bowl less than ten feet away.
There, she had stayed all night, at the foot of their bed as Amanda slumped asleep in Trevor's arms.
Trevor lay awake.
Next time, he knew, they would not send warnings.
He knew their intentions.
The message was clear.

**

Trevor was sunbathing in Bermuda. The boat had been successfully delivered.

The news had came into his office in Washington. Fiona screened the call and he took it on his way to a meeting on the fourth floor. Amanda had asked that he be informed directly by the Marine Broker.

There had been a fire. The Marina that sheltered their boat in Maine had been destroyed. The fire had caused major damage to the facility.

Their insurance broker suggested that the boat either be moved to another Marina in the vicinity for winter storage, or commissioned for a delivery to warmer weather for the balance of the winter season. Since all dry-dock facilities in the vicinity of the Marina were full, Trevor was left with only one option.

Moreover, he was advised, since the Marina had neither yet processed their boat through its scheduled overhaul, nor serviced and certified its diesel engines as required by Coast Guard Certifications, its scheduled maintenance updates would soon lapse.

It would need to be done at a warmer port. And it would have be done immediately. Hours remaining on the diesel engines would allow for one delivery trip south to Bermuda - but not much further without Inspections-compliance and re-certification.

"You'll need to sign off at delivery Trevor, and get certified inspection docs before the Charter Company takes possession of the vessel. I'll call a boat surveyor. The rest is management, maintenance and Safety requirement measurement."

"Is that what the Marina was intending..?"

"Yes. That's short for ageing use of the boat that requires upgrades or replacement...Better to start fresh. Like buying a new boat?" he chuckled.

Trevor laughed, and said he would have to discuss it with Amanda.

Bad as the timing was, Trevor told his broker that he would fly down to the Bermuda Yacht Club for a few days and sign off the billing and invoice papers. He would stay at the Bellavista Hotel and sign over the management of the boat to the charter company directly.

Amanda had concurred, and she informed her family about the boat.

As Trevor asked Fiona to make his travel arrangements to Bermuda, there was some office teasing. Their boat needed repairs in dry dock. It was a trip to the tropics for a few days in the sun, as he explained it, and the office filled with envy and laughter all round.

Fiona booked his flight.

Trevor MacDonnell had other business.

* *

Trevor could not resist one last cruise across the Sound before giving the boat to Charter Management. The helm was a pleasure to handle.

For Trevor MacDonnell, this was a Remembrance of sorts, redolent with stories told him as a boy by his father. Off Darrell's Island, he imagined the air ringing with the sound of WWII American bomber seaplanes; Catalines with rear turrets, and camouflaged naval planes preparing to launch a military strike.

The facility here had been garrisoned by Scottish Highland troops recovering from the battle of Dunkirk, a battle fought by brave hearts of Scottish clansmen from his own region.

How else to describe that period of the war, early on, when the reality of German invasions swept across Europe too suddenly to respond. Many had fallen at the Battle of Dunkirk, and they were brought here. Especially that remnant from Scotland who attempted to resist, if too late... His father was one of them.

The sea was calm.

Bermuda, that island in the sun for the brave, the un-brave and the damaged. *What was her draw?*

To this place England sent those set aside for various reasons. Sometimes for healing. Sometimes for safety. Sometimes... for prevention.

Here is was that the young and handsome King Edward VII came to live with his wife, a divorcee from Baltimore, rendering him unable to rule. He had abdicated in 1937 for her love. Or so it was announced in his Declaration of Abdication.

The truth however, was more about his own affiliations and loyalties. They were questionable, if not treasonous.

Like so many monarchs and sovereigns of Europe swept away by invading Armies of Europe, his position was suspiciously on the edge. Had he colluded with the enemy? Had he thought of making possible Alliances... He abdicated, and his brother Albert became King George VII, a speech impediment notwithstanding.

King George VII saw England through the war with Winston Churchill as his Prime Minister in Parliament. Together with Russia and America as Allies, the war finally came to an end in 1945.

Still, Winston Churchill kept the former King Edward under surveillance. His liaisons with the Germans remained worrisome, especially since *Appeasement* was a word still on the lips of many loyal Britons.

The former King, now titled Duke of Windsor, was sent to the post of Governor in Bermuda. If quartered in beautiful surroundings and royal trappings, he was kept there nonetheless - held off shore and away from English soil. Edward was sequestered here as British troops fought against German forces all over Europe and Africa in battle.

Trevor sailed the boat passed Darrell's Island, and approached the old Bellavista Hotel by attaching to its marina dockage. The dock master came running down to help him tie up the vessel.

"She needs to be fueled up and freshened below decks, if you will please?" said Trevor MacDonnell.

"Yes Sir! What a beauty!"

"Aye, she is that! Belongs to my wife. I've come to enjoy it enormously" he grinned.

The dock master smiled "That's usually the way, Sir!"
"Anyway, I shall sail her out at first light, so have her ready to go. I'll be settling my account up at the Lobby with the Hotel in advance. Please add to my account any expenses outstanding."
"Absolutely Sir!" he said, and tied off the painter at the pump station. "We shall dock her at the outside pier, End-slip, for your easy access into the channel. She'll be ready to go. The dock is closed at night Sir, the gates open at 7.00 AM. Your room combination number will unlock the gate if you need to push off before light, and enter the gates."
"Right"
"Engine Ignition keys will be left in the locker at your Captain Station on board Sir."
"Thank you!"

* *

Trevor was waiting.

The Bank Vice President came back with the Manager. Both were reluctant to concede to Trevor's request to open the vault of anyone Diseased.

"Please know Mr. MacDonnell, we are careful about who should present themselves. Mistaken identity and theft today evades detection in ways that elude us all, please understand."

Trevor nodded deferentially.

"Furthermore, it's been so long since any deposit was made in this vault for this Deposit box, we are reluctant to open it *On Demand* without assurances... We would need some kind of security clearance for opening this Deposit box. We have nobody on the premises today able to verify who and on what conditions we should open this vault."

"It was my father's vault!"

"We understand Sir. And we feel certain that your request is legitimate. You have sent us advance correspondence. But this vault is particularly under our tightest security since it cites the parties of other banks that must also collaborate and verify..."

"I understand" said Trevor.

They apologized. "We have not the authority, nor even the key code to access that vault Sir, let alone access numbers to open the account."

"Who does?" Trevor quietly asked them.

"Our man in Switzerland!"

"But the account was opened here?..."

They paused and consulted.

"Perhaps we can call over there: It is well into the night, their banking hours are closed. May we call in the morning and give you his response tomorrow Sir?"
"Very well."
Trevor went back to the hotel for dinner, then strolled out to the open veranda where the sun washed the horizon in gold hues. He took a seat at the Deck bar for a drink.
Warm air touched the fringes of palm fronds and bougainvillea, having traversed ocean trade currents much as if propelling ships to the new world.
Trevor consulted his watch. The evening light was still early, if leaving only dusk hues now across the water.
He would retire early and he ordered a final cappuccino coffee - Amanda's favorite nightcap. He pulled out his phone. He would call her tonight.
The night was still, except for music emanating from the Bellavista Hotel, tunes of big band era. It permeated the air with its melodious beat and soft luminescence. Perhaps not unlike the music of his father's time, Trevor thought.
 It seemed as if nothing had changed in over 70 years since the years of the War, or since the Duke of Windsor, formerly King Edward VIII, came to Bermuda in 1940.
Hastily arranged by Winston Churchill, the trip to Bermuda was to keep the Duke of Windsor from going to America. With him came his new bride, Wallace Simpson, an American.
The Duke of Windsor himself had been a monarch for only a year, succeeding his father, King George VI in 1936.
But the choice to marry "the woman I love" was untenable. She was an American citizen twice-

divorced. That left him no choice but to abdicate as per the dictates of royal succession to the throne.

Further, Trevor understood Churchill's concern.

During the years of WWII it was said that the former King was courted by the Nazis to be their puppet king once the Germans invaded England.

Nor did the former King make it any easier for the English people. His expression of doubts and ideology about England's ability to win was defeatist. His loyalties were suspect, and his opinions were used as propaganda by the enemy.

It particularly worried Churchill that the Duke and his wife would go to America and garner popular support against the war. America was still conflicted about entering the war, Roosevelt was unable to consolidate support as isolationist tendencies prevailed.

England was in trouble. They desperately needed the aid of America. The British Cabinet arranged to take the Royal couple by the Export Lines vessel named *"Excalibur"* It was to take them as far as Bermuda, and from there, after a week, they would be transferred to another ship for the Bahamas.

The Duke hated the appointment, he called it "a third-rate colony." Especially since he and his wife, while in Bermuda, were denied by Buckingham Palace the right of royal courtesies following his abdication, including the title of *Royal Highness*.

* *

The Bank Manager explained that he had instructions from Switzerland. He took his seat across from Trevor. The Deposit box had been sealed by certain men who were in Bermuda at the time of the early months of the war, he explained.

Trevor's father was there as Monarch of the Glen Eastern Scotland and Officer of the Dunkirk Scottish Highlanders at the time...

But only those familiar with coded information could have access to the account. If Trevor MacDonnell felt that his father was one of the men who sealed the contents of that vault box, then he should take the test to answer the necessary security question.

Trevor felt he could. The question was put to him over the telephone from Switzerland, with the bank Manager in attendance, and the Vice President.

The question was simple. *Who was the Colonel?*

Trevor knew that if he answered incorrectly, there was no way he could access the vault. If he answered correctly, he would find answers to a bequest left by his father before his death - A bequest never revealed on English soil. Here, on this Darrell's Island where he had died from wounds suffered at Dunkirk as a commanding officer, he had written his wife, Trevor's mother, offering his apologies for leaving her to raise two sons without him. With that, he had instructions and directives for the family as Head of his Clan.

One matter concerned an Account in Bermuda. It was to be opened by his heirs only. These details his wife transmitted to her sons in her Last Will and Testament. Trevor heard about them when he was a young adult, in the presence of a family solicitor, just before entering University. Only once did his mother recite his father's words.

Trevor walked to the window of the bank, his hands folded behind his back, thinking. Now was the moment to open the Deposit box as directed.

He turned to face the men at the desk.

"Warden!" he said. "Colonel Warden was Winston Churchill, a code name ascribed to him by Roosevelt for his honorary position as the Warden of the Cinque Ports - a post held by Churchill. Churchill used it only for the highest security measures."

They were staring.

Then, turning back to the phone line to Switzerland, they relayed the exact words just spoken. The response took a few minutes. They hung up and turned slowly to face Trevor.

"Mr. MacDonnell, you have access to the vault. Please Sir!"

* *

There was no question that Trevor was looking at the crown jewels of a Czarist Russia. This was a world long before the beginning of World War II.

Pictures and provenances of the satin-lined box described the items, each one couched in satin or velvet.

This was part of a collection of crown jewels brought to England for safekeeping during the Russian Revolutions in 1914, prior to the World War I.

Even beginning at the start of the century, the ancient jewels were being sent away in secret as social rebellion swept Europe, overturning the monarchies, one nation after the other.

King George V of England, the Duke's father, very much resembled in appearance his cousin, Czar Nicholas of Russia.

Distressed by all that had befallen the Royal family of Russia, and moved to avoid such riot on English soil, King George V accepted the jewels for safekeeping.

When King George V died in 1936, it was thus that his eldest son Edward VIII succeeded him to the throne.

Following the abdication of Edward, the royal crown jewels passed to his brother King George VI and Queen, Mary.

It was Queen Mary who purchased the Russian crown jewels as additions to the British collections.

It was said that Queen Mary did so to give needed cash to the bereaved Russian Royal family, many of them scattered across Europe, but related.

The jewels were chiefly worn as official Royal Dress.

From this code of ethics, the monarchy presided over its realm, symbolically, both in peacetime and in war.
Mostly worn in defiance against the enemy now, Royal displays were a source of pride for thousands of marching troops fighting for freedom of democratic rule by Parliament.
The crown jewels of the monarchy became the sacred insignias of venerated custom of trust, sacrifice and nobility for every man woman and child of the realm.

Rudely, Edward VII discovered in Bermuda that the Royal Crown jewels, serving as symbols of title nobility could not be trifled with - neither as costume enhancements nor as displays of wealth.
This occurred when the rank and file staff of the Diplomatic offices of the Island failed to pay homage to him as they had done before...
After the event of the abdication, the former King Edward and Wallace Simpson had waited a long time in France for the ratification of her second divorce. When finally they married, Edward was styled Duke of Windsor with his Duchess. It stirred him only then that he was no longer entitled to the rights and privileges of royalty, nor to wear the official symbols of title.
This, they had to explain to him.
He was angry, and lodged his complaint with the officials at the Embassy there. They waited for a reply.
Finally, he was shown the official cable from Buckingham Palace.
There could be only "One ruling monarch"
If angered, they did not show it to public.
The Press imaged the newly-wed couple in the Bahamas. He a handsome man, and she, with her elegant and strong features, a beauty.

The jewels lay there on the cachet of velvet.
Trevor went through the Deposit box in the vault held by his father. Here the small items, redolent with the battle of Dunkirk, resonated. Below it all was a second tray of valuables.
Here, he saw memorabilia from a visit to their Scottish home by the newly crowned King George V and Queen Mary at Kaverness for a Scottish Hunt. The same occasion, he remembered, when the Queen's jewels had been stolen, bringing disgrace upon their Scottish family. There was a picture even, all together...
He picked up the coronet, if broken in parts, as if to be reshaped for a new wearer in an *altered* state - no longer the traditional form seen of the picture.
And there, in a case, was the full necklace, a rope of drop-sapphires; diamonds and pearls. It matched a small coronet of sapphires; diamonds and drop pearls. The same set of necklace/coronet and tiara originally added to the Trust of the English as Crown Jewels, bought by Queen Mary from the Russian collection of the deposed Czar.
With it was a Note.
Trevor held the Note addressed to his father.

> *To Henry MacDonnell, Monarch of the Glen of Eastern Scotland..*
>
> *Forgive our household, dear Clan MacDonnell of the lands Scottish!*
> *These were purloined from your Castle on the visit of the King and his wife for the purpose of adorning a new royal beauty...*

We do return them to you now, with our humble apologies for the family disgrace that followed. You never stole them! We are instead, always in your debt for your loyal service and faithful discretion.

This, I write by the hand of an official representative, party and witness to this act of restitution."

Seal of the Duke Royal , 1940
Edward VIII

*****

Trevor was still sitting at the Deck bar on the veranda of his Hotel, a drink in his hand and his mind lost in thought.

It was dark now, and the music tantalizingly blue.

Like yesterday, the sun had set on the long white beaches of Bermuda, a few lingering honeymooners trailing along the shoreline.

The drink before him brought back lifetime memories of a family dedicated to honor, duty and wartime obligations.

Trevor's mother had done a splendid job raising two boys without a head of household; and his brother had done them proud to pick up the pieces of a family name. He himself was a careerist in the British government, and now married to a woman...

"Hello Mr. MacDonnell" said the sultry voice behind him.

Trevor turned from his drink.

The accent was unmistakable, and it shocked him.

There stood the woman at the Charity Gala in Washington who had dazzled them with a jewel of sapphire around her neck.

"Ms... *DeBerle*?" he managed, the scotch of memories and solitude still warm.

"The same" she said, stepping out of the shadow.

"I thought you were...The Russian Embassy informed me that..."

"That I was dead?"

"Yes."

"How true!" she said, a glint in her eye.

She had moved sveltely to the bar stool beside him and nodded at the barman for a drink of the same.

"You have kept my jewel, I trust?" she said.

**

Amanda had not heard from Trevor.

She was fielding questions from his office; their friends, their now social obligations if not financial matters that needed attention. He had disappeared it seemed.

It was not that she kept a tight leash. Such was the nature of their marriage. A relationship that allowed for professional courtesy when the need arose, but with intermittent periods of intimacy and friendship.

She wondered about it. Increasingly, they had come under pressure, no ebb and flow, with time offline sufficient to smooth out long days of work and intervals of intensity.

Where was he?

Yet, to a large degree that was what she cherished the most - the ability to weave in and out of a professional life and engage in domestic life with seamless transition. But only when both were cooperative. Or both, at least, present!

She made coffee.

Trevor had been gone for days.

He had left messages here and there with his secretary, Fiona. She, wonderfully accommodating, had grown accustomed to the things that mattered. Almost like an extension of family, and God knows, she had spent enough time at their home to make it her own...

But Amanda felt a certain malaise. An absence of closeness. Something cold had settled between them. She sensed it. As if it were later to be explained...but something.

Recently, there had been a lot of work, and work-related travel.

She herself had been the cause. What began as a favor, really, had turned into a gold standard that she had to perform for the Senator.

Then, what to make of the Senator?

How to explain his hot and cold temperature to something so critical?

Or more importantly, after what happened on the Hill, why expose someone to an impossible mission?

* *

Chapter 14

"Paste! It's what they called it paste!..." said the thin voice on the phone.

It was raining in Washington DC, the wind sending water fiercely against glass windows as if needing to clean-up a city in one fell sweep.

Worse, purple-grey clouds hovered all morning, darkening the sky so as to warrant a few houselights at noontime. Like the desk lamp in Amanda's study.

The phone in the kitchen had interrupted her, and she was tempted to let it lapse, for later.

However, there was so much to do and so many deadlines to achieve, that one lost call might cost her an agony of work if important...She rushed down the hallway and almost brushed off the caller who sounded like a tradesman selling a product. That is, until she heard the news.

"Mrs. MacDonnell, I am sorry to disappoint..."

Amanda could hardly believe her ears. "Are you certain?"

"I am certain. The jewel you brought in is not authentic. I have called in a number of experts from our diamond district here in Philadelphia. Even a consultant for the Museum. It is an antique piece of costume jewelry. But not an authentic gem..."

"But I thought…" she felt embarrassed. "Well, I was led to believe…"

He was patient, the caller, understanding her reaction.

"I see" she said, composed.

"Do you have it insured?"

"I was about to do so. And I will have to speak to the underwriter, of course. Can you give me a complete written assessment?"

"Of course Mrs. MacDonnell. I am sorry. There is nothing more disappointing when such a thing is discovered. After all, jewels are investments of enormous value…"

"So was the cost of insuring that thing, if real!"

"Oh, then we would be speaking about something with the value of a museum piece. No. This is not authentic. I am sorry!"

"Thank you Mr. Bernstein. I shall inform my husband immediately!"

She did. She left a message for Trevor that was informative, yet not explicit - a security precaution.

He would understand immediately.

Fiona took the message.

* *

It was dark - drizzling and windy, but quiet. She walked into the kitchen and prepared a snack, more like a late night meal. She heated a bowl of soup, tossed up a salad in vinaigrette and toasted a slice of French bread. She added wine.

She set out a place-mat and sat at a scrubbed oak kitchen table, its broad round corners nicked and grooved with years of food preparations – doubtless happy gatherings with long memories. It had been in Trevor's family for generations.

She leaned back, her neck muscles taught.

The work was done, yes, but it had been hard to concentrate. All those damned interruptions; the nature of the report, and those shadowy thoughts that fought for her attention all day...

What?

For someone with a cheery disposition whose desk turned out exceptional work, Amanda felt somehow frustrated.

What exactly, was bothering her?

The kitchen lights were dimmed, yet there stood the phone on which she had received a call from an expert jeweler in the Philadelphia diamond district. What was all that about?

Didn't Trevor say that the jewel was authentic and had been stolen from his family household when he was a child? The very same jewel hanging from the neck of the woman at the Gala?

And yes, the very woman at the Gala - who was found dead in her apartment, as the newspaper obituary said. Now there was the question!

Nothing was bothering her as much as the call she received just weeks ago.

"Please tell you husband that I have been to the police about the woman found dead. It is not the body of my sister...They are mistaken..."

Bad enough that they were harboring a Fugitive wanted by the Government for cyber-theft, if not Intelligence-related spying, but now subterfuge about the identity of a murdered Russian...?

Where was Trevor?

** **

Trevor could hardly believe the situation.

The jewel in his house in Washington DC was supposed to be the missing link in the array of treasure stolen, long ago.

Yet here she was ...LaDevine DeBerle

She had approached him.

Trevor looked at her now. How different was this situation from a whimsical event in the city when first introduced?

She moved closer, in tandem with two men half emerged from the shadows.

"We know that you would lead us to the real cache" she said.

It took him a while to grasp her meaning.

"A ploy?" he asked.

"Absolutely!" she said. "And the source of many years of secretive deposits held on this island. Offshore banking!"

"That's illegal" he put down his drink. "In fact, that's top grade Tax evasion!"

She laughed, the two men came forward. "Of course. If only you knew how many, and or how much was invested..."

"Did you report this to your government?"

She smiled at one corner of her red lips and came closer. "Allow me to introduce to you my government!"

She nodded to the two men behind her. "Again, the account number please? You surely have it?"

"And the jewel at the Gala...?"

"To match with the rest of the collection of jewels ...for corroboration!"

"So it was a fake?"

"Of course! But it did the trick. You led us exactly to the bank, or should I say, account and vault that has the balance of the Russian collection...So, again I ask. The vault combination account number please?"

He padded his pockets, and demurred. "Your plan?"

"Once the Initial code authorization was cracked from Switzerland, the account is open to whoever presents the correct combination of ownership identification."

"How long have you been doing this?"

"Oh! A long time, they tell me. Many an uncooperative depositor like you has been caught by a stray bullet, Mr. MacDonnell. Especially if related to this island where there are countless offshore and tax-free banking accounts. You may call us Collectors of ill-gotten gains!"

"A business then?"

"Yes! Since there exists no accounting or official lists of these offshore accounts... All of them tied to European and American fortunes!" She paused. "I'll take the combination sequence they gave you for identification, please!"

Trevor looked over her shoulder. "I wouldn't want to make a scene with your henchmen here... It would not do for a diplomat to be found in a bar brawl with them." He got up.

"No."

"Of course, it's in the Safe of my hotel room!" Trevor finished his drink. "What the hell? It's all insured anyway, Right?"

"Right!"

She approached the bar. "Please retrieve it. Oh, and Mr. MacDonnell, we would not want to expose your secret to the British Media for another salacious story of the stolen royal jewels, nor hurt your wife in Washington. So, Alert no one! I'll be here, waiting!"

Trevor walked to his hotel room, a two-story suite. He unlocked the bedroom floor, opened the small Safe, which was empty, and left it open.

He headed for the window at the veranda, climbed down the rose trellis and moved into the trees and down across the lawns of the hotel that led down to the waterfront.

Trevor dowsed all navigation and safety docking lights, unshipped the boat halyards from their mooring without a sound. He unfurled the jib in one clean pull off the winch and the vessel began to ghost out of the harbor in the dark.

With barely a flashlight for the chart, he navigated down the channel using depth sounding only and channel markers.

He passed through the Harbor Straight and round the Point in the dark, a skill he had learned from Amanda. By the time they discovered that he had left by boat, he would be re- docked somewhere, and gone.

**

At Government House, the conference was held in the basement where the wares and treasure had been laid out on adjoining tables for a complete accounting and inventory.

Two security officers guarded the door.

The loot was enormous. Large money amounts were fully documented; coin collections itemized. Deposits and safekeeping of items vested in these local vaults were incalculable. Many included unrecorded works of art; some known stolen since before the war. Much of it delivered with Churchill for shelter during WWII.

His father's vault was the main safe repository.

Occasionally, especially amongst the items of value in antiquities, some little item was without value at all, perhaps holding family memories. But all were the collections of depositors sending their wealth away from England in Trust.

The paperwork was still being catalogued. Some had descriptions of assets laying elsewhere. Bonds, bank notes, industrial coupons...

Others were ledgers. Titles of ownership and mineral wealth of regions unknown; including nations long ago passed by treaties into a post-war Europe and Asia. Clearly, most were the properties of estates overtaken by the war.

"What will happen to all this?" asked Trevor.

Lionel Neville, Governor of the offices in Bermuda sat across him at a white damask dining table, the view of the aquamarine sea stretched beyond them. They were having lunch at the Yacht Club.

"The cache of these offshore accounts will be itemized by the government. If traced to the rightful owners, the taxes owed on these estates can be either negotiated and paid by the owner through a mediation process, or declined by the owner and confiscated by the government."

"I agree. It's not necessary to prosecute."

"No. Besides, the statute of limitations would have expired by now. It's not our intention to embarrass people, just to receive honesty and strike a fair deal for taxes unpaid, like other hard-working citizens must do!"

"What of the Works of Art?"

"Amnesty may be considered for special items, such as museum pieces that should be exposed, and so on. How other governments will deal with their accounts is not our affair. But we have you to thank in large measure for this revelation. Especially all the intelligence coming on the bank accounts. It seems the Swiss kept records!"

"And the Irish!"

"Yes. I know you are not revealing all Trevor! I know you have more work to do. So we won't ask."

"Thank you, Sir!"

"By the way, apart from what you found in your father's account that completes the explanation of what happened to the English Royal jewels - and we do appreciate your donation of them to the rest of the royal collection, but I have to ask: Do you have any idea what happened to the original cache of all the Russian gold and treasure? They are nowhere accounted for..."

"No. I do not" said Trevor, getting up and extending his hand. "And now, if you'll excuse me. I had better catch that flight home!"

"Of course! Keep in touch."

* *

It bothered Trevor greatly, and he thought about it on the flight home.

While he had donated what small bequest was left him from his father's vault to the British collection of Royal Jewels, what was unaccounted for was the large cache of Russian treasure entrusted to the British government to deliver to America. It was part of the Lend lease Agreements, now repaid in full.

He thought about what he saw in those vaults offshore. Aside from intrinsic value, the historical and cultural value from that era were incalculable. An era in which many had been engaged.

It was a terrible war for too many. And their sacrifice should never be forgotten, decided Trevor.

Nor could not have been easy as a modern society evolving - opulent and awkward as it was, in trying to reform the role of governments; democracy and commerce: Not of all of it worthy, or Just, but they did achieve advances that paved the way for today's world, he mused.

Just as Churchill had envisioned at the first Atlantic Conference when meeting Roosevelt for the first time to "establish an order of peace in the world, which – after the war was won – would lead to a golden century with prosperity and security undreamed of for all classes of society and all peoples."

What of the cost, he wondered. Britain had to pay the Americans for their Lend-Lease supplies, regardless the losses at sea, if that were the case. The British paid dearly at a time when they were as depleted - as any other nations after the war. But pay they did! As a matter of trust and good faith - Britain paid all its national debts, Trevor knew.

And yes, it came at a cost to the people: Taken from levies and opportunities, perhaps. The cost of reconstruction had been vast.

He did not deny that tax-fairness was something non-negotiable. But it had been a long road to recovery for Britain who paid her dues, and invested in her own recovery, without exemptions.

Here, the accounts were endless. Worse, discovering that wealth hidden offshore had been siphoned off systemically by an underground black market was bad enough.

But what of the Russian treasure? There were rumors. Rumors that it had been shipped and sunk by U-Boat action in WWII. Rumors that it never left England. Rumors even, that it was recovered by the Russians.

On any losses documented, all liabilities had been picked up the British.

Regardless, one thing was certain. The British had paid all its obligations for Lend-Lease from the Americans. Much of it out of the Bank of Scotland, even Trevor's own Bank.

Plus, they had compensated for deficits owing by the Russians. Indeed, Britain had more than compensated for any debt structure owed to the Americans by Russia, their ally in war.

If ever found, such share of restitutions paid out by the British should be refunded to the British. Of that there was no doubt.

* *

Trevor was driving through the city of Washington DC.

Traffic Stop-signs were planted on every corner for tourists. Plus, traffic wardens were on the alert.

He decided there was only way to unearth the Russian treasure.

He needed the list of accounts of the Irish banks that cited, as collateral for loans, all gold shipments promised.

But such bank information was in the hands of the European Central Banks at the moment, still finding ways to pay out creditors for a failed Irish banking system!

There was only one other list existing. He must retrieve it in full. The Irishman had not given it over entirely. His point of contact, evidently, was Amanda!

The woman Ladevine DeBerle knew something more about the location of the treasure, of that he felt certain. There was a greater cache, somewhere.

If the treasure was cited as *collateral* for loans made to individuals holding offshore accounts in Ireland...then it was up to him to find the connection to that collateral.

But it was dangerous, he knew.

The Russians took the matter seriously enough to kill for, that was clear.

Plus Trevor had put Amanda in danger.

Then the woman herself, Ladevine. "Many an uncooperative depositor has been caught by a stray bullet, Mr. Trevor..." she had said.

No. He must intercept their quest... if on behalf of the Irishman! Amanda had become embroiled to a degree that not only compromised him, but endangered her life. He had to be careful. Bad enough that he was trespassing on an underground trade that was old, dangerous and undocumented. But he could not let his wife be the scapegoat!

Above all, Amanda must remain without knowledge of illicit depositors, he decided. Even if the Senator's own integrity was not without blemish. He must keep her unawares of the details. Otherwise, she might be an unwitting guide to claimants seeking offshore retribution, including the IRS!

It was not a position with many options. The offshore banking world was a world without laws, protection or accountability.

How to meet Ladevine?

Not in the United States, she was too recognizable.

Trevor had packed and was out the door when the housekeeper arrived. She was being dropped off by her husband Eduardo Carlos. It was Thursday.

"Good Morning Signor MacDonnell!" she sang out, waddling up the pathway. "How are you? I come to leave with you a very nice clean house!" she grinned happily.

"Good Morning Mrs. Carlos!" The door he was about to close, he now held open. "It's very nice to see you! How is the family?"

They bantered, he came back in with a few instructions and apologies about where stuff was strewn.

Mrs MacDonnell wanted some things cleared away, he explained. Especially when she returned, he told her.

Mrs. Carlos nodded amiably, knowing that with the owners out of this house, she could take her time, clean it as thoroughly as she wished, and be handsomely rewarded for it.

"You leaving now Mr. MacDonnell?" she said, seeing his luggage.

"Yes. I'm on my way to the Airport now. I've left a Note for my wife when she returns tomorrow, and I should be back in a few days!"

Smiling, Mrs Carlos looked at him askance.

"You leave a nice message for the Mrs. MacDonnell, Si?"

"Of course!" he grinned. "Tell her that I love her!"

She howled, raising her hands to her chest in approval.

"Goodbye Mrs. Carlos!"

"Si, Signor MacDonnell"

The taxi appeared and he left his housekeeper waving cheerfully from the door step of his Washington home.

National Airport was amongst the most comfortable airports he knew, Trevor decided. It was easy to access, and not far outside the city on the Potomac River. Better known as *Ronald Reagan Airport* since it was upgraded, and it boasted the very best of facilities and glamour for its size and air-carrier capacity. Nowhere near the size of Dulles Airport in Virginia, nor the Baltimore-Washington Terminal in Maryland, but it held its own both in convenience and elegance.

Trevor passed the check points and entered the Lounge for first class passengers. He had a strategy.

He would post the matter of his re-discovered royal necklace and jewels in the newspapers of London. Specifically, for historical integrity and public information value.

He would show the sapphire pendant itself, and describe it as precious, valued at a worth of many millions.

Most readers would appreciate that the old matter of the loss was to be finally put to rest, restored and returned to its owners. An Auction, perhaps. A private donation to charity, even. Or a fundraiser for a Museum piece.

Only one person would recognize it as a calling card: The person who wore it, most certainly, who knew that the sapphire was a fake. Bait.

Thus, just as the gem had lured him in at the Gala and led them to the vault of Bermuda, the gem described now would bring her out to him!

It was a brilliant ploy, he decided, since she would be undoubtedly informed of the publicity it would generate in the press. Certainly the advertisement was ample...

"Announcing passengers on Flight 282 to London leaving Washington now. Boarding at Gate No 1"

Trevor finished his whiskey, picked up his bags, and boarded his flight.

* *

Trevor was in the Tower of London.

The Keeper of the Tower History at the Royal Armories was conducting a tour, and for Trevor MacDonnell, it was thrilling.

"The windowless form and restricted access suggest that it was designed as a strong-room for safekeeping of royal treasures and important documents..."

This was the stuff that Amanda had anticipated for her own celebrated little Tower in Newport, Rhode Island. Of roughly the same period, he thought. *She would have loved to hear this!*

"The White Tower was a Keep, a place also known as a "donjon." Here, fortification held lodgings for the King and his treasure. Known by medieval kingdoms, this was the largest Keep in the Christian world."

The crowd was standing in wonder.

"The most complete eleventh-century palace in Europe..." said the Keeper.

Trevor looked about. The resemblance was striking. Kingly or not for its enormous size, this Tower of London was 36 by 32 meters, but still fit the same purpose of design that Amanda asserted for Tower in the new world. This, Trevor later shared with the tour guide Tower Keeper.

"My wife's monument, The Tower of Newport that stands in the new world bears similarities in function with this one. Three stories high, a basement floor, an entrance level and an upper floor with an entrance above ground facing south. Access – perhaps - via a wooden staircase which could be removed in the event of an attack..."

"It is possible. When was the Tower built?" asked the broad-faced Keeper.

"1635"

"Well now. My! That *is* interesting for the new world!" He carried on.

 "In Henry II's reign, more battlements were added to the south side of the tower, now lost..." he grinned. "But as you can see, each floor was divided into three chambers, the largest in the west, a smaller room in the north-east, and the chapel taking up the entrance and upper floors of the south-east..."

"A chapel...*of course!*" said Trevor. "I must tell her!"

The recess indentation in the stone structure of Amanda's Tower at the first floor level was an *Altar*. Was that possible?

To Americans, the cavity looked vacantly without purpose. Here *was* the purpose - something of medieval veneration for that period. A place for an icon of Christianity!

How wonderful... Not that the Tower of Rhode Island built in 1630s was anything like the Tower of London, but custom and tradition in architecture had a way of persisting through time, even on smaller scales...

And Amanda was right. What if it had *wooden* beam structures appended to the stone tower placements - timber construction of the 17th century would have made for a larger structure?

Trevor was fascinated. He must bring Amanda here!

"At the west corners of the building are square towers" continued the tour guide Tower Keeper "while to the north-east a round tower houses a spiral staircase. At the south-east corner there is a larger semi-circular concave protrusion which accommodates the Apse of the chapel." Trevor had to smile. Perhaps he was imagining too much. But this was a world populated by ambition and expansion and trade and battle...

The crowd moved on. "The building was intended to be a large residence hall as well as a stronghold, cisterns were built into the walls, and four fireplaces provided warmth..."

Trevor thought of Amanda's words. She did say there was evidence of a grain storage facility perhaps that was something prized, a food source, a commodity to defend.

"As was most typical of most Keeps, the bottom floor was an undercroft used for food storage. One of the rooms contained a well..."

That then, should be the point of exploration for the next archaeological exploration of her tower, decided Trevor.

He asked the Keeper where he could consult them for more information. He might have further need of reference for identification purposes, he said.

"Of Course Sir. My office will see to it that your queries shall be answered!"

Trevor looked at his watch. It was almost time for his rendezvous. His brow hardened at the thought.

There was another agenda that brought him here.

He proceeded to St. John's Chapel where bare unadorned stone masonry told of a Norman period. Only later, in the 13th century, during Henry III's reign, was the chapel ornamented with gold-painted icons and stained glass windows depicting the Virgin Mary and Holy Trinity.

He stopped.

That's where he saw her, kneeling at the front pew of the Chapel...

Ladevine DeBerle.

A far cry from the elegantly dressed diva of the Washington Gala, or the racketeer in Bermuda, she knelt devoutly, her head down and her hand enclosed around a pyx.

He approached. "Hello Ladevine."

She looked up, smiled, and stood upright in a skirt and suit of black leather.

"I am glad you agreed to meet me" said Trevor. They walked. "I need some information from you."

She nodded, her gambits and deceptions gone.

An ornamental jewel-sized pyx, bearing the disk of the early Catholic, now hung from her neck.

She fondled it frequently as they strolled amongst tourists, rubbing at the inscription.

"*Justitia Virtutum Regina*..." she said

"Justice is the Queen of Virtues" he finished. "Also, known as the motto of the Worshipful Goldsmiths presiding over the Trials of the Pyx!"

She looked at him bleakly. "I never know what it meant."

He thumbed his hand at the Tower of London. "The Tower was once a Treasury Mint of the realm where Trials of the Pyx proclaimed the true value of coins. Rather apt?"

"I am sorry Mr. MacDonnell" she said. "I am nervous to be seen...It was a mistake to come. But I tell you this only once. When the sapphire was detached from the collection, long ago. Or, not so long ago since it visited Scotland...we saw the pictures in the newspapers, and forged the sapphire."

"And do you know who stole the jewel then?"

"No. We have no idea."

"We know the jewels are Russian, and kept by the British. We want them back..."

"Russian jewels have also been cited by the Swiss authorities examining old bank accounts in proceeding. There may have been more?"

"If there was, then it too should be ours" she looked down.

"There were rumors that the Germans got the Russian trove before it got to America. Or rather, were supposed to...But they never succeeded. Just rumors though, I don't know for sure."

"Where did these rumors come from?"

"I'm not sure. My uncles were Polish in London during WWII. They said they worked in the docks and ships. They heard those rumors from spies."

"Spies?"

"Is ...wartime! Churchill he fail to give Poland again from the Russians after the war. My uncles, they lose everything! Lubin Committee make Polish became communists, and my uncles no more wanted to pay Americans for aid..."

"I see. So, you don't know what happened?"

"No. Only that they spoke also of ports and docks of Wales, or Ireland. They had spies too."

"I am sorry Ladevine. History is never easy. You should know though, that we have long paid the debt to America without it, regardless. For all that was promised as payment for supplies, or for safekeeping, the British completed all obligations. Even assuming it to be all lost at sea. So, if it were to be discovered, I doubt the Americans would pay back the money. Therefore the treasure, by default, would revert to its keepers' authority!"

She got up to leave. "Then know this, we will never give up searching for it" She walked off.

Thieves never do, he thought.

He would report to his office in the morning. He would look up old intelligence reports, those he had access to, at least.

That night he called home. There was no response.

Trevor looked down at the brochure and made a mental note to share it with Amanda. He could visualize her now, her bright face engaged in things that held meaning in life...

How fortunate he was to have her as his wife, he thought.

Towers were the Keep, or place of valuables. Like arms, jewels, coin and precious metals plate...

God, how he missed her!

He picked up the phone and left a message.

"I think I know where the loot is!" he laughed, chatting in his message.

His account had been terminated.

* *

New York City

The Division for Delinquency cases was in New York City, not far from the Commercial Center of Finance and Trading. Here, a collaboration had been established between the US Treasury; the Internal Revenue Service and the Investors Association.

For years now, the matter of offshore accounting had come before them. How to deal with illegal deposits made in foreign banks from profits made on US soil. Taxes were taxes. Everybody hated them. But at the end of the day, they were the lifeblood of society.

As leaders in a global network of high finance and corporatization, the gold standard was now subordinate to the American dollar. Taxes of today dictated the rules of public finance policy and international trade agreements.

But as experts liked to point out, it was the wrong policy to bail out the banks in 2008 to stem a financial meltdown - a moment in history never before seen when Congress passed a bill to lend $600,000,000 in TARP money. The money was all paid back.

This meeting was held in the Ruthamond Federated Central Bank, 10th floor.

"Shall we begin?" asked Percy, the man chairing the meeting, waiting for all to take their seats.

"...then good, let's do so!" He put on his spectacles and picked up the tear sheet before him.

"Well Gentlemen, as you know the Bank Secrecy Act requires U.S. Taxpayers to file a Department of the Treasury Form 90-22.1 Report of Foreign Bank and Financial Accounts (FBAR). That is, each person, including a bank." He paused, looking up.

"So, 'subject to the jurisdiction of the United States having an interest in, signature or other authority over, one or more bank, securities, or other financial accounts in a foreign country must file an FBAR if the aggregate value of such accounts at any point in a calendar year exceeds $10,000. (31 CFR 103.24). A recent District Court case in the 10th Circuit may have significantly expanded the definition of "interest in" and "other Authority."'

He looked up, and took a deep breath.
"Questions?"
None came.
"Good, we got that out of the way, now let's talk..."
"Gentlemen, as you know, we are in a changing world. Our government asserts that it needs to bring home its capital. As you know, half the world's capital flows through offshore centers. Tax havens have 1.2% of the world's wealth, including 31% of the net profits of US multinationals. An estimated £13-20 trillion is hoarded away in offshore accounts. Swiss banks alone hold an estimate 35% of the world's private and institutional funds... The Cayman Island some 2 trillion US dollars in deposits, etc. etc. ...*Need I go on?*"

He looked up, and he saw a room of malcontents, if polite enough to listen. He proceeded.
 "Assuming conservative estimates alone, if these assets earned an average of just 3% a year in income for their owners taxable at 30%, then the offshore funds would general some £121 billion in tax revenues alone! Of course, that's also assuming that these funds have no taxes owing!" It was getting hot, and he tugged uncomfortably at his tie. He looked up, relieved to find a question.

"Yes, Mr. Mundy, you have a question?"

"Sounds like Socialism to me! Why not confiscate everything and have a world Marxist regime?"

The room bloomed into laughter.

Percy rolled his eyes.

"Right! We are all taking a look at who is using these accounts. Clearly, many of them are illicit."

"Since when?" asked one.

More laughter.

"September 11th, 2001. The US PATRIOT Act authorizes the US authorities to seize the assets of a bank, where it holds assets for any criminal activity. The EU has agreed to sharing information between jurisdictions; and the OECD is cracking down on tax evasion."

They looked down, the specter of that horrible day etched forever in their memory.

Someone raised their arm.

"Ok. So there are ways in which offshore banking is legitimate" he pushed at the table. "Is this more political bullshit by failing administrations, or true reform of the laws?"

"That depends on where your accounts are!" chirped in a grey-suited man. Now everyone roared.

Percy continued. "OK Gentlemen, it's the oldest – or almost the oldest - trade in the world to hide your money. All's we're saying is this: Play by the rules, and you're fine!"

"So, what are we all in here for?" said one.

"There's been an Informer. One of the failing banks needing a bailout is selling critical information that, if leaked out, taints the whole barrel. So, I'm here to inform you that you need to do your accounting and be in compliance with the law. Tell your clients that where they must, they pay tax. That's all. Got it?"

“Where is this informant?”

“*Safe!* I can promise you that. The Fiscal authorities in Ireland, Belgium, Finland, Greece, Italy, the Netherlands, Norway and Sweden are all willing to share information for the betterment of the system. India remains out there, but many clients are stepping forward voluntarily. Action is likely; reparations will be demanded. Further, there is a proposal to place fees on transfers of currency, and to place taxes on business activities outside their jurisdiction.”

“Are there any *good guys* in this play?”

“I don’t know what you mean by good guys, but yes, there are some zones that have immunity from scrutiny. Panama, for one. Other critical or bottleneck centers too...”

“Hey, lucky the Scotsman Darien who founded Panama, and banking with his investor’s money!” said the first man seated to the left of Percy.

“Too bad the English King turned him down!” They chuckled.

“So, we’re adjourned then. Give me your thoughts, your paperwork, and your feedback before I deliver the Compliance Regulation and proceedings. Ok Gentlemen. We’re done!”

It took them all an hour to empty the conference room, but on the way out, one manager was hailed over by Percy. He intonated his office down the hall.

In his own quarters, Percy checked with his Secretary for call, and walked over to the Coffee alcove where he brewed himself a cup of fresh coffee.

“Care for a cup?”

“Oh, no thanks. Just ate!” said the manager, a middle aged executive with dark rimmed glasses.

They sat down in Percy’s office.

While every investment banker in New York was eager to be perceived as an honest broker and in compliance with the laws, they were nonetheless investment bankers looking for business.

This building could hold all the meetings it wanted on behalf of the IRS, but this brokerage firm was the office of an individual broker with his own means of dealing, and his own means of collecting...

"What's at stake?"

"Well, let's just say that in 1914, Russia held the world's largest gold stock until 1921 when the reserves in Moscow just ran out" said Percy. "Associated with the Crown Jewels, much was taken overseas. Some of it deposited into the State's owned Depository of Treasures. They looted private property across Russia, confiscating everything off the aristocracy; the bourgeoisie, the Church and the banks...."

"What a world, huh...?"

"Yeah. Many considered it wholesale communist betrayal. Others considered it the hijacking of a culture. Worse, they sold art and treasure from Russia to pay bills."

"Some of it however, *didn't*...get lost!"

"What are you saying Mike?"

"The Russian cache is still out there and unaccounted for. It's ours for the taking! We find it, we bank it, and we keep it out of sight, right?"

"Right."

Percy opened his lap top and swiveled the screen around.

"Follow this man. He's Irish. He knows everything, and he's trying to make contact. Find out where he is, who he knows and why. He's *ours!*"

"Name?"

"Ian Kendall"

* *

Washington DC

The color, tissue, shape and imagery was magnificent. Several mounted specimens, drawings and editions were extraordinary collections of engravings, discoveries and stories of tales of adventure...
The Library of Congress had preserved them all.
Amanda discovered volumes of bound books ornately inscribed, some illuminated in the original. Many had personal annotations by Her Imperial Highness the Czarina of Russia, cousin to Queen Victoria of Great Britain and now wife of Czar Nicholas II.
Some books were Christmas presents to the children stamped with the Russian seal of the Czars Palace, evocatively illustrated in its telling as the story itself.
Amanda was fascinated.
One book in the exhibit, Louisa M. Alcott's *Little Men* was inscribed with the words *'For darling Tatiana from Papa and Mama, January 12, 1909."*
Less than ten years later, Amanda knew, at Ekaterinburg, such a world would be silenced forever. It happened in the summer of 1918, after their capture at Tsarskoe Selo. The Russian Royal family were assassinated by a firing squad of Revolutionaries.
"Ms Wells?" asked the attendant, her voice soft "Your boxes are up for your perusal..."

The Request for Research was unusual.
Amanda began with two key questions. Who survived the massacres that brought the old regime to its end, and, what happened to their belongings?
There were several sources of information. The Hoover Institute at Stanford University in California; the

Bakhmetev Archives at Columbia University in New York, the Houghton Library at Harvard University and the State Archives of Moscow.

The Romanov's treasure, as it was known, and the Russian wealth that fled the country prior to the Revolution needed verification. She was to provide an inventory. For Assessment purposes the items were to be valued and catalogued.

As far as Amanda Wells was concerned, wealth began with knowledge. Books. Literary works would hold the highest value of assessment to anyone collecting. So she went to the Library of Congress.

Following the collapse of the Royal Imperial Family, a hemorrhage of valuables from Russia began with the Exodus of *White-Revolutionary* émigrés, who fled to Europe and sold them.

The Bolsheviks, needing to finance their overseas propaganda, decided to sell as much Russian Imperial wealth as they could find.

Decisions were made to export Russian assets for cash, and the new Soviet Regime secretly arranged for sales of state-owned jewels to Western Capitals, including those of the Romanoff family. That included heirlooms and crown jewels of Russia, all kept in the Palaces of the Imperial Families.

Within a decade and half, the Soviet authorities sold hundreds of paintings by Rembrandt, Titian, Raphael, Van Dyck, Romney, Watteau, Tiepolo, Velzasquez, Hals, Botticelli and Veronese.

Andrew Mellon alone purchased over seven million dollars in paintings from the Hermitage in 1930, accounting for a third of the Soviet sale.

In 1931, the New York Public Library acquired some 2,200 volumes of books from the library of the Grand Duke Vladimir Alexandrovovitch, the Czar's uncle.

Others who purchased from the libraries at Gatchina, Anichkov and Tsarskoe Selo included Harvard University and the Hoover Institution.

Years later, when revolutionary fervor had abated, even the Russians decried the loss of their cultural treasure, calling the policy "ignorance and stupidity."

By then, a total of 757 volumes had been sold to Israel Perlstein, a Polish naturalized American book-dealer, all of them now in the Library of Congress.

When finally Amanda looked away from browsing, she focused on the research at hand which she stored on her laptop computer.

That night, she developed her framework and prepared notes.

By far the greatest portion of Russian wealth unaccounted for, was their Reserve of gold.

National gold holdings in Russia, like any other sovereign state, could only be amassed by two means.

The first was produced from its gold mines, the other as revenue money from a trade surplus of exports paid by other countries.

Just prior to WWI, at the time of the Czars, Russia was in full supply of both.

As a Sovereign state, she did not hesitate to expend her hoard of gold to develop her nation and to pay for her defense with ammunitions and other wartime equipment from her Allies. It was the terms and conditions under which the gold was paid for her provisions that remained in question. The mystery lingered, where was the gold delivered?

Amanda's task was to research the question.

Why the request had been made, she was uncertain. Only that it came from a party in New York through the Senator. Not that she was on the warmest footing with him. After all, the Committee on which they worked had been dissolved. He had sent her a terse note of dismissal. *"Your services are no longer required."* At least he apologized for not showing up at the Hearing – a Hearing that ended in a power-failure and utter closure of the investigation to allowing new opportunities to engage the markets in economic growth...

That, plus her last conversation with him. She had confronted him with the revelation that there had been information forthcoming about his investments overseas.

He brought everything to a halt - his parting remarks suggesting merely that he'd like a chance to talk with Trevor...

But that was it. No answers. No explanations. No acknowledgement. It left Amanda wondering about his integrity. *What was he so afraid of?*

Still, he had called on Amanda to furnish a research report for an investigation at the Department of Justice. Research was what she did, perhaps it was his recommendation that gave her the business.

Regardless, she picked up the phone and dialed her business partner. She left a message.

"Hey Barbara, we have some work to do. Are you free to help on the topic of Research related to Russia?"

Two days later, Amanda was in New York.

"Has Trevor any interest in this?" asked Barbara, licking at a cone of ice cream in Downtown Manhattan. Amanda looked away. "No."
"You mean... there's trouble at home?"
"That's not what I said. I just said... Oh, never mind."
"So, you're marriage is in the PAUSE mode?" she licked. Amanda shrugged.
"That's bullshit. He's mad about you!"
"He's away..."
"So..." said Barbara with her annoying New York impunity to search matters of the heart. "Still..." she continued, crossing the street with Amanda in tow as a cab came to a halt not six inches from her coat "...there is no getting out of this one! Here, you will see things of beauty that you never thought possible; things that will make your heart sing..." A second taxi screeched by and splashed dirty street water on their boots "...or your eyes tear in anguish... This way!" she beckoned.
They crossed the street.

It was true, the Art in this private gallery was the most incredible collection of Russian jewels Amanda had ever seen.
Faberge Eggs made of a filigree gold took her breath away. Two of the fabled Eggs pictured in frames were those recently returned to Russia as Museum exhibits by Queen Elizabeth I of England.
Amanda nudged closer and read the inscription.

> "Acquired by Queen Mary in 1929 and 1924. A Tsar's Faberge Easter Egg, The *Colonnade Egg*, had been presented to Alexandra his wife in 1905 to commemorate the birth of the heir to the throne. The *Mosaic Egg* was made in 1914.

Of the fifty six Easter eggs made for Alexander II and Nicholas II by Faberge only fifty four were in royal hands in 1917."

Amanda was awed. She understood the poignancy with which the Russians felt bereaved of their cultural treasure. Barbara stood beside her.

"Your family came from Russia, didn't you say..?"

"Yes. A century ago!"

They toured. Displays of jewels, gems, clothes, porcelain, art, silver, gold religious iconography, paintings, sculptures were impressive.

"It's amazing..." said Amanda.

Barbara remained quiet.

The exhibit ended with a large plaque, printed and framed. It stood firmly in the center of the chamber that was the last room of the private gallery. It framed a printed news bulletin from 1918.

> "The Bolshevik government nationalized all banks and took over the [private] accounts of "rich" people, including a special decree on 13 July 1918, nationalizing all the property of the Emperor: All private property of Nicholas and his predecessor Alexander III, including investments in Russia and abroad, now belong to the Russian Socialist Soviet Republic."

* *

Chapter 15

Amanda had not heard from Trevor in three days. Not that such a condition was unusual. Many ranking officials could be called away on sensitive matters – often absent and kept off limits even, if the occasion called for it.

Trevor was never one to keep things from her, let alone keep her guessing.

Further, when such absences did take place, even relating to some political imperative or government crisis that would warrant his attendance, he gave her lots of advance warning...

He had left without a word.

She had returned from Boston to find the Housekeeper finishing up... Then Carla announced that she had seen Trevor leaving on his way to the airport!

She did not know where, said Mrs. Carlos, but that Trevor said he had a message for her: To tell La Signora that he love her!

They laughed of course, and Carla left.

But that was it. Amanda found no message. No Note. Nothing.

She searched the house. Nothing in the study...Nor a playful mystery *billet doux* with a hint or clue or promise to bring back a tourist gift or prize in endearing fashion.

It was chilling.

She later even talked with Mrs. Carlos. Again, she knew nothing.

The next day it was grey. She walked the dogs, pursued a few obligations at her desk, but the house seemed empty, the day quiet. Her life felt still...

She almost burst from her seat when the doorbell rang. Perhaps it was a special delivery from Trevor, a courier with something to inform her - a message, flowers or a surprise of some kind.

Instead, it came as a shock when three men introduced themselves as Special Agents from the Immigration Offices. They showed her their official identity shields. She let them in and answered their questions. Did she know the whereabouts of her husband?

The picture of Ladevine DeBerle was on the table, presumed dead. *Yet here she was!*

Did Amanda know anything at all...? What was the last known conversation or contact that they had...*Who* had called her, exactly...?

The query was put to her over and over. Finally, they asked her about the boat.

That was the question that most disturbed her. Not because she had no answer beyond what the broker told them, but because of the pictures on the table.

Here was Trevor in Bermuda, with a woman at the bar of a hotel...

The second depicted a highly modern looking Ladevine DeBerle in London, touring the London Tower, again walking in the company of Trevor!

How could Amanda *not* know anything? Especially since the photos were less than a week old.

"And this..." they said, laying a note on the table for her to open and read.

Gradually, the conversation turned from DeBerle to Trevor himself. They had questions about his activities. Where was his desk? His portfolio? His accounts? Could they take a look around?

What were his work habits? Whom had he visited, seen or called recently? Why was he missing? Did he usually go missing?

Amanda kept her nerve. It was all she could do by the time they left. She would have called their Attorney. She wanted to flee to the phone...

She could have called Barbara. Or Fiona.

But she paused.

As Amanda closed the door, she sensed that it was not even the Irishman who was under investigation, his name never even came up, nor was the death of the woman found in the apartment.

At first they wanted to know who the woman was, *what* she wanted, and *why* she was known to Trevor.

It soon became obvious that Trevor himself was the object of their attention.

In fact, after they left, she realized that Trevor had been the object of their attention for quite a long time. The photographs told of their interest. He had been under surveillance...

Her cell phone rang.

She approached it carefully as if it were an object of suspicion.

Pick up? Defer...?

She threw back her hair suddenly, and in a normal sounding voice answered the phone "Hello?"

"Hello" said the voice on the line. "Are you alright?"

She swiveled around, unnerved. *Was someone observing her?* She waited. "Have they left?"

"Yes" she said.

It was Ian.

"I am sending you something" he said "The location of the gold is marked by the Celtic Cross. If you have to, use it to save yourself!" then he hung up.

She rushed upstairs, grabbed her raincoat, a few items for travel, and left the house by car, her thoughts a mess.

"*My Darling,*" said the Note still on the coffee table.

"*As you know, I'm at a Conference in Munich for the European Finance Roundtable.*

I shall stop in London this weekend and meet with someone - someone you know. I do not wish to alarm you, but the women supposedly murdered in Washington is not the Ladevine DeBerle we met at the Gala.

In fact, I am meeting with her again...There are reasons that I shall fully explain. But I think you may know already.

Please understand, my dearest, how distressing this business is for me. I shall explain everything to you in person when I see you next..."

Trevor

* *

Amanda went jogging. She was looking around her. No sign of being followed. No eyes watching her through Rock Creek Parkway. No Ian lurking in the shadow...

Her cell phone rang.

No, this was not a moment for Barbara's life coaching, thank you!

With every beating of the pavement, her thoughts revolved around the same question. Had she *missed* something?

What was Trevor trying to say? Had there been some omission somewhere?

More like, how could she be so stupid...?

I am meeting with her again..

What threw her so suddenly?

What made her feel so... so full of doubt, so lacking in value? Was it the note? Or the Agents showing up at the door? The photographs of Trevor with another woman...

Run. Run!

Breath. Breath.

She stopped. *What was going on?*

Had she carved out selective attention to details that only served self-doubt?

Run. Run!

Breath. Breath.

"But I think you may know already..."

That's impossible, she decided. She and Trevor had a wonderful relationship. There is no way that the officers implied infidelity by Trevor. No way!

Run. Run!

Breath. Breath.

There had to be an explanation! She refused to believe what she saw in those photographs. If they thought to foster self-doubt, then they were wrong...

These people should not be intruding. There was something else going on.

Right?

Or was there?

She would ask him. Was there room for improvement in their marriage? Had she missed his needs?

Run. Run.

Breath. Breath.

She stopped.

Jesus! What had happened to them suddenly?

The jewels, the woman, the murder...Ian, the inquiry...the missing message apparently left by Trevor - A Note never found. *Was that the Note he had left for her?*

She thought about it. So, if he had left a Note that she never found, that meant that it had been lifted between the time that he left...even after Carla left, and before the time she got back.

Who had access to the house?

She stopped abruptly.

She knew who, and the thought shocked her.

Right then she made a decision.

* *

Chapter 16

Mrs. Carlos lived at the bottom floor of the courtyard of a building in Alexandria, Virginia. It was an older apartment building filled with tenants also from South America. Here, the building management was glad of residents who paid their rent – even if the age of the building, its amenities and sanitation were less than ideal.

Washington DC had seen a boom in growth. Inflated house prices, a financial crisis notwithstanding, brought new construction. This was a local liberal government with an open bank book.

Most Latino women were housekeepers.

Since Alexandria, across the Potomac, had affordable housing, renters commuted by rail into the city. Further, the building had a large swimming pool where children passed the summer months splashing and playing in the swings and park grounds.

At night, music emanated rhythmically from apartment windows and balconies everywhere. It made for an ethnic neighborhood.

Amanda found Mrs. Carlos in tears. Especially when confronted about the Note left by Trevor.

She sobbed.

Evidently, the three men at Amanda's door had been there already to speak to Mrs. Carlos.

They had grilled her with questions: Did she know *anything* that would tell them where Trevor MacDonnell was?

She had given them his Note left for Amanda. Mrs. Carlos apologized profusely, and she labored with her weeping.

Amanda remained calm. "Who were these people?"

"I dunno Signora MacDonnell. They show me badges and papers and they say they with the INS. I tell them I know nothing...I do as they say, the government" she cried. "Please Signora, I mean no trouble."

Amanda needed no further explanation. It was easy to imagine how these things went. The woman before her looked fearful.

Amanda smiled at her. Then she added "Did anyone threaten you, Mrs. Carlos?"

The woman looked up, dried her eyes and walked over the windows. She drew the curtains.

"I say nothing Signora MacDonnell. I have green card. I work hard, si?"

Amanda nodded.

"I sorry Mrs. MacDonnell. I sorry I not-tell you..."

"That's OK. You were coming to the house tomorrow, right? I am sure you would have told me then, right? It's just that I was visited by those men who surprised me with... what you gave them. I had to come here to ask you why you did that. You understand?"

"Si, signora."

"Look. As difficult as things are, it is best to do things correctly. And to be honest."

"Si Signora"

"I understand, Mrs. MacDonnell. You see that I steal *Notata* of Mr. MacDonnell - and I give to police. You right to say that I not to be scared, that I behave so with police...I must to be *fiducia* and *securita* with employer, si?"

There was little more that Amanda could add.

"That's alright Carla. We'll get it sorted out. We'll discuss this later in the week, alright?"

Mrs. Carlos smiled. "Thank you!"

Amanda made her way to the car and decided she was glad to have confronted the housekeeper. The matter was explained.

*****

It sailed off across Broadway like Mary Poppins' umbrella. Everybody laughed.

Amanda giggled. She was wondering what she would call it. Later, when she and Trevor could be finally alone, they would chuckle about the *'windblown event.'* "And in more than one way..." Trevor would add, referring to the longwinded speeches.

In actuality, the wind gusted with such velocity that the platform shook, freeing loose the awning above them, and shuddering the support rafters.

It was May, and ostensibly, a mild spring in full bloom. But that was not the reason for Amanda's bright hat. She and Trevor had giggled all the way Downtown in the back of their taxi. Their ordeal was behind them.

"It's all that screwing around..." she admonished softly, leaning into him.

He grinned triumphantly. "That'll teach you to be such a hussy..." he whispered back.

Amanda was pregnant. They were going to have a baby.

"The UN!" announced the Cab driver, stopping.

"Right!" said Trevor, fishing into his pocket for a twenty dollar bill. "Keep the change...We're celebrating!"

"No place like New York to Celebrate!" said the cab driver.

Amanda could not resist the challenge as she slid out of the seat and landed on her feet on the street "We are going to have a baby!" she announced.

"Congratulations!" said the New York cab driver. "Joy and best wishes to you both!" he added, infected by her cheer.

"There! I've said it, Trevor MacDonnell. We are going to have a baby!" she heralded, her arms aloft.

"Err...We still have work to do?" he reminded her in coy fashion.

He led her across the street and to the conference room where they would meet with their parties.

If their minds were operating, their feet were hardly touching the ground. Trevor looked at her from time to time, his mild manner distracted by a beautiful wife and child on the way...

As the Americans completed their Report, they explained their conclusions. It was a momentous day for Kendall. For all of them, really. And they relished every detail.

They had made the case, the attorneys explained. Not so unusual really, considering the history of the colonies, but arguably a tenet for possible dispute, as he phrased it.

Based on our 1884 Act of purchase of bonds by Treasury for independent venture in America, they had to default into earlier assumptions...absent clear evidence, they had said.

Further, recognizing independent trade in the colony of Rhode Island – a central Port for the region as being *independently* financed (meaning, not by the Crown) and endorsed by local law of Admiralty Court... It therefore came down to reconstituting antecedent precedence of the historical laws!

A sort of grandfathering clause: In the case of earlier acceptance for barter as legal tender, the decision had been made for a finding that allowed for a modern Business Exchange center to be built in the region...

The Senator had clearly scored big.

The argument was made that that while those laws would be another local provision and establish groundwork, the agreement was made to allow them a grant for market development. Hence, recognizing its statutory standing prior to the Revolution!

"Well done!" said the attorney facing Amanda. "You're a worthy historian. You have established precedence to support the law case..."

Amanda smiled.

Were it not for the battles of the colonists and their Parliamentarian ideals of independence, none of the present economies could have existed, said the Administrator. Well argued, they grinned.

Amanda was pleased.

It was the Tower of Newport as Treasury and Watchtower for defense; seceded from the Crown and other foreign invaders that established the precedence of regional trade and exchange, even as England went into civil war, she knew.

The Tower, its past largely unknown, had inspired a people to settle here; its central function speaking volumes as it lay there in ruins, surrounded by plantings.

They strolled, she and Trevor.

She decided to keep the picture of the Tower framed in her study at home, she said.

Near the soft padding of April's bed. Beside her office desk, she said.

* *

Ireland

The crew that showed up at the old Church Monastery arrived in a convoy. They included two large eighteen-wheel hauling trucks; six rough-terrain paddle pick-up trucks; one flatbed with road anchors for a backhoe and a forklift...

Ten men wearing construction helmets and insulation suits emerged to cordon off the Church yard with tape and fencing, curtained with tarps. Behind them a dark minivan of personnel unloaded equipment and long range antenna.

With the perimeter secured, a small tent was erected inside the graveyard, and a second covering over a cluster of gravesites, not far from the church priory.

Once the equipment was unloaded, the minivan opened up, and several men emerged in dark suits with berets and bulky uniform. They took their positions at the far extensions of the enclosure, and stood guard.

Above, a rotation visit by a helicopter appeared.

Off the coast, two small high speed military craft patrolled.

Inside the Church, the Pastor and his Office Clerk handed over documents to the CO who set up a table and a Communications post. The minister and his staff were escorted from the premises, and the church secured from the public.

The British Government had arrived to retrieve its treasure of gold since WWII, hidden in the Church grounds.

* *

They dashed across the street still holding hands.

It wasn't cold. The sky was a clear cistern-blue, the sun draping sultry shadows on all who passed beneath its glare.

But the wind blew in noisily, and traffic was intimidating. The combination made for less than clear reflection.

A VW van waved an angry finger at them and came to a screeching halt.

"Tourists!" muttered Trevor.

Amanda giggled, her hair wet still and her toes slippery in her deck shoes.

They made another dash and reached the café across the main street of Newport, the main road teeming with pedestrians.

It was the high season for sailing, and the town was packed...

To be up here again, the year gone, for more frolic on the boats was a moment to relish, if not an anniversary celebration. They had made it! Less the matter of sailing and a sporting event, but more the relief that they had sustained a long ordeal. More importantly, their relationship had survived. That was the source of joy.

It was a playful day.

"*Café au lait*, croissant and anything else that looks good!" she smiled.

"Make that two servings of scrambled eggs; juice and bacon too. Plus a couple of those over-the-top scones..." pointed Trevor.

"Bob's scones?"

"Bob's scones, filled with all those things in it, please!"

"You got it" said the waitress, folding the menus and walking off with a full list of items that told her they didn't much care what they ordered, or how much it would come to, just make their breakfast full, fun and fast...

"My second season here, and already, I'm a veteran!" Amanda smiled, then with a straight face said with her lips silent "I love you."

"Mmm" he said, looking down, afraid of meeting her gaze in public.

She felt below the table and squeezed the hand on his knee.

"Behave!" he admonished.

"Yes" she said, pursing her lips and repressing a smile.

In fact, the whole harbor was alight last night with boats and tenders rowing around everywhere. Many were rafted together to make space for incoming contenders.

Already, the year had passed since they were last here enjoying Race Week in Newport Rhode Island.

"Hello! Are you racing tomorrow Trevor?" asked a man making his way to a table close by. He had a boat in their class.

"Not really...Just here for the Sendoff..."

"Oh, that's right. You're officiating for the Yacht Club on the Committee Boat..."

They laughed. This year, they were having fun.

A day at the Yacht Club and shopping. Or, sailing with friends, then dinner on lobster and shellfish at Benjamin's Restaurant.

Added to a night full of partying in the harbor, it had been nonstop action. Plus a good New England summer squall and squeals of laughter coming from everywhere...

-And now breakfast at the Bayside Café.

Everyone knew everyone. Even tourists joined in.

From Australia, one team showed off their race on a large ipad. The New Zealand team and the American teams knew better, they said...

Nothing however, could compare with the night they had together, she and Trevor.

It had been a long time - a distance between them because of tension, suspicion, work and absence – There had not been the trust to be close.

The night sea calm and the sky sparking with silver dots, they viewed from the deck of their boat only that which was illuminated by twinkling harbor lights, and the shadows of the rigging on the water. At aft-deck, with only a few strains of faraway music, Trevor took her into his arms.

"I love you" he murmured, and they moved with the music.

Below decks, for Amanda, no star could be quelled, no thought strayed. She was with the man she adored...

They had let go of their city inhibitions, and Trevor touched Amanda with a passion that made her feel as if he were holding her very heart in his hands.

Together, they rediscovered new tenderness. Between them, there was a trust.

Perhaps it began two days ago, when Amanda and Trevor walked up Truro Hill to visit the Tower.

There, where the Historical Society cared for the stark and sturdy stones of the Tower, where all that pruning and weeding for tiny clusters of flowers, a plaque explained its historical significance.

They would talk to someone, they decided. But for now, they were happy to gaze at the medieval structure, its sturdy pillars firmly implanted and its curvature unchanged for centuries. They sat on the park bench. Here, early settlers of the new world had built the Tower.

From the seventeenth century until now, it kept its mission. Had it served its task, wondered Amanda? All those tightly fitted stones placed carefully into the mortar, did they achieve their telling, still? Or was there yet much for it to say?

Regardless, they were content to sit on the public park bench, and they enjoyed the sun setting on the Atlantic from this vantage point on Truro Hill.

The woman in her late sixties appeared across the green wearing a gardening apron. She was lost to her little word of greens and things, picking up a twig here, a blown off blossom there...

She inspected the trees, and from her apron pocket a small shovel appeared, such that she dug around the iris bulbs and pruned unyielding leaves. She tugged at the weeds, and smoothed over the soil. Then she toddled across the green and knelt by a mound of woodchips. She inspected the patch of earth carefully, then pulled up more weeds.

She smiled at them, thinking them to be tourists until something caught her attention, a blown piece of trash that threatened to land in the circle of the Tower. Sternly, she swooped it up and stuffed it into a plastic bag that unfurled from her apron pocket.

Mrs. Smith and her husband were members of the Historical Society, she explained. There were others in town who tended to the little historical site. And they were very pleased with the border fence that rimmed the flower beds, she beamed.

They had planted bulbs, she said, just two weeks ago. She was checking if they had emerged. "No hurry. There's lots of time!" she said.

They had a Tower *Newsletter* and a website, she explained. For tourists, if they were interested...

Trevor and Amanda introduced themselves, and she called her husband on the cell phone. He came over with Trevor's letter in his hand.

He was a tall man wearing a floppy Tildy sailor's hat, his pink face and round spectacles intensely interested. They sat on the bench and talked at length.

Yes, they said, they would be glad to accept his donation. They exchanged cards to further communicate, and they shook hands.

"Thank you!" he said.

It was Amanda's idea to donate the item to the Historical Society. The Pyx of the Chamber was a rare antiquity, a gift Trevor had brought back from England for Amanda.

The members of the Historical Society of the Tower were delighted, and Trevor explained what it was.

The Pyx was an egg-like metal encasing, like a covered tankard of pewter. Surrounded by a disk, when closed the two disks joined perfectly. Inside the cavity was a prescribed sphere used in medieval England to measure the purity and weight of ore to mint coinage. A Trial of the Pyx pursued.

If the Trial in the Chamber of the Keep agreed that the ores in the Pyx had true worth and value, then they presented it for blessing, and coin was minted for circulation by the Crown. If the trail in the Chamber found the metal in the Pyx wanting, or impure, then the coin was not minted and the metals rejected.

"The Tower was the Keep" said Trevor "You should have the symbol of its significance. After all, it was the aspiration for opportunity in the new world that drove them across the sea!"

Mr. and Mrs. Smith were grateful. They would address the full membership with this.

Amanda smiled.

Money, if pursued with purity of heart, could vanquish all things. It was the pursuit of nobility, she and Trevor. For this, she decided, they had come to Newport!

* *

They were all standing there in a row, tucked into coats and shawls for what had been a punishing cold winter, unyielding to blossoms and buds in spite of it all.

The SEC was represented. The IRS. Attorneys from Washington. A few diplomats. Especially Kendall... He could attend the dedication ceremony - on his way to the Airport for extradition with his escort of designated officers – Kendall could stand in the background, they conceded.

The handiwork of Barbara was never far away.

A short press conference would announce the success of the Boston Business Center Project.

But there was more to this event.

At the same time, the IRS was getting a full account of Tax information from 'cooperative informants offshore.'

They would be repatriated funds. A bonanza of sorts, in exchange for indemnification and extradition of a party so far unnamed, later to be handed over to the authorities.

Kendall had given the Americans all the intelligence he could. Trevor supervised the transition of information. But there was more to this, they knew. Something even Kendall could not verify.

Trevor understood.

Today, as the city of New York flew past him in the cab, Trevor saw a sobering world. Here, once the center of the world, things had changed. Here, he knew, were undertones of eves-dropping, spying and intelligence-gathering.

And he was fearful. Fearful not just for his national interest, but for all who had fallen victim in the past.

Except that the debts had to be repaid. And they were un-repayable. Life must continue in the spirit of trust and cooperation, he said, when he spoke on the podium.

This was intelligence-gathering of the most insidious sort, without precedent, laws or defense. It represented new tactics of money collectors, spying on all who could pay, should pay, and might have to pay for the debts of others...

This was more than uncollected taxes and offshore accounts. This was about uncollected and massive debts with exposure to electronic transfers of unprecedented risk. . This, he knew, would have to be tamed within the context of a huge and growing world population.

Still, Trevor kept these thoughts to himself. For now, the Americans were satisfied with the legal resolution of the deal for Kendall.

It was a happy ending of sorts, and only a few reports, friends and personnel attended the small outdoor gathering, windblown and blossoms notwithstanding. This, Barbara saw to.

Still, as the tiny celebratory event progressed, it was becoming obvious that an outdoor event in New York had been ill-advised in this weather. Even if NBC held an outdoor studio year round, regardless the weather.

Across their faces where expressions of discomfort. Some asked whose idea it was to have this little ceremony on a podium that shook with the wind gusting. Or why.

In actual fact, only underlings were present, if truth were known.

Representatives, rather than principles or even official spokesman were present. So it was part token, part tourism, and part politics, they knew.

The platform itself had been there since last Fall. No repairs needed, said the Park Service. Nor had the event been much advertised.

Security, explained someone.

As Amanda looked behind her briefly, her scarf fairly slapping her face, and she smiled at Kendall.

There was something about his face that alarmed her. It was anxiety bordering on panic. His eyes did not stop sweeping the crowd, that is, the two or three dozen that assembled for the event.

They stood on their grey-planked platform, hardly worth the media, in fact. And across the park, there was little traffic. But that changed nothing.

The bullet was intended for Amanda.

There were several shots, when they dropped to the deck. Then it was over.

The only sounds were distant and dry, wind and dust still blowing. Kendall was badly damaged. Trevor was hit.

The chaos that followed was immediate. Police cars surrounded them, and Fire Protection Patrols were deployed.

This was a city experienced in crisis-management. A shooting was a killing, New York had zero tolerance for those who thought they should break the rules...

An flood of investigative police arrived on the scene. Then local and Federal agencies of law enforcement managers, forensic image technicians, ambulances and officials...

Mercifully, the press were held at bay, and for good reason.

Trevor's leg had been shattered. He was taken off in an ambulance. They offered to take Amanda along with him. She could follow, she said.

But it became clear there was a greater need for her attention.

Seeing Kendall's condition, prepped to enter another ambulance, she walked over to him.

Kendall did live a few minutes more. He uttered words which were directed at Amanda. She leaned over him, Trevor's blood still on her face and clothes.

"For you, Amanda. I did good?"

"Yes" she said "Thank you!"

"My son?.."

"He is ...successful. I promise!"

* *

Kendall, evidently, had barged forward. Something he saw made him leap with a ferocity nobody could have anticipated.

Perhaps he was expecting reprisal of some form. Perhaps he even knew it was coming, or had been warned. Perhaps it was a trade-off, a deal he had reconciled with...

 He was hit in the chest even as he lunged, they said. Trevor had turned into Amanda to shelter her from danger and received a small caliper bullet under his arm that lodged in his collar bone. His leg received worse.

It had been a strange scene, recounted dozens of time to the investigative police. But one thing became obvious. Kendall had seen it coming, and shielded the two persons he wished the most to protect - with his own body.

It was just over a week when Trevor was released from hospital, but only on the grounds of a two-month recovery

Heroic acts like Kendall's was something that only a few could recognize, perhaps rooted deep within the feelings of loyalty and belonging.

 "And speaking of going back to traditions" said Trevor one evening, referring to his home in Scotland "We need to get back...I have much to do there!"

Amanda chuckled, knowing that the time for recovery was finally coming to a close.

"That makes three of us!" she said, patting her tummy.

"Come here my beautiful. Will you be my chatelaine?" She smiled.

"Oh..."she said, a decision made "I have news for you!"

"You do?"

"Yes. You are having a son. I wanted to surprise you. But I also want you know..."

Trevor looked away, far away.

He turned to her and took her hand. "My dear" he said tenderly "You have provided me with a Laird of the Castle!"

"True. And one of the first things he shall learn is how to sail a boat!"

"Aye!" he grinned.

* *

They spent time together. A luxury, really. Never had their lives enjoyed quietness and peaceful contentment for very long...

They talked a lot over the next six months, Amanda feeling compelled to absorb everything, share everything, as if time was ticking.

Trevor was taking stock of his life. He had a calling, he said. It was as if he were rehearsing his thoughts with his wife

"One of the things that challenges me the most," he would say on one of their afternoon walks on the moors of his home in Scotland " that as we modernize, we forget the basics...the fundamentals of how important the simple things are to people: And how the sovereignty of independence is something to be cherished...Like a gift to be valued and protected."

Amanda noticed that on some days his thoughts were fluid and easily articulated. He was above all, a government statesman.

"For without solvency, a sovereign state cannot offer its citizens the very thing they need the most. Shelter. Identity. Belonging. "

He was talking with thoughts of his return to Parliament, she knew.

"But without sacrificing the will of the individual..." she squeezed.

He smiled.

"Of course. Without sacrificing the will of the individual" he said.

"So how to strike a balance then..." he would proceed, his cane leading the way across grass and outcrops of the Scottish highlands.

Long into the night they would talk, Amanda growing in size..." and wisdom," he added, feeling very pleased with his wife having a baby.

And his own health was improving by the day.

One Friday evening, just as the summer lark was making its last call, they were in the drawing room of their bastion, as Amanda called it, a joke that only began to describe the size of the medieval dwelling they resided in.

Trevor's mother, Lady Marshand and Amanda were seated in deeply couched highback armchairs either side of the hearth.

The summer evenings could be chilly even in summer on the Locks of Scotland. But today had been particularly kind, and the windows remained open to the terraces. Trevor sat at his desk, with soft music emanating from the hallway sound system.

Amanda wanted to laugh, the three of them enjoying a lazy evening together, like part of nature.

More than anything they were pleased that Trevor's health was so improved, even as his planned his return to London.

"I can't wait to get back..." he said, "I shall make notes!" he grinned "Ideas. Concepts. Hopes. Dreams...Stuff that only the Americans say.."

Amanda looked at him.

His mother looked at him.

The orator.

"Why not call it a Treatise?" said his mother peering above her eye glasses, a touch of the poetic in her tone.

"And thus I shall!" he teased back.

"Then, as you prepare to change the world..." proceeded his mother "Amanda and I ...have important things to do. Like the knitting of our mittens!" She leaned over. "How is yours coming along dear?" She looked down at the delicate thread on her fingers "I'm afraid I've missed a row of pearl stitches...can you help me fix it?"
Amanda smiled graciously.

The next evening, Amanda Wells was delivered of a child.

* *

END